'... did
n... ery
unp...

AUTHOR NOTE

I hope my readers will enjoy this new Regency. I love writing, and always hope my books will give as much pleasure to my readers as they do to me. I have well over sixty books published with Mills & Boon® and am still going! Although many of my books are Regency, I'm also enjoying *The Melford Dynasty*, which began in the Medieval era and is coming down the generations through different time periods. The most recent in this family saga is A STRANGER'S TOUCH, and I'm about to write number eight.

Sarah's story in HIS UNUSUAL GOVERNESS is a fun one, so sit back and enjoy the romp with a heroine escaping from undesirable suitors only to find herself falling into an impossible romance.

Love to all.

HIS UNUSUAL GOVERNESS

Anne Herries

... the imagination ... bearing the ...d by any ...ncidents are

...n in whole or ...gement with ...blication or ... in any form ...photocopying, ...or otherwise,

This book is sold subject to the condition that it shall not, by way of trade or otherwise, be lent, resold, hired out or otherwise circulated without the prior consent of the publisher in any form of binding or cover other than that in which it is published and without a similar condition including this condition being imposed on the subsequent purchaser.

® and TM are trademarks owned and used by the trademark owner and/or its licensee. Trademarks marked with ® are registered with the United Kingdom Patent Office and/or the Office for Harmonisation in the Internal Market and in other countries.

First published in Great Britain 2013
by Mills & Boon, an imprint of Harlequin (UK) Limited.
Harlequin (UK) Limited, Eton House, 18-24 Paradise Road,
Richmond, Surrey TW9 1SR

© Anne Herries 2013

ISBN: 978 0 263 89818 7

Harlequin (UK) policy is to use papers that are natural, renewable and recyclable products and made from wood grown in sustainable forests. The logging and manufacturing process conform to the legal environmental regulations of the country of origin.

Printed and bound in Spain
by Blackprint CPI, Barcelona

Anne Herries lives in Cambridgeshire, where she is fond of watching wildlife, and spoils the birds and squirrels that are frequent visitors to her garden. Anne loves to write about the beauty of nature, and sometimes puts a little into her books, although they are mostly about love and romance. She writes for her own enjoyment, and to give pleasure to her readers. Anne is a winner of the Romantic Novelists' Association Romance Prize. She invites readers to contact her on her website: www.lindasole.co.uk

Previous novels by the same author:

THE RAKE'S REBELLIOUS LADY
A COUNTRY MISS IN HANOVER SQUARE*
AN INNOCENT DEBUTANTE IN HANOVER SQUARE*
THE MISTRESS OF HANOVER SQUARE*
FORBIDDEN LADY†
THE LORD'S FORCED BRIDE†
THE PIRATE'S WILLING CAPTIVE†
HER DARK AND DANGEROUS LORD†
FUGITIVE COUNTESS†
BOUGHT FOR THE HAREM
HOSTAGE BRIDE
THE DISAPPEARING DUCHESS**
THE MYSTERIOUS LORD MARLOWE**
THE SCANDALOUS LORD LANCHESTER**
SECRET HEIRESS
BARTERED BRIDE
CAPTAIN MOORCROFT'S CHRISTMAS BRIDE
    (part of *Candlelit Christmas Kisses*)
A STRANGER'S TOUCH†

*A Season in Town
†The Melford Dynasty
**Secrets and Scandals

And in the Regency series
The Steepwood Scandal:

LORD RAVENSDEN'S MARRIAGE
COUNTERFEIT EARL

I would like to dedicate this book
to the memory of my great friend Paula Marshall,
whom I loved dearly, as did so many of you.

Prologue

'**W**hat was so important that you summoned me here?' Lord Rupert Myers arched a languid eyebrow at the Marquess of Merrivale. ''Tis an unseasonable hour and I was up late last night.' He smothered a yawn and levelled an elegant gold-rimmed eyeglass at the older man. Seeing that the marquess looked strained, he dropped the air of boredom and said in a very different tone, 'What may I do for you, sir?'

'Good grief, sir,' his uncle said, looking at a coat that had so many capes it made Rupert's broad shoulders look positively menacing. 'Where did you get that monstrosity?'

'Uncle!' Devilish eyes mocked him. 'My feelings are deeply lacerated. Don't you know I'm a very tulip of fashion? I dare say at least six young idiots have copied this cape only this week, for I saw Harrad's boy wearing one with nine capes and this has only seven.'

'More fool him,' the marquess grunted. 'Sit down, m'boy. You make me feel awkward, towering over me like an avenging dervish. What happened to the eager young fellow I saw off to war six years ago?'

'I dare say he grew up, sir,' Rupert replied carelessly, but there were shadows in his eyes as he sat in the chair opposite and his mouth lost its smile. He did not care to be reminded of that time for the memories were too painful. 'Is something bothering you?'

'I fear it is,' the marquess said. 'I'm in somewhat of a pickle, m'boy—and I'm hoping you'll sort me out.'

'Anything to oblige. I do not forget that you stood as a father to me when my own…' Blue fire flashed in bitter regret, for the late Lord Myers had been a rogue and a cheat and had brought his family almost to the edge of ruin. That Rupert had been able to save himself and his sister from disgrace was in large part due to this man. 'No, I will not go down that road. Tell me what you wish, sir, and if it is in within my power I shall do it.'

'It's Lily's children,' the marquess said with a heavy sigh. 'You know my daughter's story,

Rupert. She would marry that wastrel. I warned her that he would run through her fortune and break her heart. She wouldn't listen and he did all that and more—he killed her.'

'You can't be sure of that, sir.'

'He drove her out into the rain that night. Her maid told me of the quarrel between them. Scunthorpe broke her heart and she stayed out all night in the rain. You know what happened next…'

Rupert nodded for he did know only too well. Lily Scunthorpe had died of a fever, leaving a daughter of six years and a son of three, but that had been more than ten years previously and he could not see what the urgency was now.

'You took the children when Scunthorpe deserted them, installed them in Cavendish Park with a governess, tutor and the requisite servants—what has happened to throw you into a fit of the blue devils?'

'The governess and tutor both gave notice last month. I've tried to find replacements, but with very little success. I fear my niece and nephew have acquired a reputation for being difficult. I have managed to find a woman who is prepared to take them both on—I suspect because she has no choice—but I'm not sure she'll stay above a few days.'

Merrivale cleared his throat. 'They need a

firm hand, Rupert. I fear I've spoiled them. If I read them a lecture, they would apologise sweetly and then go straight back to their old ways. Would it be too much to ask you to stand as mentor to them for a while? The boy may go to college at the end of the year and the girl… well, she ought to have a Season next spring, but I fear I shall find it hard to secure the services of a woman influential enough to give them a good start.'

'Play bear-leader to a girl on the edge of her come-out and a rebellious youth? Good grief, Uncle! Have your wits gone begging? I'm hardly a role model for either of them. Besides being a tulip of fashion, I'm a notorious rake— or hadn't you heard?'

Merrivale ran nervous fingers through his white hair. 'I know you have your mistress, but I'm not suggesting you should take her with you to Cavendish.'

'Thank you for small mercies,' Rupert said, the light of mockery in his eyes once more. 'She would take it as an invitation to marry me. Annais is too greedy for her own good. I have been looking for an excuse to finish the affair and I suppose one is as good as another…she has no love of the country.'

'Do you mean you will do it?' A look of such relief entered the marquess's eyes that Rupert laughed out loud. 'I should be so grateful, m'boy.'

'I'll do what I can for them,' Rupert said. 'But I must have a free hand. Discipline is never popular and I dare say one or the other will write and complain of my high-handed behaviour or some such thing.'

'Lily was very precious to me and her children are all I have left—apart from you, m'boy. Francesca is very like her mother, but I think the boy may be more like his father. I hope John won't turn out to be a rogue like Captain Scunthorpe—but that is why he needs a firm hand now, to knock him into shape a little before he goes to college. I suppose I should have sent him earlier, but I preferred to educate them at home—some of those schools are very harsh to boys, you know.'

'We've all suffered at the hands of bullies at school,' Rupert said. 'John needs to learn to stand up for himself. I could teach him to box, gentleman's rules—and perhaps fencing lessons. I'm not sure about the girl, but perhaps the governess will be what she needs.'

'I pray she will be suitable. Her references from Lady Mary Winters were good, but Lady Mary's daughter was leaving for finishing school in France so she may just have wanted to get the woman off her hands.'

'How old is this governess and what is her name?'

'She's in her late twenties, I think, and a sensible woman. Her name is Miss Hester Goodrum and she teaches the pianoforte as well as French, literature and needlework.'

'Miss Goodrum?' Rupert nodded. She sounded sensible enough, though her skills were limited. 'I'm not sure what help she would be to John. He needs rather more than that—but for the next six months he shall have the benefit of my knowledge, such as it is.'

'I'm not sure what you mean.' The marquess looked puzzled. 'I thought you would just run an eye over them, give them both a lecture and then pop in once in a while?'

'I hardly think that would do much good, sir.' Rupert arched his right eyebrow. 'I've been feeling jaded for a while and this sounds like a challenge. I shall reside at Cavendish Park until the boy goes to college and by then you will have found someone to take Francesca on, I imagine. I can be John's mentor and tutor and keep an eye on this governess until Christmas. After that I dare say I'll be thoroughly sick of it all, but I've never refused a challenge.'

'Then take my hand on it. If I can be of service to you, you have only to ask, m'boy.'

'You have done more for me than I could

ever repay,' Rupert assured him, clasped his hand firmly and smiled. 'It will be a change for me. My estate is in good heart and almost runs itself these days. Besides, I shall be no more than a day's ride from my home if I'm needed.'

'I fear you may find they do not take kindly to authority, Rupert.'

'I dare say John may kick a bit at the start, but he'll gentle to the bit in time.'

Rupert waved his uncle's gratitude aside carelessly. After all, what trouble could one young boy and a girl on the brink of womanhood be to a man of the world? He hoped the governess would be presentable and not one of those sour-face spinsters, but whatever she was like they would bob along together easily enough....

Chapter One

'It was so good of you to take me up with you, Miss Hardcastle,' Hester Goodrum said as she climbed into the comfortable chaise. 'Lady Mary promised to send me to Cavendish Park in comfort, but she was called away to her sister's bedside and forgot all about me. I have to be there by the end of the week, because the marquess sent word the young people would be alone by then, except for their servants, of course.'

Sarah Hardcastle looked at the woman sitting opposite her and nodded. Hester was in her late twenties, attractive, though not pretty, and kind-hearted. She had heard of her predicament and been moved to offer assistance.

'Well, I'm returning to my home in the north

of England and we must pass within twenty miles of Cavendish Park. It is no trouble to take a detour, Hester.'

'My fiancé told me I was a fool to agree to this position,' Hester went on as she settled in her seat. 'He wanted me to give up work and go home to Chester and marry him.'

'Why didn't you?' Sarah asked and caught at the rope as the chaise moved off with a lurch. 'I fear Coachman is in one of his moods again. If he continues this way, I shall have to call a halt and give him a scolding.'

'Please do not do so on my account,' Hester said. 'I should like to get married, miss. I've been saving for years, but Jim needs more money to set up for himself in an inn. He's got some savings, but we both know we need to wait for another year at least.'

'That's a shame...' Sarah looked at her thoughtfully. She'd been told the governess's story and it was part of the reason she'd offered her the ride in her chaise. 'How much more do you need to save?'

'I suppose a hundred pounds might be enough...' Hester sighed. 'If we both save hard this year, we may just manage it, though I contribute very little and it may take much longer.'

She was not a young woman. Sarah felt sympathy for her, because time was passing her by and her youth was fading. It was so ironic that Hester should be longing for marriage, but did not have enough money while she, Sarah Hardcastle, was doing her best to avoid being married because she'd had rather too much of it.

Was her plan too outrageous to have a chance of success? She'd thought about it all the previous night and her stomach was tying itself in knots. No doubt Hester would think she'd run mad.

'Supposing I offered you two hundred pounds and gave you two of my best dresses in return for your reference from Lady Mary and the gowns you have in your trunk? Would you change places with me? I mean, let me take your place as the governess at Cavendish Park—and you go home to marry your fiancé?'

There, she'd said it out loud. Did it sound as mad as she imagined?

Hester was staring at her in bewilderment. 'What did you say, miss? I don't think I heard right.'

'I offered you two hundred pounds to let me have some of your clothes and the reference Lady Mary gave you. You can do what you wish with the money.'

'You want to be a governess? Why?' Hester was stunned. 'You're a rich young woman,

Miss Hardcastle. Why would you wish to be a governess?'

'I need to disappear for a while and it seems an ideal situation to me. Your employer has never seen you. The girl is almost seventeen so will be easy to manage and the boy is going to college in six months—so how could I go wrong? My tutors considered me a bright pupil. I imagine I can teach the boy mathematics and geography and the girl music, literature, French, Latin, drawing and dancing. What more does she need to know?'

'Nothing, I shouldn't think,' Hester said, but looked anxious. 'I don't know what to say, miss—it doesn't seem right. We should be deceiving my employer...'

'But if he didn't even bother to interview you he can't be that bothered about his grandchildren. All he wants is to keep them out of his hair—and I can do that as easily as you.'

'Perhaps better, miss. You've a way with you. People pay attention when Miss Hardcastle speaks.'

'That is because my father left me a fortune invested in mills and mines and I've run them myself since he died when I was just nineteen.'

'How old are you, miss—if you don't mind my asking?'

'I'm five and twenty,' Sarah said and sighed.

'My aunt and uncle have been trying to marry me off for months. They say I need a man to help me and they're afraid I shall die an old maid.'

'Do they bully you, miss?'

'No, I shall not lie. Aunt Jenny is kind and my uncle is well meaning, but I have no intention of marrying simply to please them. I came away because my uncle would not let the subject drop.'

'What will happen to your mills if you're not there, miss?'

'I have managers and a man of business I trust. I shall keep in touch with him by letter—and it will just be for a short time, until I've made up my mind about something. After that I'll give notice and your pupils will have a new governess. Surely my influence cannot harm them in that time?' Sarah leaned forward. 'Will you think about it today? This evening when we stop at the inn you can tell me. If your answer is yes, we'll change clothes. In the morning I'll send you on in my chaise to Chester—and I'll go by post-chaise to Cavendish Park.'

'I don't know what to say...' Hester looked worried, clearly torn between taking this wonderful chance and fulfilling her duty. 'It's such an opportunity for me. It would mean the world to my Jim to have his inn this year instead of waiting.'

'Well, the choice is yours. I shan't twist your arm. If you say no, I'll simply find another way to disappear for a while.'

Hester nodded, settling back against the squabs with a sigh. She was obviously tempted and Sarah crossed her fingers under the folds of her elegant travelling gown. Being a governess would be a safe environment for a wealthy heiress to hide in until she could shake off the feeling of being persecuted for her money.

Why had her father had to die in that accident at the mill? Tobias Hardcastle had always been a hands-on employer, not above taking off his frock coat and rolling up his sleeves. He'd started out with fifty pounds left to him by his grandfather and built up his huge business using his brains and his ability to work twenty hours out of every twenty-four for years.

Before she died, Sarah's mother had complained bitterly that she wasn't sure when he'd had time to give her a child. It wasn't true, of course, for he came home for meals and occasionally had Sunday off, but he'd certainly put in long hours to ensure that his business empire was solid. Sarah couldn't claim to do the same, but she had a knack of choosing her employees well and of inspiring loyalty. She'd taken up

the challenge at the start because it was there
and she did not wish to hand over her father's
empire to someone who might abuse it. However, she had begun to grow a little tired of the
constant rounds of meetings and bookkeeping
that were an ever-present part of her life. It was
time to sit back a little, for her life was slipping
away and some might already consider her as
being past the age of making a good marriage.
Her managers would make sure the mills continued to prosper during her absence and also
the two copper mines she owned in Cornwall.
It was on her return from her biannual visit to
the mines that she'd stopped off to visit her own
governess and there met Miss Hester Goodrum.

Something about the young woman had appealed to Sarah immediately. Had Hester been a
woman who wanted a lifetime career she would
have offered her a position as her companion,
but Hester had confided her hopes for marriage
and that had set Sarah's quick mind working.

It was a little deceitful to pretend to be
someone she wasn't, of course, but she wasn't
harming anyone. She wouldn't steal the silver
or teach the children to swear and drink gin.
A smile touched her lips, for the idea of being
the children's mentor was pleasant. Sarah had
worked hard since her father's death, giving
little thought to pleasure of any kind. She'd

been asked to dinners and evening affairs at the homes of her father's friends, but since she knew that the ones with wives wanted to buy her mills and the widowers wanted to marry her to get them cheaply, she normally found such evenings tedious.

Even at school she'd been aware that she wasn't really one of the gentry. She was the daughter of a rich man who'd bought the right to live in a big house and own land, but she wasn't one of the blue bloods. The other girls were friendly to a degree, but she'd felt the barrier between them and knew that they laughed at her northern accent, which had all but disappeared now. Sometimes, if she was upset, it returned, but her teachers had earned their money. Mr Hardcastle had wanted his daughter to be a lady and to all intents and purposes she was—except that she wasn't fully accepted into their society. They welcomed her on the boards of their charities and they were even friendlier towards her money, which they grabbed as soon as it was offered, but she was seldom invited to an intimate affair at their homes. Occasionally she would be invited to a large dance because of her influence, but she wasn't the kind of woman that gentlemen thought of marrying.

Well, that wasn't quite true, either, Sarah mused, glancing out of the window. She did have one rather persistent suitor. Sir Roger Grey had asked her to marry him three times now and he didn't like being refused. Sarah was aware that he was in financial difficulty, though he'd managed to hide that fact from her uncle and most of his acquaintance. Sarah had asked one of her agents to make enquiries and his report was disturbing. Sir Roger gave the appearance of being wealthy and respectable, but in reality was a rake and a gambler, and the last man she would ever wed. However, he was difficult to shake off, for he seemed to have taken it into his head that she would come round to the idea if he continued to press her. Unfortunately, her uncle was completely taken in and believed him to be a man of his word.

It was Sir Roger's tactics at the charity ball in Newcastle that had made her decide to leave for Cornwall a month earlier than usual. He'd tried to kiss her and he'd fumbled at her breasts. She'd had to fight him off and had scratched his cheek in her efforts.

'You little hellcat.' He'd put a hand to his cheek in shock. 'You will be sorry for that, Sarah. I'll teach you to respect your betters.'

'I do not consider you my superior, sir,' she'd retorted. 'I have no intention of being seduced. If you thought to compromise me and force me into marriage, you are far off the mark. I would rather have fingers pointed at me in the street than marry you.'

That was perfectly true, for she would rather die than marry a man like him, but it was also true that she didn't wish to lose her good name. Nor would she care to be whispered about or pointed out as an object of shame.

'If you would marry Sam Goodjohn, or Harry Barton, you'd be safe from rogues like that,' her uncle had told her when she'd told him what had happened. 'They're good men and run mills of their own so you could stay home and be a wife and mother as you ought. It's time you married and thought about a family, Sarah—unless you want to die an old maid.'

'I know you want to protect me, Uncle William,' Sarah replied. 'But I should hate to be married simply for the sake of my fortune. When I find a man I love who loves me, I'll get married.'

'Love,' her uncle scoffed at the idea. 'When did love ever get you anywhere? You need a man to protect you and look after your business, young woman. Don't leave it too late or you may find that even money won't get you the kind of man you need.'

Her uncle's scolding had jerked her from her complacency. It was true that time was slipping by and she was no longer a young girl. If she wanted a family she must marry—and Sarah had begun to realise what she might miss if she did not.

Was she so ill-favoured that she needed money to buy her a husband? Sarah knew she wasn't beautiful by any means. Her hair was dark brown, and her nose was straight. Her mouth was bigger than she liked and she wished she had thin lips like Hester. Miss Goodrum was prettier than she was, but Sarah didn't feel ugly. When she dressed in her best she was attractive enough and people said she had a nice smile.

Was it impossible that she would find love?

She felt she might have more chance of it if she were not her father's heir. When men looked at her they saw the rich Miss Hardcastle and they wanted what she could give them. The hard-headed ones wanted to build up her business and get richer; the spendthrifts wanted a ticket to the easy life.

Sarah wanted… A little sigh escaped her. She wanted a man who would make her laugh. A man who appreciated music, poetry and beautiful gardens…someone who would love her for who she was, not for her money.

Was she asking too much? Perhaps her uncle was right. It might be sensible to accept one of her suitors and have the lawyers draw up a contract that gave her the right to retain control of her business and protect her fortune.

It was the simple way out of her predicament. A business arrangement that would protect her from fortune hunters and unscrupulous businessmen who wanted the vast wealth her father had bequeathed her. Until recently, Sarah would have thought it a perfectly sensible idea, but for some reason she had begun to feel a slight dissatisfaction with her life as it presently was. She had not thought of marriage whilst her father lived and in the first years after his death she'd been too wrapped up in her work to consider it. Of late she'd begun to notice children playing in the parks and sweethearts walking together in the sunshine. If she did not marry, she would miss so much.

Was she lonely? Certainly not! She had friends and loyal employees and was too busy to be lonely.

Yet surely there was another way to live? She must have time to consider, to decide what she wanted of life. What Sarah needed was a place to escape, to hide and to be someone else for a while....

'Yes, I'll do it, miss. Like you said, it can't hurt anyone—and Jim will be so happy to have me home....'

Sarah blinked, dragging her thoughts back

to the present. For a moment she couldn't believe that Hester had agreed, then, as she saw the other woman was in earnest, she smiled.

'Thank you so much, Hester,' she said and leaned forwards to touch her hand. 'You won't regret it. I shan't do anything that could harm your good name, I promise you.'

'Lord, miss, as if you would.' Hester laughed, looking younger as her eyes lit with excitement. 'I can't thank you enough for giving me this chance—and I hope you'll get on with your charges. Lady Mary arranged it for me. She said they're a little bit difficult, but I'm sure you'll be fine.'

'Yes, I'm certain I shall,' Sarah agreed and laughed. 'How hard can it be to look after a young lady and a boy of thirteen?'

Chapter Two

'Why do we have to have a mentor as well as a governess? I thought you said it would be all right when we got rid of the last two? You said Grandfather would give up sending us tutors and take us to live with him in London.'

'I said he would take me. It's time I had my come out,' Francesca Scunthorpe said and made a face at her brother. She was a pretty girl with soft hair and bright eyes, and a mouth that was wide and sensuous. Her yellow-silk gown was attractive, but not as fashionable as she would like, and made for her by a local seamstress. 'You will be going to Cambridge after Christmas. It looks as if I'll be stuck here on my own with some stupid governess.'

'I don't mind going to college,' John said

and threw a paper dart at her across the school-room. He was a sturdy boy, attractive with dark hair and eyes and a stubborn chin. His tutor had given him a list of Latin verbs to learn to keep him busy until the new mentor arrived, but John was bored with lists. His tutor had given him new lists every day for the past eighteen months, but he hadn't explained anything. His lessons consisted of setting a new exercise and then tests to see what he'd learned. 'It would be better than staying here on our own.'

'It was all right at first,' Francesca said. 'When we were younger we had Miss Graham and Mr Browne. I liked her and she taught me lots of interesting things, but she left and the last governess was useless. She couldn't play the pianoforte or the harp and she chose all the wrong books.'

'And she didn't like frogs in her bed,' John said, a gleam of mischief in his eyes. 'I've never heard anyone scream as much as she did when she saw that grass snake.'

'She thought it was poisonous.' Francesca looked scornful. 'She didn't know it was a grass snake and harmless.'

'Anyone knows the difference between a viper and a grass snake,' John said and looked up at his sister. 'What are we going to do, Fran? I'm so bored—aren't you?'

'Yes, some of the time,' Fran agreed. 'I like to read poetry, but I know you'd rather play games or go fishing.'

'Can we go fishing today? He will probably stop us having fun when he gets here—and your governess will say it isn't a fit occupation for a lady.'

'We'll outwit them somehow,' Fran promised. She picked up a volume of poetry she'd been reading earlier, then threw it down with a sigh of discontent. 'They are both supposed to arrive later today, though not together. We'll go fishing this morning and come back when we feel like it.'

'Grandfather's letter said we had to be on our best behaviour—to be waiting in the parlour when they arrive.'

'Well, he should have come down himself and stayed for a few days.'

'He said it was getting a bit much for him. Do you think he's ill?'

'I don't know.' Fran's brow creased because she worried about her grandfather. The marquess was all they had—the only one who bothered about them anyway. Her father had gone off abroad somewhere when his money ran out. His house and estate had been put up for sale and the marquess had brought them here. At first he'd spent time with them, but of late he hadn't bothered to come down other than at Christmas, though he always sent birthday gifts. 'I hope he isn't, because I don't know what would happen to us if he died. We haven't any money of our own, John. Everything comes from Grandfather. If I get my Season, I'll marry a rich lord and then we'll have money. I'll look after you then. You won't have to work for a living.'

'Do you think Grandfather will leave us anything?'

'I don't know. I don't want to think about that…' Fran's throat caught at the idea that they might be forced to leave this house. She'd loved it from the moment they came here and didn't want to live in a horrible little cottage like some of the children on the estate. 'Come on, I refuse to be miserable on a lovely morning like this. Let's get some stuff from the kitchen and go down to the stream.'

'Yes.' John grinned at her. 'At least we've got each other. I'll put frogs in her bed and you can think of something to do to this lord whatever-his-name-is…'

'Lord Rupert Myers,' Fran said. 'Don't worry, we'll think of some way to get rid of them if we hate them. Let's go fishing. It will serve them right if there's no one to greet them when they get here.'

* * *

Sarah got down from the chaise and looked at the house. Cavendish Park was a pleasant country house, much the biggest one she'd ever visited, larger and more impressive than her father's on the outskirts of Newcastle. She'd visited a few country houses as the guest of her school friends, but never one quite like this. It was so beautiful that for a moment all she wanted to do was to stand and stare at the mellow golden walls and long windows that sparkled like diamonds in the sunshine.

'If you'd like to come into the house, Miss Goodrum.'

Sarah came to herself with a start. The housekeeper must have been speaking to her for a few minutes, but she'd been lost in thought—and it was difficult remembering that she was no longer the wealthy heiress, Miss Hardcastle. She'd packed that particular persona into her trunks and sent them back to her home with a letter for her uncle explaining that she was taking a little holiday and they were not to worry. All she had with her was a small trunk containing the clothes she'd purchased from Hester.

She was wearing Hester's best gown, because she'd been assured it would be expected for her first arrival. It was pearl-grey with a slender skirt and tight bodice, and it had a white lace collar. Sarah had fastened a small silver brooch at the neck to cheer it up a little. Hester's other gowns were not as good and certainly not what Sarah was accustomed to, but she would get used to them—and it was only for a few weeks or so.

'Yes, thank you, Mrs Brancaster. I was just thinking what a lovely house it is. You must enjoy living here?'

'It's a nice enough house, Miss Goodrum, but…' The housekeeper hesitated and then pursed her thin mouth. 'Things are not quite what they ought to be. His lordship doesn't come down often enough and the children are left to do much as they please. The house needs a master or a mistress, if you ask me—preferably both.'

'Yes, I expect it does. A big place like this takes some running and it shouldn't be left to the servants.'

Unaware of the odd glance her remark had brought from Mrs Brancaster, Sarah walked into the house by way of the kitchen entrance. Since she made a habit of visiting her kitchens regularly at home this did not make her uncomfortable. She might be wealthy and she'd been educated as a lady, but Sarah knew she was a long way from being one. You could take the girl out of Newcastle, but you couldn't take

Newcastle out of the girl; it had been one of her father's favourite sayings and made her smile. She'd been so close to her father, his right-hand man, and she missed him so very much.

She supposed she was looking for someone she could admire and respect as she had Tobias Hardcastle. If such a man were to present himself, she would not hesitate to hand over her person and the day-to-day running of her business to him—but as yet she'd never met anyone who came close to filling his shoes.

'I'll take you straight up to your room,' the housekeeper was saying. 'You can settle in and then come down to the kitchen for a nice cup of tea. Miss Francesca and Master John were supposed to be here to meet you, but they slipped off early this morning. I suspect they went fishing in defiance of the marquess's instructions that they should sit in the parlour and wait for you and their mentor.'

'Their mentor? I thought the Marquess of Merrivale was their grandfather and guardian?'

'So he is, Miss Goodrum. Mr John is to have a tutor and he is to be their mentor. As I understand it, he's to be in charge here and we shall all report to him.'

It was the first Sarah had heard of this arrangement and she wondered if Hester had known. This new man might enquire more closely into her background than she'd imagined and she was glad she'd asked for the reference as well as Hester's clothes.

'I see. Do you know this…mentor's name?'

'I wasn't listening properly when Mr Burrows told me,' the housekeeper admitted. 'I'd just discovered that the pair of scamps had disappeared again and my mind wasn't on it, but I'll find out when he arrives and let you know.'

'Thank you, Mrs Brancaster.' Sarah was thoughtful. 'Do you think I could leave the tea for an hour or so? I should like to take a walk about the grounds before I unpack—get my bearings.'

'Well…' Mrs Brancaster looked a bit put out. 'I'm sure it's up to you, miss. I thought you might want to see the schoolroom?'

'When I return you can give me directions or I'll ask one of the footmen. I don't want to take up too much of your time, because I know you have so much to do in a house like this—and with two new visitors it must have turned your routine upside down.'

'It has…' Mrs Brancaster nodded. 'Well, off you go then. Your trunk will be taken up and you can find your own way here when you're ready, I dare say.'

'Oh, I'm sure I shall. I'm really quite capable, you know.'

Sarah left the housekeeper staring after her. She knew that she had perhaps risked offending her new colleague, but she'd felt as if she must escape before she did something stupid. All at once the enormity of what she'd done—and what she was attempting to do—had hit her square in the face. In her comfortable chaise with all her familiar things about her it had seemed a clever idea. She'd imagined the children were left much to themselves with just their grandfather's servants—but who was this new mentor and what would he be like?

If he was just another superior servant, she might manage to get away with her masquerade by keeping her own counsel. If, however, he'd been placed in charge of the children's future by the marquess, he might want to know too much about her. Sarah couldn't afford for him to dig too deeply into her background. Should he discover she was lying, he might imagine her to be a person of low integrity and dubious virtue.

Her stomach was fluttering with nerves as she strolled through the kitchen garden, noticing how well everything was kept. If she'd expected to find an air of neglect here, she was far off the mark. What if this mentor had met Hester Goodrum in the past?

Oh, this whole thing was madness! She should go back to the house, ask for directions to the nearest post house and leave. What on earth had made her think she was capable of carrying out a masquerade like this? She hadn't been thinking clearly, of course. Sarah wanted time out of her life, time to come to terms with what she needed from the future: should she marry for the sake of companionship or should she wait until she fell in love?

A smile touched her mouth. There was no guarantee that the man she chose would reciprocate her feelings. Sarah knew that she wasn't the prettiest girl in the world and if she found someone she wanted, he would probably not be interested in her.

She must not rush her decision. Looking about her as she walked, Sarah fell in love with the beautiful rose gardens, the herbaceous borders and the sweeping lawns. Some of these trees must have been here for centuries. Hearing the sound of laughter coming from what appeared to be a small wilderness, she turned instinctively towards it and then stopped as she saw a young woman of perhaps sixteen years and a boy some years younger. They were sprawled out on the grass, watching as a fish cooked slowly over a smoking fire.

The camaraderie between them and the sound of their laughter caught at Sarah's throat, making her aware of how much she missed in not having a family. They were so beautiful, so wrapped up in themselves and their amusement that she hesitated, not wanting to intrude. If she introduced herself now they might resent her intrusion into their private time and she would start off on the wrong foot. No, it would be better to wait and meet them later when they had washed the dirt from their hands and faces. Yet how she longed to be a part of that scene.

Turning away, Sarah felt the ache inside her. She had been thinking it best if she made some excuse and went away, leaving the new mentor to arrange a new governess for his charges, but now she'd changed her mind again. Something inside her called out to the young people she'd discovered having fun and she wanted to stay. She had no wish to harm them and she would keep her distance from their mentor, be friendly but reserved, as a proper governess should be.

Lifting her head, she took her courage in her hands. Her father's lawyers had advised her to sell her father's mills to the highest bidder and not to think of trying to run them herself. She hadn't listened to their prophecies of doom and gloom, and, though she'd come up against prejudice and men who resented a woman in their midst, she'd overcome their opposition and her business was thriving. She wouldn't turn and run at the first obstacle now.

It was time to have that cup of tea with Mrs Brancaster. Sarah wouldn't lie more than she had to, to sustain her masquerade as a governess, but she wasn't going to walk away from those delightful children, either.

Rupert was getting down from his curricle when he saw the woman walking back from the gardens. The sun was shining on her head, picking out the red tints in her dark hair and giving her a kind of halo. From her dress he guessed her to be the new governess and surmised that she'd been for a little walk to acquaint herself with her surroundings. He knew very little about her, except that she had been recommended by Lady Mary Winters.

Well acquainted with Cavendish Park from visits to his uncle as a young man, Rupert had no desire to follow her example. He'd known his uncle's grandchildren when they were all younger, but it was years since he'd seen them. He wondered whether they were waiting dutifully in the parlour, as they'd been bidden, or, as he would have done in their place, escaped for a last day of freedom.

'Your lordship,' Burrows said, his face wreathed in smiles as he came out to greet him. 'It is a pleasure to see you, sir. I've been informed that you intend to stay with us for a few months.'

'Yes, until John goes to Cambridge,' Rupert replied. 'It's Burrows, isn't it?'

'Fancy you remembering that, sir.' The butler looked gratified. 'Most of the staff are still here, though some of the maids and footmen are new.'

'Is Mrs Brancaster still with you?'

'Yes, sir. She'll be up in a minute…ah, here she is now. I dare say she was busy…'

'Are Francesca and John in the house?'

'They went off early this morning, sir. Shall I send someone to look for them? One of the gardeners thought they'd gone fishing.'

'Perfect day for it. Wouldn't have minded a spot of fishing myself this morning. No, don't make them feel guilty. We'll soon have a routine established once I've had time to sort things out. I think I should like some cold ale if you have any and a bite to eat—didn't stop for nuncheon.'

'Lord Myers—' Mrs Brancaster looked stunned as she came up to him '—how are you, sir? I didn't realise it was you coming down today. I've prepared the wrong room. I thought…' Her cheeks turned pink. 'Forgive me, I'll have your own room ready in half an hour.'

'Plenty of time,' Rupert assured her, amused by her obvious embarrassment. 'I should like to

meet Miss Goodrum. I believe I saw her return
to the house a moment ago?'

'Yes, sir. She went for a little walk to get used
to her surroundings. We were just about to have
a cup of tea when I was told you'd arrived and
it set me all of a fluster.'

'No need to stand on ceremony. I'm the same
as I was when I came here as a lad, Mrs Brancaster.'

'No, that you're not, sir. We all heard how
you were decorated for bravery for what you did
over there in France—and you were wounded
in the leg.'

'Which is so much better I hardly know it
happened. It's only when the weather turns cold
that I feel it.' Rupert's smile dimmed. He did
not like to hear himself praised for something
he felt best placed in the past where it belonged.

'I'll tell Miss Goodrum to wait on you in the
front parlour immediately, sir.'

'Please request her to visit me there when
she has had time to take her refreshments. I
should wish to be on good terms with the young
woman. Tell me, Mrs Brancaster, what are your
first impressions?'

'Of the new governess?' Mrs Brancaster
frowned. 'I've only just met her, sir, but…she
seems very calm and sure of herself.'

'Do I detect a note of disapproval?'

'Oh, no, sir, nothing like that I assure you.' The housekeeper was thoughtful. 'It's just… she isn't quite like any of the others we've had. They usually have a look about them…sort of resigned and disappointed…but she's not like that at all.'

Rupert quirked an eyebrow, amused. 'I see. An unusual governess. How interesting. I hope she is intelligent enough to know that you cannot keep a girl of Francesca's age always in the schoolroom. However, we shall see.'

'You mustn't take against her for anything I've said, sir. I've only just met her and I'm sure she's perfectly respectable.'

'Oh, I'm certain of it. Lady Mary would not otherwise have employed her. She comes with impeccable references. I am quite looking forward to meeting her.'

'I'll send her along in about ten minutes— and your refreshments will follow as soon as they're ready. I'll have your room prepared immediately.'

'Thank you. You always did spoil me, Mrs Brancaster. I can see I've been missing a treat by not coming down more often.'

Mrs Brancaster positively glowed and scurried away to set everything in motion. Rupert smiled to himself as he went into the house. Nothing much had changed here. It still smelled of roses and lavender; the furniture was mostly good oak and polished to within an inch of its life, though in the main salon he recalled seeing some mahogany Chippendale pieces.

It was what it had always been, a pleasant country house, comfortable rather than elegant, and he could feel its welcome as he made his way to the parlour. Vases of flowers stood everywhere and the smell of roses was even stronger in the parlour. Merrivale had good servants and it was a pity the marquess didn't spend more time here, but Rupert supposed the memories were too strong for him. He'd grieved for his wife for years and the loss of his daughter had nearly done him in, bringing on a heart attack that had left him with a weakness. Rupert suspected that the old man found it too upsetting to visit often for reasons of his own, but it hadn't been wise to let the children run wild. Francesca in particular would need to be schooled in the manners she needed for society and he could only hope that he would find some support in the new governess—because he was more used to dealing with ladies of a different kind.

Rupert laughed softly in his throat. His latest mistress had been most disappointed to hear that he was leaving town and did not expect to return for months.

'What am I to do without you?' she'd asked, as she ran her long nails down his naked back. 'Do you expect me to languish here alone?'

'I expect you to take a new protector within a week,' Rupert told her with a mocking smile. 'We both know this was merely a convenient arrangement for us both, my dear Annais. You will find yourself adequately compensated by my parting gift, so do not pretend to feel more than you do.'

Her nails had scored his back, her eyes glinting with temper. Rupert had known she was angry at being given her freedom to find a new lover, but the diamonds he'd gifted her should soon dry her tears and he was aware that she'd been casting glances at Lord Rowley for a while now. He would bet that the gentleman found himself in her bed within the week. His own feelings were not touched. It was a long time since he'd found more than a fleeting pleasure in the arms of a woman—since Madeline had broken his heart before he went off to fight for his king and country.

A picture of Madeline's beautiful face and long blonde curls passed through his mind and was ruthlessly dismissed. When she'd married the old Duke of Marley for money, he'd put her out of his heart and mind. At first he'd been angry, bitter, broken by her scorn and her betrayal, but then he'd found something more worthwhile—and that was the camaraderie of his friends. It was only when he'd lost them that his heart had become encased in ice.

His one-time friends believed that he had done something careless that had led to the deaths of several of their comrades. Rupert knew that he was innocent of their charges, but he refused to explain or to tell them the truth about what had happened that night. If they could see only what was in front of their noses, then they were not worth bothering over—they were certainly not his friends and not the men he'd thought them to be. Where was the trust that should have existed between them? Where was the respect he believed he was entitled to expect? Since they had chosen to believe evil of him he would not defend himself. Let them think what they chose. He'd shut out the memory of their friendship, becoming in truth the man society believed him: a hardened rake and a ruthless card player.

'You wished to see me, Lord Myers?'

The voice was soft, but there was just the trace of an accent. Rupert turned to look at the young woman who had entered the parlour as he stood gazing out at the park. Although no beauty, she was of medium height, slim, attractive with dark hair that he knew carried tints of red in the sunlight. Her eyes were a bluish-green and her mouth pleasantly full. She carried herself well and there was a hint of pride in her face—also something else?

Did she seem wary? A little uneasy, perhaps?

'You are Miss Hester Goodrum?'

He thought there was a slight hesitation before she inclined her head. 'I am the new governess, sir.'

'Miss Goodrum?'

'Yes.' This time her voice was firm and without hesitation. 'I believe you are to be the children's mentor?'

'My uncle has requested me to be John's mentor until he goes to his college. I am also here to see that Francesca is ready to enter society next Season. She will be seventeen then and I believe arrangements will be made for her to stay with a suitable lady next spring. Until then you are here to keep her from getting into mischief.'

'I dare say I can find ways to do that, sir. Once I have established the level she has reached in her studies, we can plan a new schedule.'

'I hardly think you can expect to keep a young woman like Francesca in the schoolroom all day, Miss Goodrum.'

'I would not be foolish enough to try,' she

replied, her head up, eyes meeting his. All sign of the hesitation had gone now. 'Perhaps some poetry, music and dancing lessons would not go amiss. I imagine she already has some knowledge of French, Latin and drawing. We can find some way of making the lessons more interesting, I dare say. John may need more tuition, but I think that will be your province, Lord Myers. I am prepared to give him certain lessons if you wish, of course. I could take history and literature and mathematics. However, geography and the sciences were never my strong point, though I am willing to attempt them should you wish?'

'I am amazed you are able to offer such a wide curriculum. I am sure my uncle did not tell me you were so accomplished.'

Did he detect a hint of colour in her cheeks— a lessening of her confidence? Why? He'd just paid her a compliment, yet he seemed to have made her uneasy. For a fleeting moment she looked uncertain, but then her head came up and she bestowed a cool smile on him.

'I dare say you are able to take the boy's education to a higher degree than I could, my lord. However, I am willing to help should I be required.'

Rupert's instincts were alerted. She certainly was an unusual governess. Her manner was far from that one might expect of a woman in her late twenties who had little expectation of life other than to work for a succession of employers until she retired. This young woman did not look a day over four and twenty and she had a confident manner beyond her years, which was strangely at odds with her calling. Something about her did not ring true.

'I understand you have been employed by Lady Mary Winters for some years?'

'Yes, sir. I was her daughter June's governess until recently. Miss June has gone to Bath for a visit with her mother and aunt. She no longer requires a governess, which meant that I was free to take this position.' He noticed that her eyes seemed to be fixed on a spot beyond his left shoulder.

'Fortunately so was I.' Rupert smiled. 'We must try to keep these young rascals in order. They have been allowed to run free, I fear, and their last tutor and governess left at rather short notice.'

'I was told they might be a little difficult at times?'

'I do hope you are not frightened of frogs? John apparently has a habit of putting them in the governess's bed.'

'Ah, I see.' She smiled. Rupert caught his breath. There was something very engaging about this young woman, a way she had of hold-

ing her head and of sometimes looking straight
at you. 'Thank you for the warning. I do not dislike the creatures, but would not wish to find
one in my bed. I shall make sure to inspect it
each night before getting in.'

'If you find something unpleasant, let me
know. I'll deal with the culprit.'

'Oh, I dare say I can manage,' she said. 'My
cousin was forever playing such tricks when we
were both children. Uncle William was glad to
pack him off to E…to school.' A hint of pink
touched her cheeks. She drew breath, lifted her
head and met his curious gaze. 'Do you wish
me to prepare a curriculum for you to inspect,
sir?'

'Good grief, no. I shall leave Francesa's lessons to you. However, I think we should arrange
for her to have dancing lessons—perhaps someone will know of a local man who could come
in once or twice a week.'

'I would be happy to play the pianoforte. If
there is no master to be found, you might supply
the lack. I can teach her the steps if you would
practise with her.'

'Is there no end to your talents?'

'I…have an interest in music and dancing,
also deportment. I think I may be able to teach
Francesca how to enter a drawing room in society and how to conduct herself, to engage oth-

ers in conversation…enough so that she does not feel strange when she meets her chaperon next spring.'

'Indeed? I would not have thought you would have had much experience in the drawing rooms of society hostesses?'

Rupert saw her colour deepen and knew he'd scored a hit. It was perhaps a little unfair of him to say such a thing to her, but he had not been able to resist it. This confident young woman had aroused his curiosity. He was quite certain that she was not what she was pretending to be. Governesses did not meet the eyes of their employer so boldly nor did they have much experience of society.

'I have acted as companion to a lady of quality,' she replied, her head up. 'Besides, one is accustomed to being with ladies and young women of…breeding.'

'Tell me, Miss Goodrum—where were you educated?'

'I…my father employed a governess for me and I went to Miss Hale's school in Newcastle for young ladies for a period of two years. It was a highly respectable academy, I assure you.'

'What manner of man is your father?'

Her body stiffened. 'My references are all

in order, sir. I have them to hand if you wish to see them.'

'I am not your employer.' Rupert's gaze moved over her. 'It was just idle curiosity. You are not obliged to answer me.'

'My father ran a mine, sir. We were respectable and he was able to give me benefits that not all girls of my class receive. He died a few years ago and…I was obliged to earn my living.'

'The manager of a mine and from the North of England, I think?' Rupert nodded, pleased because he'd detected the slight inflection in her voice, especially when she was disturbed. 'You *are* an unusual governess, Miss Goodrum. I believe we shall rub along well enough—providing that I do not discover you have lied to your employer and to me.'

Her head came up at that and her eyes flashed with temper. Rupert was tempted to laugh. He'd thought her merely attractive at the start, but he was beginning to see that there was much more to Miss Hester Goodrum than met the eye. He would swear that there was fire banked just beneath the surface.

'Was there anything else, sir?'

'Oh, yes,' Rupert replied with a smile. 'I believe we've only just begun, Miss Goodrum. However, we shall leave it for the moment. You

will do me the honour of dining with me this
evening, I hope?'

For a moment she hesitated, then she gave
him a straight look that took the wind out of his
sails. 'As I am sure you know, that would not
be appropriate, Lord Myers. A governess may
be asked to dine with the family on occasion,
but only when the mistress of the house is present—and certainly not alone with a gentleman.'

'How disappointing. Now you are being a
proper governess. I had hoped we might get
to know each other better. Besides, Francesca
and John will be dining with me. Did you really
imagine I was asking you to dine intimately,
Miss Goodrum? I assure you I would only do
that if I had seduction in mind.'

Now the colour was high in her cheeks. She
took a moment to control herself, as if afraid
of speaking too quickly and betraying herself
into unwise words.

'I think you like to mock, sir. I am certain
you had no such thing in mind. Why should
you?' She hesitated, then, 'If Francesca is to
dine with you, perhaps I should also be present. You may be here as John's mentor, but you
are a single gentleman and Francesca is an impressionable young girl. I think I must act as
her chaperon.'

'How wise of you to change your mind,' he

murmured softly, adding, as she left, in a voice she could not catch, 'And who, I wonder, will chaperon you, Miss Goodrum?'

Chapter Three

Sarah went straight up to her room. Mrs Brancaster had asked her to return to her sitting room after the interview, but she needed a little time alone to calm her nerves. When she'd suggested that she change places with Hester Goodrum she had not dreamed she would have to run the gauntlet of those steel-grey eyes and that razor-sharp mind. Lord Myers was a man of the world and very intelligent. As herself, Sarah would have felt his equal, well able to parry any darts he fired at her, but she was at a disadvantage because she was here under false pretences. Lord Myers had warned her that he would not take kindly to lies on her part and she could imagine what he would think and say if he discovered the truth.

Cold chills ran down her spine. What on earth would she do if she were exposed as an impostor? It would be so very embarrassing and could ruin her reputation. For a moment she was tempted to turn tail and run away now before she was dragged into something beyond her control, but pride would not let her.

No, she was doing nothing wrong…not terribly wrong anyway. Having embarked on her masquerade, she could at least stay to greet the children. If the challenge became too much for her she could always hand in her notice and leave and no one would be any the wiser. Besides, it was unlikely that anyone she knew would visit Cavendish Park and, providing she gave good service, her employer would have no cause for complaint.

Having calmed her fears, Sarah changed into a fresh gown. It was clean, neat and clearly the kind of plain no-nonsense dress that a governess would be expected to wear. She pulled at the bodice because it was a little tight across her breasts. Although of similar heights, she and Hester were of a different build, Sarah being rather more curvy.

However, the dress fitted well enough and perhaps she would have time to let out the seams a little. Had she been impersonating a maid there would have been a uniform but governesses were expected to provide their own gowns.

Sarah wondered how much Hester had been promised as her wage. It was one of the many things she hadn't had time to discuss and now regretted. Money was not a problem for the moment, because she still had several guineas in her purse and would need very little while she stayed here. She might miss her clothes and favourite pieces of jewellery, but had decided to have her trunks stored until further notice. Had the housekeeper decided to investigate her closet, it would not have done to have a dozen silk dresses hanging there. Mrs Brancaster would have immediately thought the worst, because there was only one way a governess could come by such gowns.

Hester Goodrum had given her the reference from Lady Mary, also the schedule she'd intended to set for Francesca and John. A swift perusal had left Sarah feeling that it was sadly lacking in imagination and she made a few notes in the margins of lessons she thought a young woman might enjoy.

Making her way downstairs to the kitchens, she heard voices and, since her name was mentioned, hesitated outside the door.

'What do you think of her, then?' a woman's

voice asked. 'Will she last longer than a month, do you think?'

'Well, Cook, all I can tell you is that she seems very sure of herself—and that's what I told his lordship. She's not like any of the others so she might just succeed where they failed.'

'I hope as you're right, Mrs Brancaster. Those young devils were in here earlier and they took all the cake I'd baked yesterday and I had to start all over again.'

'Well, let's hope she can keep them in order—' Mrs Brancaster broke off as Sarah opened the door and walked in. 'Ah, there you are, Miss Goodrum. We were just talking about you, wondering whether you would settle here.'

'It is a lovely house and the grounds are magnificent,' Sarah said. 'Have Miss Francesca and Master John returned yet?'

'I believe they went upstairs just a few moments ago. His lordship said we're to serve tea at the normal time—and he asked that you should join them in the drawing room. Says he's going to introduce you to your pupils.'

'Oh…' Sarah's heart hammered in her breast. 'I thought I was to have tea with you, but if I've been summoned… Where is the drawing room, please?'

'You recall the parlour? Well, the drawing room is at the far end of the corridor and looks out over the park. Shall I send one of the maids with you?'

'No, I dare say I can find my own way.'

'Well, Miss Goodrum, I'm pleased you've come,' Cook said, wiping her hands on her apron. 'In my opinion it's time those youngsters were taught some discipline.'

'I shall do my best to make them behave, but I can't guarantee it.' Sarah smiled. 'I think Lord Myers will soon have Master John under his control. I hope I may have some success with preparing Miss Francesca for her future role.'

'She's been allowed to run wild and that's the truth of it,' Cook said. 'Their grandfather has spoiled them too much in my opinion.'

'Well, perhaps they just need someone to take an interest in their needs. If you will excuse me, I shall find my way to the drawing room before they ring for tea.'

Sarah left the kitchen and walked up the back stairs, letting herself out into one of the back halls. For a moment she looked about her, trying to get her bearings. Had they turned left or right for the parlour? It was a large house and if she took a wrong turning she might lose herself.

'If you're looking for the drawing room, Miss Goodrum, you turn to the right,' a voice said. Sarah turned and found herself being addressed by a footman. He was young and attractive, with dark blond hair and blue eyes and his smile was friendly.

'Oh, thank you,' she said. 'I visited the front parlour earlier, but couldn't quite recall which way to turn.'

'It's easy enough once you get used to it,' he said. 'I'm Trevor Bent, Miss Goodrum. Your name is Hester, isn't it?'

'Yes, but I don't like it,' Sarah said, her cheeks faintly pink. She hesitated, then, 'My father called me Sarah. I prefer the name, if you don't mind.'

'I don't mind,' he replied and grinned. 'May I call you Sarah—or am I being too forward?'

'I don't mind at all,' she said. 'Thank you for your help, Trevor.'

Turning in the direction the footman had pointed out, Sarah was pleased by the respectful admiration in the young man's eyes. He seemed to like her and it was refreshing to know that he had no idea that she was rich. She was tired of being courted for her fortune—and, of late, a certain person's pursuit had been nothing short of menacing. He was determined to push her into marriage and she was equally determined to resist—but her uncle and aunt were on his side, forever telling her what a good husband Sir Roger would make.

'He's a gentleman,' Uncle Matthew had told

her. 'He won't interfere in the running of the mills, but he'll be there at your side to give you more authority. A woman alone can't hope to mange everything your father left you.'

'But I told you what he did—that he is a rogue. How can you say he would make a good husband for me?'

'Reformed rakes make the best husbands,' her aunt had told her with a foolish and rather coy smile. 'I dare say he got carried away a little at the party by his love for you, Sarah. Gentlemen can be like that sometimes.'

'Love is neither here nor there,' her uncle had said. 'A woman should be married and caring for her children, not managing the mills. Sir Roger has mills of his own and would take the burden from your shoulders.'

It was no use telling her uncle that Sir Roger left his mills to the care of neglectful overseers and was in danger of losing them—or that she would never subject her people to the kind of treatment they received from Sir Roger's managers. Of course, Sir Roger never went near them himself. He was far too busy enjoying himself in London—and no doubt he imagined her money would allow him to continue with the life he desired.

Sarah had bitten back the hasty retort that rose to her lips. She had been managing her mills alone quite well, with the help of her managers. It was true that she had found it time-consuming, giving her little leisure for herself, which was why she'd decided to take this time out. Yet she would hate to relinquish them to a man like Sir Roger.

As she approached the drawing room, she heard the sound of voices raised.

'Why doesn't Grandfather come himself?' a girl's voice said on a truculent note. 'John and I are tired of being given boring lessons and told to get on with them. We want to see other people—to have some fun.'

'Well, you have me now. I think John is old enough to start fencing lessons and I'll teach you how to shoot—and we'll go fishing and play cricket, but of course you will have to do some lessons. Your governess will take you for those, but I'll take you both for drives into town. If you behave yourselves, that is.'

'What about me? Why should John have all the fun while I get stuck with a boring governess?'

'I'm afraid that is a woman's lot in life,' Lord Myers said, but with a teasing note in his voice. 'I dare say Miss Goodrum may allow you some fun if you behave.'

'We don't need her here. Why can't we just have…?'

Sarah walked into the room. A very pretty fair-haired girl and an equally attractive youth were standing in front of the open hearth with Lord Myers. They looked cross and upset, a contrast to the carefree children she'd observed in the grounds. The girl's English-rose colour heightened as she turned and saw her.

'Ah, here is Miss Goodrum,' Lord Myers said into the hushed silence. 'As you can see, ma'am, the truants have returned. I have decided they will receive no more than a warning for this day's escapade, but I shall not be so lenient in future.'

'I dare say no harm was done,' Sarah replied. 'It was a perfect day for fishing after all. Since we did not arrive until half the day was done, it would have been a shame to waste it all indoors. I am hoping to walk with you both on pleasant days. There is no need to sit at a desk to learn. We can observe nature and practise our Latin verbs while on a walk, John—and I think you, Francesca, may find the discussion of your favourite poets as interesting in a meadow as a musty schoolroom.'

The girl's cheeks went white and then pink. She was clearly undecided whether to show appreciation or hold on to her reserve.

'Mr Morton made me spend the whole morning doing exercises while he sat in his chair and read a book,' John exclaimed indignantly. 'I want to play games and do things.'

'So you shall.' Sarah and Lord Myers spoke at the same time. 'There are many ways to learn,' Sarah finished while the mentor looked at her through narrowed eyes.

'What about me?' Francesca gave them a sulky look. 'What am I supposed to do?'

'Learn some manners for a start,' Lord Myers said. 'You've neither of you welcomed Miss Goodrum to Cavendish Park.'

'She didn't have to come here.' Francesca said rudely. 'I'm too old for the schoolroom.'

'That is why I intend to teach you to dance,' Sarah said, unruffled by the girl's sulky manner. 'We should discuss society and what kind of people you may encounter—and the conversations you may have with friends and acquaintances. Also, you will need to know how to spot a rake and how to avoid being compromised by ruthless gentlemen.'

Francesca's eyes opened wide. She stared in disbelief, her mouth slightly parted. 'What did you say?'

'We shall naturally discuss poetry and literature and you will need to practise your drawing, embroidery and the instrument of your choice—but learning to dance, to enter a room, to curtsy and to hold your own when a gentleman flirts with you is very important. You will need those skills before you have your Season.'

'You don't want me to write an essay on the decline of the Roman Empire or conjugate French verbs?'

'I imagine you've had a varied and extensive education. We can discover the boundaries of your knowledge together in conversation. A young woman of fashion must be able to converse intelligently, do you not agree, my lord?'

Sarah risked a look at Lord Myers, who was watching her with narrowed eyes. She was not sure whether they expressed suspicion or disbelief.

'Most young ladies of my acquaintance are too missish to say boo to a goose. They repeat phrases parrot-fashion and then lapse into embarrassed silence if asked a question.'

'Too harsh, my lord!' Sarah laughed, her face lighting with amusement. 'Well, I shall hope that Francesca will have more to say for herself on her debut. If she has not, I shall have failed in my duties.'

'Remarkable...' Lord Myers's eyes held a look of calculation. 'Francesca, I think you have been more fortunate than any of us imagined in your new governess. My only question is—how did Lady Mary ever bring herself to part with you?'

Sarah refused to lower her eyes. He was probing, trying to get beneath her skin, but she would not allow him that privilege.

'Lord Myers is using mockery, Francesca,' she said in a calm and composed manner. 'Were I a young woman of fashion I might do one of two things. If I wished to encourage him, I might give him an enigmatic smile and flirt with my fan—or, if I wish to discourage his advances, I should raise an eyebrow and move on without answering.'

'Here endeth the first lesson,' Lord Myers drawled. 'It is actually good advice, Francesca. May one ask which you would have chosen, Miss Goodrum?'

'I shall leave that to your imagination, my lord,' Sarah replied, but was relieved when the door opened and the housekeeper entered accompanied by two maids, each of whom carried a tray. 'Ah, here is our tea. Would you like to play the hostess, Francesca?'

Francesca shot her a nervous look, but took her seat next to a small occasional table. Mrs Brancaster set up her butler's tray, exchanged a few words with Lord Myers, looked curiously at Sarah and left, taking one of the maids with her.

'You are aware that you begin with the lady of first rank,' Sarah told Francesca as her hand hovered. 'However, since I am the governess, you should begin with Lord Myers and then me and then your brother. Were there several ladies of rank you should attempt to serve the highest rank first and then, when all the ladies are served, go on to the gentlemen and begin again in the same way.'

'Miss Goodrum may be correct,' Lord Myers said. 'But in my opinion ladies are always first—of whatever rank. You may serve Miss Goodrum tea first, Francesca.'

Sarah shot a look at him, but did not contradict him. 'I take my tea with lemon, no milk or sugar,' she said and smiled as Francesca lifted the heavy pot. The girl's hand trembled slightly but she accomplished the ceremony without accident, handing the cup to the maid who delivered it to Sarah, and serving Lord Myers next. He asked for milk and one sugar and then accepted a sandwich and fruit tartlet from the hovering maid.

After everyone had been served with tea and cake, Francesca looked at Sarah. She inclined her head and the maid was dismissed.

'Did your last governess take tea with you both?'

'No, she preferred to take hers in the kitchen,' John answered, a trifle indignant. 'Fran and me had most of our meals in the nursery together. The only time the drawing room was used was when Grandfather came down and we had guests. Mrs Brancaster served us then—or sometimes Cousin Agatha.'

'Fran and I,' Sarah gently corrected. 'Your cousin visits you from time to time?'

'Only at Christmas,' John said. 'We've been on our own for years, haven't we, Fran?'

'Yes.' Francesca sipped her tea. She had crooked her little finger in an affected way, but as she looked at Sarah and saw that she held her cup in a more relaxed manner she did the same. 'We're both bored. Why can't we have friends here to picnics and dances?'

'We might have a dance on your seventeenth birthday. It's a few weeks before Christmas,' Lord Myers said. 'If you attend to your dancing lessons and whatever else Miss Goodrum has to teach you, you may be ready then. We might start to entertain a few visitors, though—just to dinner and cards or some such thing.'

'The weather is beautiful,' Sarah said. 'I think a picnic for your neighbours would be ideal as a way of letting people know we are receiving calls and visits. The best way to become accustomed to company is to invite them into your home. Does a picnic appeal to you, John?'

'Can we have games and races? We went to the fete at the vicarage last summer—Fran and I won the three-legged race. It was fun.'

'I am sure something could be arranged, but you must ask Lord Myers. I am just the governess. I can suggest, but it is not for me to decide.'

Sarah opened her eyes at him, inviting him to respond, her manner carefully controlled. His frown deepened and his gaze narrowed, as if he were trying to read her thoughts. Lord Myers was clearly not convinced that she was a governess.

Just how far would he go to discover the truth?

'A picnic?' His gaze moved from one eager face to another and then back to Sarah's. 'I seem to have been outnumbered. A picnic it is, then—but I shall expect you to write the invitations, Miss Goodrum. And you will organise the games, if you please.'

'I'll help you write the invitations. I know where Grandfather keeps his list of people to invite for Christmas,' Francesca volunteered. 'And we'll both help with the games, won't we, John?'

John looked at his sister and nodded. He was very much under her influence, Sarah realised. If Francesca gave the new governess her approval, half the battle would be won.

They were talking excitedly about what they wanted at their picnic. Sarah smiled inwardly while helping herself to a dainty almond comfit. This was exactly how she saw family life in the country and she was enjoying herself. However, she knew the battle was not yet won. At the moment the children were getting their own way and were therefore prepared to be amenable, but at the first hint of authority they might change like the wind.

Sarah was very conscious of being scrutinised by Lord Myers. She felt that he did not know what to make of her and was taking his time in deciding. Sarah found herself wishing that she was the governess she professed to be, because she wanted to stay here and be a part of this charmed circle.

A little shiver started at the nape of her neck as she imagined what they would say and think if they knew she was the rich Miss Hardcastle escaping from the pursuit of an overeager suitor. Would they feel betrayed or angry? Of course they would, because she'd lied to get her position here. She had no qualifications for her position as a governess, other than the fact that she had herself been schooled by an excellent governess and spent two years at a finishing school for young ladies.

Sarah hoped that Lord Myers would not discover just how expensive her school had been, because he would wonder how the daughter of a mine manager could afford the fees.

'Will you teach me to waltz?'

Francesca brought her mind back to the present. 'I shall do my best and when you're ready you may practise with your tutor.'

'My tutor?' Francesca gave a little laugh. 'Lord Myers is my cousin,' she said, making the situation clearer. 'Grandfather is his uncle.'

'We are second cousins,' Lord Myers told her. 'Your mother was my cousin.'

'Oh…' Francesca nodded. 'It's the same thing. My last governess told me that all the aristocracy were part of the cousinry—everyone is related to everyone else through marriage, if not by blood.'

'I've heard it said.' Lord Myers inclined his head. 'I'm not sure it's true—though many are related in some way. You don't have a male cousin, Francesca. I'm your nearest male relative apart from your grandfather. I have a married sister. Have you met Lady Meadows at all?'

Francesca shook her head. 'Grandfather asked her to stay last Christmas, but she refused.'

'Jane was having her first child at about that time. She had been married just over a year and wanted to rest to make certain there were no accidents.'

'Will she come for my birthday dance?'

Francesca's expression was uncertain, a little pleading, and Sarah's heart went out to her. She was surely in need of female company and advice.

'I shall certainly ask.' He looked thoughtful. 'You must not worry, Francesca. In a few months you will be out and you'll meet lots of people—ladies and gentlemen.'

'It's so long to wait.'

'You must learn patience,' he said. 'A properly brought-up young lady does not expect everything to happen to suit her. It will not be like that when you are married.'

'If I ever marry,' Francesca said and sighed.

'You will when you're ready,' Sarah assured her. 'Marriage is to be expected and hoped for in your case, Francesca—but there is no hurry. You should enjoy being courted and meeting people. Once you're out there will be dances and lots of exciting things to do. One day you will fall in love and marry the man of your dreams.'

'My last governess said I should be required to marry for money and position.' Francesca tossed her head defiantly, as if to challenge them.

'Why should you? I think that was a foolish thing to say. A girl like you will be able to take your pick. When you are invited into society you will meet lots of gentlemen, and I'm sure you'll find one that will make you happy, if you give yourself time. Do not throw yourself away on the first to ask you.'

'Have you been asked more than once?'

'Yes, several times…' Sarah answered without thinking. 'I refused because…I wasn't in love.'

'Love?' Lord Myers snorted his disgust. 'Marriage is for property and money, Francesca. Do not expect too much from life and you will not be disappointed.'

'Is that true, Miss Goodrum?'

All eyes turned to her and Sarah felt warm. She guessed that her cheeks were very pink.

'Money and property are useful, but I would prefer to live in a cottage with a man I loved than be a fine lady in a manor.'

She had given her pupil a false impression by implying that she cared nothing for money. Her own situation was entirely different—and yet she would not advise marrying for position alone.

'Of course having money is very useful,' she added conscientiously.

'I think I shall marry for love. I want more than just a convenient arrangement,' Francesca announced and her head went up as if defying her cousin to challenge her.

'I think you are wise. You should think carefully before committing yourself.'

'I shall not marry unless I fall in love.'

'You cannot throw yourself away on an adventurer,' Sarah said. 'But I would hold your heart in reserve until you find someone who will show you love rather than mere affection.'

Francesca was silent, but obviously thoughtful. Lord Myers was frowning, perhaps shocked by the new governess's unconventional opinions. Sarah realised that she was speaking her mind, but perhaps in a way that might not benefit her pupil.

'Of course you would wish your husband to be a gentleman and of reasonable fortune.'

'So love in a cottage might not be everything after all?'

Lord Myers threw her a mocking look that stung Sarah. She wanted to retort sharply, but decided she had been indiscreet enough for one day and merely inclined her head, as if acknowledging his hit.

After tea, Sarah asked to be taken up to the schoolroom and both Francesca and John accompanied her, leaving Lord Myers to do whatever gentlemen did until it was time to change for dinner.

Sarah glanced at some of the work her pupils

had done, thought it uninspired and dull, but made no comment. They looked at the books that had been provided and she shook her head over the lack of history and literature.

'Does the marquess have a library here?'

'There are shelves of books,' Francesca said. 'The last tutor spent most of his time there and told us it was off limits, because the books were too valuable to be touched by ignorant children.'

'Good gracious!' Sarah was shocked. 'How could he have been so impolite! I feel his attitude showed a lack of both manners and sense. I shall ask Lord Myers if we may use the library for our lessons when there are no guests staying. This room is too isolated and dark. If the library is on the ground floor, we can have the windows and doors open on nice days and take our books outside.'

'You're different,' John said, looking at her oddly. 'Not like a governess at all. Do we have to call you Miss Goodrum?'

Sarah hesitated, then shook her head. 'In company it might be wise to do so—but when we are together you may call me Sarah if you wish.'

'I thought your name was Hester Goodrum?'

'My father called me Sarah and I prefer it.' Sarah felt the open-eyed scrutiny of the young girl and guilt struck her. She had not given enough thought to this escapade before changing places with the governess. It felt uncomfortable to lie to this girl, more so than the eagle-eyed man who was here to overlook their education.

She wanted to be Francesca's friend. She sensed that the girl was lonely and needed the love of a mother or an elder sister. Sarah would like to give her friendship, to have her trust and like her—but their friendship must be based on a lie, and that hurt.

She would make up for her deceit somehow. As she heard the eagerness in the young girl's voice, Sarah vowed that she would do all she could to make her happy and to prepare her for a life in society. If things went as she hoped, no one need know that she was not Hester Goodrum and when she left them no harm would have been done.

Chapter Four

Sarah lost no time in changing for the evening after her pupils had gone to their own rooms. John was clearly excited at the prospect for it was the first time he had been allowed to have dinner in the dining room, with the exception of Christmas dinner, which was always earlier so that the staff could enjoy a little free time in the evening. Francesca was pleased, but trying hard to be grown-up and take it all in her stride.

Having changed quickly into a simple grey-silk gown, which was the only one of her own that Sarah had brought with her and suitable for dinner should she be summoned to dine with the family, she went downstairs to find Lord Myers. One of the footmen directed her to the library and she found him perusing the shelves, which were set out on three sides of the room. There were several long windows to let in the light and a set of French windows, which might be opened to allow access to the garden. A perfect room for studying.

'Forgive me for disturbing you, my lord,' she said in what she hoped was the tone a governess might use. 'I see you enjoy reading, which may make you more disposed to granting my request. I find the schoolroom inadequately provided for my pupils' education and I hoped we might have permission to use the library for an hour or two each morning.'

He turned to look at her, his eyes narrowing as they studied her. Sarah wondered if her gown was too smart. It was the simplest she had and she would not have worn it had he not made it impossible for her to refuse to dine with him.

'I am not sure what my uncle would think about his privacy being invaded should he decide to come down—but while he is in London I see no reason why we should not share the facility. I like to read in the evenings when we do not have company, but I shall be busy in the estate office in the mornings. Shall we say from nine-thirty to eleven-thirty the library is yours and the children's?'

'That is most generous, my lord.' Sarah approached the shelves. 'Is there a good poetry section? I dare say there is little new here…'

'Oh, I think you may find enough to keep yourselves amused. My uncle may not visit often, but he is a collector of books. You will not find books bought by the yard here. All of them have been read and handled—and there are a few new novels here. I imagine my uncle bought them for his niece.'

'John told me their last tutor forbade them the use of this room.'

'Then he exceeded his authority.' Lord Myers looked annoyed. 'It seems to me that my uncle has been ill served as regards to his grandchildren. They were neglected, Miss Goodrum. I do not intend that it shall happen again.'

'John will benefit from your tuition, sir. I hope I may do the same for Francesca.'

'She admires you.' His gaze was stern, his sensual mouth set in a hard line. 'You will not let her down, Miss Goodrum. I shall be watching her progress.'

'I hope to prove my worth to you.' Sarah raised her head. 'Thank you for your generosity.'

'The library should be available to all.' His gaze intensified, dwelling on her in a way that sent little shivers down her spine. 'I am not sure who you are, Miss Goodrum—but I intend to discover the truth.'

'I am not sure I understand you.'

'Do you not? Then perhaps I am wrong—but I sense a mystery. If I discover that you are not what you profess to be, I shall be merciless. As I told you before, I do not take kindly to liars.'

Sarah found it difficult to suppress the shiver that ran through her. Had she given herself away already? How could he know that she was not a governess—and what did he imagine her to be?

'Francesca is an impressionable young girl,' he continued. 'She has begun to trust you. Please do not give me cause to dismiss you. I should be loath to destroy her faith in the first person to offer her friendship.'

'I have no intention of harming either John or Francesca.'

He moved towards her, staring down into her face for a moment before reaching out to tilt her chin so that she was forced to look into his eyes. Sarah felt a tingle of some strange new sensation; it started low in her abdomen and spread throughout her body, making her feel hot. Her cheeks were warm and she wanted to jerk away, but held her ground.

'Are you an adventuress?' he asked, quirking a dark eyebrow. She could not help noticing that his mouth looked perfect for kissing and she trembled inside. A man like this was dangerous. Despite his sensual appeal, he had a look of iron about him and she feared what he might do if he guessed she had deceived them all. 'What do you hope to gain by coming here? Did you think you might capture yourself a wealthy husband? Had you heard Merrivale was a lonely old man who might fall for your charms?'

Sarah caught her breath and then the absurdity of his question made her laugh. It was so far from the truth that she felt her tension melting away.

'You have a vivid imagination, Lord Myers,' she said. 'I do not count my charms so high that I would ever seek to advance myself in the way you suggest. I am sorry I have given you such a poor opinion of my character. I assure you it is undeserved.'

'Indeed?' He bent his head and kissed her, his mouth soft and yet demanding, evoking a swift response. For a moment she felt lightheaded, her heart racing as he deepened his kiss, and she wanted to swoon into his arms. Something inside her longed to respond to his demand and she felt a rising need, a sweet heat between her thighs that she had never experienced before.

Suddenly realising that her response must be confirming his opinion of her, she placed her hands against his shoulders and pushed him back. As anger replaced the feeling of bliss, she raised her hand and would have slapped him as hard as she could had he not caught her by the wrist.

'So there is fire beneath the cool calm exterior,' he murmured and there was devilry in his eyes. 'You intrigue me, Miss Goodrum. I am not usually wrong in my first impressions and I know you have not always been a governess. You are hiding something, but I shall find you out.'

'You are no gentleman, sir,' she replied coldly. The look she gave him had quelled the mill managers who had tried to dismiss her authority when she took over her father's business empire. They had sought to cheat and ridicule her, but she'd faced them down—and she would put this rogue in his place. Even if she had felt close to swooning at his kiss—but that just showed she was a foolish spinster starved of a man's love. What on earth was she thinking of to have allowed it to continue before pushing him away? He was far from being the kind of husband she needed, were she to decide to marry. 'I am aware that you have a privileged position in this house but that does not give you the right to question my morality or to attempt seduction in this manner. If you ever behave this way again I shall give in my notice—and I shall make it plain to the marquess why I was forced to leave.'

'She has claws,' he said, looking amused. 'Come, Miss Goodrum, you did not find the experience so very unpleasant, I think?'

'You insulted me and then tried to take advantage of me. I should like to make it plain that I will not stand for such behaviour. If you feel me unsuited to the position, you may dismiss me.'

'Dismiss you?' His gaze burned her to the core and her stomach clenched. 'Oh, no, I have no intention of sending you away until I discover the truth. I thought I might find an extended visit to the country a trifle boring, but it is no such thing. I shall enjoy crossing swords with you, Miss Goodrum.'

'I would prefer that you keep your distance. We must remain on good terms for the sake of the children, my lord—but I see no reason for our paths to cross other than in their company.'

'Do you not?' He smiled oddly. 'You rest on your dignity, but it was a different matter when I kissed you. Yet I would not harm you if you are truly what you claim to be. We shall endeavour to be polite to one another for the sake of

John and Francesca—but you are the most un-usual governess I have ever met.'

'Is that necessarily a bad thing?' Sarah raised her eyes to his. 'I give you my word that I am not an adventuress, nor did I come here to en-trap anyone into marriage.'

'Shall I believe you?' He looked at her steadily. His strong features had relaxed and there was a teasing light in his eyes, as if he were playing with her, as a cat with a mouse. 'Yes, perhaps I shall. So what is it you are hiding? Are you in trouble? I might be able to help you if that is the case.'

'I am perfectly capable of looking after my own affairs.' Sarah raised her head proudly. 'I believe that was the dinner gong. We should go in or we shall keep the others waiting.'

He inclined his head, offering her his arm. 'As you say, Miss Goodrum. Please accept my apologies if I have wronged you.'

Sarah hesitated and then placed the tips of her fingers on his arm, her head high as they walked towards the dining room. She could only keep her distance and hope he would do the same.

The last thing she'd expected when she came here was to find herself having to fend off the advances of a man she suspected was a rake. Charming and undeniably attractive, he would make most female hearts flutter, but Sarah had come here to escape from the unwanted attentions of a similar man.

Had she been less stubborn she might have fled the next morning, but she had no intention of letting Lord Myers drive her away.

Rupert watched the governess across the table as she talked and laughed with her pupils. She seemed very at home, very much as if she were accustomed to dining in style, and showed no hesitation in choosing the correct glasses and silver. Her manner was calm and assured, and, apart from the dark looks she sent his way now and then, she seemed perfectly at ease. He knew himself at fault for that kiss, but she'd looked at him with such a challenge in her eyes that he'd been tempted. If she were truly what she claimed, he had wronged her, but his instincts told him that she was far from the downtrodden drudge that most women in her situation became after a few years.

The dress she was wearing this evening was far too stylish to belong to a governess. It was plain and simple, but in perfect taste, and must have cost as much as she would earn in a year. How could she possibly own a dress like that if she were what she claimed to be? It must have been given to her, possibly made to fit her—and who would give a governess such a gift? Yet it was not what he would have purchased for a mistress. Instead it had an understated elegance that a lady with refined taste might choose.

The gown had made him think she must be an adventuress, which had led him into that foolish kiss. He was here to mentor his uncle's grandchildren and the last thing he should contemplate was an affair with their governess. Perhaps a grateful employer had given her the gown, as a gift?

If that were the case, he had definitely wronged her, but it did not explain her manner. Summoned to eat with their employer, most governesses would show reserve or some awkwardness even if their manners were excellent, as hers were. No, she was accustomed to dining like this—and she felt it her right.

Only a woman who felt assured of her place in the world could be so at home in the situation he had forced her to accept. Had he met her in society he would not have placed her in the upper echelons, but she would certainly be accepted. Why, then, was she a governess? Had her family fallen on hard times? Yet if she were in desperate need of a job she would not be so confident—so assured. His suspicion deepened. Rupert had reason enough to distrust the female sex. His heart broken when he was no more than a lad, he'd never offered it again. Since then he'd amused himself with ladies of a certain kind, most of them married or widowed. A few of his mistresses had been courtesans, prepared to sell themselves to the highest bidder, and were usually not to be trusted.

Miss Goodrum did not follow the pattern for a downtrodden governess, which made him certain that she was not what she claimed. It followed that she was hiding something—but rather than fear he'd seen a challenge in her eyes. And she had responded to that kiss.

Her manner had aroused Rupert's hunting instincts. He found her intriguing, and, yes, had he met her in other circumstances, he might have attempted to make her his mistress.

Who was she and why was she here? Their eyes met across the table and he smiled, seeing the uncertainty in hers. Had he made an enemy of her? Rupert suddenly found himself hoping that he could recover the lost ground. She looked so right somehow as she laughed and teased John and encouraged Francesca. He experienced a strange emotion that he could not place—as if he had found a place of content, of belonging.

For the first time in an age he wanted to be a part of that family scene. It struck him then that Miss Goodrum was more like an aunt or an elder sister to Francesca, and the smile on her lips was both generous and sweet.

Yet there was a mystery here. He'd sensed it from the start and he took hold of his emotions, reining them in. A woman's smile could deceive so easily. He'd been burned as a young man, his pride ripped to pieces and his heart damaged. Since then he'd chosen carefully and made sure that none of the ladies he took to his bed had buried their claws in his skin.

The governess had claws. There was passion and fire beneath the cool exterior. It would certainly prove amusing to discover who she really was and why she'd come here.

What was she hiding from?

John was sent to bed as soon as dinner was over. Francesca was allowed to drink a dish of tea in the drawing room with her governess, but as soon as Lord Myers joined them, he sent her off to bed. Sarah immediately rose to her feet to follow. He caught her wrist, as she would have passed him.

The candles were burning low in their sconces and the fire had ceased to burn fiercely. Shadows seemed to creep over the room, making it feel intimate and tempting her to stay— but she must not!

'There is no need for you to leave, Miss Goodrum.'

'I think there is every need, sir. Please allow me to pass.' Sarah's heart raced at his nearness, the mystique of his scent powerful and attractive. She ran the tip of her tongue over her lips, knowing that this was a dangerous situation. She must go before he tried to seduce her.

He let go reluctantly, his expression odd and almost regretful. 'I am sorry for what I said earlier. I was testing you. You must admit that dress is not the usual attire for a governess.'

'No, I suppose not. It belongs to the time when my father was alive. He bought it for me as a gift. My father was careful with his money, sir, and he spent it on me.'

Sarah avoided his searching gaze, though her words were not far from the truth. She'd purchased the gown when her first period of mourning was over with the money her beloved father had left her and because it was a favourite she'd kept it. Had she worn some of her other newer gowns she could not have hoped to keep her secret.

'Then I apologise for casting aspersions on your character. Come, Miss Goodrum, will you not forgive me?'

'Consider yourself forgiven, my lord. I only wish to be on good terms with you.'

She deliberately made her voice flat, calm and emotionless, hoping that her reserve would make him step back.

'Then I shall not tease you again. We must not allow our charges to sense animosity between us.'

'No, that would be unfortunate,' she agreed, bringing her eyes up to his. His expression set her heart thumping. She had seen that look in a man's eyes before and it disturbed her. Normally she had no hesitation in dealing with unwanted seducers, but this man was different, more powerful and compelling than any other she'd met. 'We shall try to be easy in one another's company for their sakes.'

'May I not be counted as a friend?'

'I think you ask a little too much, sir. I hardly know you—but perhaps in time we may progress to friendship.'

'Very well. I was wrong to assume you were an adventuress—but my offer remains. If you are in trouble, I should be glad to be of service.'

'Thank you. I shall bear that in mind. Now, if you will excuse me, sir.'

'Very well. I shall not detain you against your will. I shall take John riding first thing in the morning, but he will be back in time for his lessons.'

'You must do as you think fit, sir. I believe

he has a great deal of energy that needs an outlet. Riding, fencing and other sports may help him to settle to his studies.'

'I believe so. Goodnight, Miss Goodrum. Pleasant dreams.'

'Thank you.'

Sarah inclined her head and walked on past him. Her heart had raced at his touch, but she had clamped down on her foolish emotions. Gentlemen in his position too often took advantage of female employees who could not easily escape their attentions. He had promised not to bother her again, but the look in his eyes had said something different.

She could not deny that she had felt the pull of his attraction, but he was not for her. As Miss Hardcastle she might attract proposals from gentlemen who needed a fortune to finance their extravagant lifestyles, but if she was not prepared to buy herself a husband, she certainly had no intention of becoming any man's mistress. Sarah might choose marriage if the right opportunity presented itself—but not to a man like Lord Myers.

She did not know his fortune, but she recognised the sensuality of the man, the attraction that must make him popular with ladies of his own class—and others. Sarah had no doubt that he was a physical man who took mistresses whenever he chose—and that was not the kind of man she needed in her life. Such a man could not be trusted. As charming as he was, she would never be certain that he would not stray into another's bed. Sarah knew that only a very beautiful and clever woman would capture the heart of a man like that, and she could not hope that he would want more from her than a brief affair to enliven a dull stay in the country.

Nor did she wish it, of course. When Sarah married, if she ever did, it would be to a quiet man who enjoyed books; a man who would be there if she needed him but also be content to stay in the background and allow her to continue to run her mills, should she wish to do so. Sarah had fought for the right to run her mills, but was not sure whether she wished to continue. Were she happily married with a family she thought she might be content to let her husband take over her affairs. However, she did not intend to be dictated to and told she must relinquish them entirely. She could not imagine that Lord Myers would ever be content to let his wife do something he would consider beneath her dignity.

He was a very attractive man, but his character left much to be desired from what she'd seen thus far. He would not make a suitable husband for Miss Sarah Hardcastle and might run through her fortune in an instant, given the opportunity.

She had not run away from one fortune hunter to fall into the arms of another, even if she did find him attractive. No such thing! She was not truly attracted to him.

It was merely that she had been lonely since her father died, of course. Her father had been such a loving companion and what she really wanted was someone to take his place, to care for her and watch over her, but demand little other than warm affection.

Lord Myers would not have received more than a moment's fleeting attention from her had they met in company. It was only that she was forced to live in what was undoubtedly an intimate situation with him.

What had brought him here? He did not seem the kind of man to relish the obligations that his uncle had asked of him. She would have thought him more at home in the drawing rooms of London society, rather than playing mentor to a young boy. Why should he give up his time and his way of life to come down here?

He accused her of hiding, but perhaps he too had something to hide? What had made him the man he was? Sarah wondered if some secret lay in his past. He was of an age to have been married for some years. Surely he must want a wife and children of his own—though of course she was assuming he had not for she knew so little about him. However, Francesca would surely have mentioned it if he had a wife?

So why had he stayed single? What had brought that hard glitter to his eyes and the brittle layer that hid the real man from the casual eye? He had a sense of humour, she knew—so what had made him so suspicious of her? Was it just that he did not trust women in general?

Oh, this was ridiculous! She must dismiss him from her mind for it was dangerous to allow a man like that into her thoughts.

Despite her determination to be sensible, Sarah found her thoughts dwelling too often on the handsome Lord Rupert as she undressed. She pulled down the covers on her bed, looking for any unpleasant objects that a teenage boy might have placed there as a prank, but found nothing untoward. Obviously, she'd passed her first test with the children at least.

She would forget their mentor and concentrate her thoughts on them. She was here to be of service to the children.

Francesca wasn't a child, though. She was on the verge of womanhood. In past centuries she might have been married by now; she might even have had a child of her own. To treat her as a child would be foolish. Sarah had taken to the girl and, as she slipped into bed and leaned forwards to blow out the candle beside it, she was determined to do what she could to make her life better. She would enjoy getting to know her charge and she would find it pleasant to share her own love of reading, poetry, history and even the occasional novel.

There was a wealth of books on the library shelves, including some with pictures of mythical beasts that she thought might appeal to John. Perhaps she wasn't a conventional governess, but she was quite capable of giving them both an education. Sarah loved to play the pianoforte and she thought Francesca might enjoy playing a duet with her.

Life here could be extremely comfortable and pleasant. She would be able to walk first thing in the morning if her lessons were not to start until nine-thirty. She would have liked to ride, but wasn't sure that privilege would be granted to a governess.

For a moment she felt a pang of regret. Her own horses would miss her and so would her dogs—and some of her servants. She had written to reassure everyone that she was quite safe. She would have to make sure that she kept in touch with her agents or they might become anxious about her and set up a search to find her.

Closing her eyes, Sarah drifted off to sleep, though her dreams were unaccountably disturbed by the look on a man's face.

'Who are you?' he asked. 'I shall find you out…you cannot hide from me…'

Rupert frowned as he brooded over his glass of wine after the governess had gone up. The shadows seemed to fold about him and he was aware that the room seemed empty. He was a fool to allow the woman under his skin, because very likely she would turn out to be the adventuress he'd imagined her at first. Yet something about her had captured his interest and he'd wanted her to stay after the children had gone up.

It was years since Rupert had enjoyed feminine company—other than in bed. Most society women bored him and he was wary of foolish young misses who were out to capture a husband. To have sat talking into the night with an intelligent woman would be pleasant, he thought.

In London he was seldom aware that he was lonely because he spent his evenings either at his club in the company of male friends, drinking, gambling or talking of politics and the price of stocks, or with his mistress. Had his uncle been here he might not have realised his lack, but in this situation it had come to him forcibly that his life was far from satisfactory.

As a young man Rupert had imagined that he would fall in love, marry and rear a large family, but a woman who preferred money and a superior title had shattered those dreams. He'd taken his bruised heart and damaged pride off to war and had for a time found content with his fellow officers—but when they turned against him...

Rupert's mind shied away from the memories. Mixed with the pain of seeing his men broken and dying, their blood spilling out on the hot dry earth, what happened later was too painful to contemplate. He'd shut away his pain and hurt, just as he'd shut out the humiliation he'd received at a woman's hands, determined to rise above the petty spite of others. And he'd succeeded so well that he'd come to be what he wanted others to think him—careless, stern and reserved. Rupert needed no one's approval. He was his own man, ruled by principles of iron and he answered to no one. Only a few ever saw the other side of him—a side he had almost forgotten.

Once he'd known how to enjoy the small pleasures in life. He'd known how to love, to show caring and to give and take joy from being intimate with another.

That was years ago, before he'd learned that no woman was to be trusted. They were all the same—greedy, grabbing, jealous little kittens that liked to be stroked and given a saucer of cream, but would scratch you if you annoyed them.

Undoubtedly, the governess was exactly the same, though for the moment he confessed to being more than a little intrigued, if only by the mystery he sensed in her past.

Yet she had reached out to him in a way few other women ever had, arousing feelings of need and desire with just one flash of her gorgeous eyes.

Sarah awoke when a maid drew back the curtains. She yawned and stretched, her mind still lost in dreams as she said, 'Good morning, Tilly. Have you brought my chocolate?'

'It's Agnes, Miss Goodrum—and you told Mrs Brancaster you would take breakfast downstairs.'

'Yes, of course,' Sarah said, the realisation of where she was returning with a rush. She had given herself away and could only hope the maid would not repeat her words to others. 'If I go down immediately I shall be finished by the time the family is up. I do not see why you should wait on me.'

'I've brought your hot water, miss—as Mrs Brancaster told me.'

'Thank you, that was kind.' Sarah threw back the covers. On waking she'd thought she was at home and her own maid was bringing her the hot chocolate she took every morning before she rose.

It would be a while before she accustomed herself to the life she had chosen—a very different life, but one that had its own compensations.

After Agnes had gone, Sarah washed, dressed in one of Hester's sensible gowns and, on looking from the window to see the sun was shining, decided against a shawl. Since she was walking on private grounds she saw no reason to wear a bonnet and left her room without one.

She found her way down the back stairs to a side entrance that led into a walled garden. The bricks were faded, trailed with roses and clematis, and would look a picture in a few weeks from now. However, she was accustomed to long country walks near her home and left the pleasant garden to explore more of the estate. She had insufficient time to walk as far as the village she'd seen, but would certainly do so on her day off. Hester had been promised one a month, which could be saved and taken together for visits home. Sarah would require only a few hours of freedom, perhaps in the early mornings or at night. If necessary, she might have to visit her home to reassure her anxious friends—if she continued here for more than a few weeks, of course.

Should Lord Myers discover her true identity she might find herself summarily dismissed. Sarah would be truly sorry if that happened. She had a lovely house herself and friends, but at home there was always the sense that she was being watched...that people were waiting for her to make mistakes.

She would forget her worries and enjoy her walk. The air was fresh and there was a hint of real warmth for later. Sarah walked as far as a small lake, where she watched ducks and swans gliding on its still waters. There was an intriguing wood to the right of the lake and a summer house that looked interesting. Perhaps she had found the site for their picnic, she mused as she returned to the house.

Her walk had made her hungry and she entered the breakfast room, thinking she would have it to herself, but a little to her dismay she discovered Lord Myers sitting at the table. He got to his feet as she entered, came round the table and pulled out a chair.

'I was hoping you might join me, Miss Goodrum.'

'I thought I might have finished before the family came down.'

'You will not disturb me. I enjoy company at meals and I am an early riser, unlike most of my friends, who rarely show their faces before noon.'

Sarah's cheeks were warm. She kept her back towards him as she looked beneath the silver covers and chose from scrambled eggs, kedgeree, devilled kidneys and bacon, making her choice before returning to the table.

'I did not wish to make more work for the maids by having my breakfast brought up. Mrs Brancaster thought it would be suitable for me to take my meals here since you invited me to dine last evening.'

'Why make more work for the servants? I've told John and Francesca that they may join us for all meals. We are a small family, Miss Goodrum, so why not make the most of each other's company?'

'It seems ridiculous to have meals taken to the nursery when we do not intend to spend much time there.'

'Exactly. Others may find the practice unconventional, but I can see no reason why the children of the family should not join their parents—unless they are ill-behaved and would annoy the guests.'

'We have no guests....'

'How perceptive of you, Miss Goodrum,' he said and there was a gleam of mockery in his eyes.

'Do you enjoy mocking everything and everyone?'

'If one could not laugh at the world it would be a dull place, do you not agree?'

'Yes, perhaps.' Sarah's mouth was unaccountably smiling despite her determination to keep her distance. 'Do you intend on inviting guests to stay?'

If he did so she would need to change her arrangements, for guests would not expect to see the governess at every meal.

'We may have that picnic John was so keen on and we shall encourage people to visit for tea—but I think no house guests at the moment. Unless my uncle decides to visit; he might come down at any time, of course.'

'You were not thinking of holding a dinner?'

'Not for the moment. Unless, as I said, my uncle decides to visit his grandchildren. He told me he has no intention of it until Christmas, but he might change his mind.'

'Yes, I can see that would change things.' Sarah swallowed a little scrambled egg and a piece of kidney. She touched the napkin to her mouth and glanced at him. 'Would it be rude of me to ask why a gentleman like you would agree to be John's mentor for six months? I should have thought you might prefer to be in town—or have business at your own estate.'

'Should you?' His brows rose. 'I see no reason why I should answer your question, but I shall tell you that my estate is within a day's ride should I need to visit it—and I do have agents and managers to run it for me.'

'Yes, of course, but there is always some little detail needing attention, do you not find? Things that only you can decide...' Sarah dipped her head as his eyes narrowed in suspicion. 'My father always said he could not leave his business for long...'

'I thought you said he was a mine manager?'

'Yes, he was,' Sarah agreed. 'He was always very busy and had little time for his family. Especially after my mother died.'

'Was that long ago?'

'I was twelve at the time. I grew closer to my father and sometimes accompanied him on...' She had been going to say journeys, for her father had travelled between the mine and the mills. 'On his way to work,' she finished lamely.

'That was before you went to school?'

'Yes, I had a governess. She did not approve of me spending so much time at the m...mine.'

Again she had been going to say mills and bit back her words. This was a dangerous subject and if she were not careful she would betray herself.

At that moment the door opened and both John and Francesca entered. After exchanging greetings with Sarah and Lord Myers, they went to the sideboard and began to choose from the various dishes. John was clearly impressed by the choice and spent some time filling his plate.

'Can you eat all that?' Sarah asked. 'You must remember that we shall eat nuncheon later—unless we just have some fruit and biscuits? I thought we might ramble later this afternoon. We can collect wild flowers and stones, things that we can draw or make into a collection. If Lord Myers has no other plans?'

'I couldn't resist,' John said honestly. 'We never get all this in the nursery. I should like to go rambling if Rupert has nothing else planned.'

'As a matter of fact, I had planned that we should start your fencing lessons after nuncheon. We shall spend an hour teaching you the first moves and then I had thought you might wish to play a ball game on the lawn. However, you may go walking after the fencing lesson if you prefer.'

'No, I'd rather stay with you,' John said and

attacked his food as if he had been starved for the past year.

'Better slow down a bit,' Lord Myers advised and John immediately sat back, chewing more thoroughly.

'I'd like to play ball games,' Francesca said. 'I'd like to watch the fencing, too—but it may be best if I wait until John has learned a few moves. We could ramble for a while and then come back and join the others, couldn't we, Sarah?'

'Yes, of course,' Sarah said and saw Lord Myers's brows shoot up. 'I told Francesca she might use my preferred name when we are alone, my lord.'

'Indeed, Miss Goodrum?' He looked at her through narrowed eyes. 'I thought your name was Hester?'

Sarah felt her cheeks growing warm. 'I never liked the name and my father had a pet name for me. It was my mother's name also....'

'I see. Are we all allowed to call you by this…pet name? Or is it only for Francesca?'

'In company I think it would be best if I remained Miss Goodrum. I leave the rest to your good sense, Lord Myers.'

'Ah, I see.' A gleam appeared in his eyes. 'I shall give the matter my full attention, Miss Goodrum.'

Sarah felt her cheeks flame. Had they been alone she might have made a sharp retort, but decided to change the subject.

For the remainder of their meal, she addressed her remarks to John and Francesca and was relieved when Lord Myers got up and excused himself.

'I have some estate business to attend to while I am here,' he said. 'I shall see you after nuncheon, John—and we shall play some kind of ball game on the lawns at about three this afternoon.'

Soon after he departed Sarah left the others to finish and went to the library. She had chosen the books they were to discuss by the time Francesca and John arrived. Having found a bestiary for John to peruse and some poetry books that she thought Francesca would like, she spent the next half an hour reading poetry. As she chose a poem that told of daring deeds and men's lives laid down on the field of battle, she was not surprised that John paid full attention to her reading.

'It was a brave thing Horatio did in laying down his life for the men he fought with, wasn't it, miss?' he said when she put down the book. 'I think I should like to be a soldier and fight for honour and glory.'

'Perhaps you will when you are older.' Sarah smiled at him. 'Now I am going to read a romantic poem for Francesca's sake. You may wish to peruse your bestiary, John—but I should like you to write me a short piece about the battle scenes we just discussed in your own time. Can you do that for me?'

'Yes, miss. May I write it as a story?'

'If you wish. Yes, I think that would be an excellent idea.' She opened her book and smiled at Francesca. 'This is Colonel Lovelace's letter to Lucasta on the eve of Battle. Although it has the same theme, it is romantic and I think you may enjoy it.'

She began to read, noticing that although John had opened his book, clearly disgusted at the idea of a sloppy romance, he soon began to listen to the poem and the others Sarah read to them.

'For your essay I would like you to write about what romance is—and what you think Lucasta meant to Colonel Lovelace to make him write such a poem, Francesca.'

'Oh, yes…it was so romantic,' Francesca said and sighed. 'Love is a wonderful thing, is it not? Have you ever been in love, Sarah?'

'No, I haven't. I loved my father, but I think being in love is very different.'

'How does one know whether love is real?'

'I am not sure—but I think when it happens one feels it in here.' Sarah placed a hand over her heart. 'If you think it is happening to you one day, you must give yourself time to be sure, Francesca—but I think you will know in your heart if it's real.'

'Men can let you down, though, can't they? I heard about one of the servant girls...' Francesca glanced at John, who appeared to have his nose firmly in his book. 'Something happened to her and she was sent away in disgrace. I asked Mrs Brancaster why and she said a man had let poor Alice down. I wasn't sure what she meant.'

'Ah...' Sarah swallowed hard. She hadn't realised the girl was so innocent. 'That is something we ought to discuss another day—perhaps in private.'

'It meant she was having a baby and she wasn't wed,' John said, proving that his ears were still listening even if his nose was in the book. 'Timothy the groom told me Alice wouldn't say who the father was, but he thought—'

'Yes, well, perhaps it is best if we do not speculate on such matters,' Sarah said. She herself had learned from her old nurse where babies came from when she was sixteen and one of her father's maids had also been dismissed for having committed the terrible sin of lying with one of the grooms.

'I sort of knew that,' Francesca admitted. 'But not why she was in trouble... I mean, what made her?'

Sarah's cheeks were warm. 'There are a few books on anatomy, which might explain how it works. However, making babies happens when a man and a woman make love—and that starts with kissing. There is more, which it would not be appropriate for us to discuss at the moment—but it is the reason your mama would have told you not to let men kiss you, if she were still here.'

'Mrs Brancaster said something of the sort, but I didn't understand her. If people are in love, why is it wrong to kiss and make babies?'

'I dare say it is not wrong. In fact, it is perfectly right and natural—but society and the church say that it must only happen when the man and woman are married. That is why Mrs Brancaster said poor Alice had been let down by a man. He may not have wished to marry her after...afterwards.'

'Then he was unkind and cruel,' Francesca said. She frowned. 'I think I should like to read those books on anatomy, please.'

'I will find them for you.' Sarah got up and went to the shelves. She ran her finger along them and took out two, which after looking at the pictures, she judged to be matter-of-fact tomes, which dealt with such matters. She handed them to Francesca. 'This explains how it happens and the workings of a woman's—and a man's—body but not why. If the attraction is there, feelings are aroused...but you should never give in to them before marriage. If you did so, you would lose your reputation and you would never find the kind of husband your family would wish you to have. Also, you would be shamed and many hostesses would not admit you to their drawing rooms.'

'Yes, I see.' Francesca put away the books along with with her poetry volumes just as the bell sounded for nuncheon. 'I should go to my room first. Thank you, Sarah. I've learned more this morning than I did in all the time my last governess was here.'

'But I saw some of the work you did with her. You can write quite well in French, Francesca, as well as being advanced in your Latin verbs.'

'What good will such things do me in life?' Francesca asked. 'Someone told me gentlemen do not like clever girls. I need to know about love and having children.'

Sarah made no reply. The morning had proved more eventful than she'd intended and she was busy with her thoughts as she ran up to her room to wash her hands. Both of her pupils had lively enquiring minds and it seemed they were thirsty for knowledge. She had answered their questions honestly, but she wasn't sure that her teaching was exactly what their uncle might wish them to learn.

Nuncheon was a pleasant interlude. No one was particularly hungry and Sarah noticed that Francesca followed her lead and ate mostly fruit, drinking a pleasant cordial and eating some gooseberries that were deliciously ripe and stewed with a rich pastry crust and custard.

After the meal John departed with his mentor to begin his fencing lessons and Francesca took Sarah on a long ramble about the estate, showing her parts of it that she had not yet ventured to alone. As they walked, Sarah explained more of how babies were made and what she knew of love, which was, she admitted, very little.

'I have felt tempted,' she said when Francesca pressed for more. 'But I knew it was wrong. I have been asked to marry, but as I had no feelings for the gentleman I refused. I should not want him to kiss me—or do any of the other things of that I have been told, but have no experience.'

'I just wanted to know what Alice had done to be sent off like that,' Francesca said. 'It

doesn't seem fair that she lost her job, but he—
well, she wouldn't tell anyone who it was.'

'She was being loyal to him, but I think it a
mistake. If he promised her marriage, he should
have been made to wed her.'

'But he might have lost his job, too. Mrs
Brancaster said that the maids were not allowed
followers.'

'You can understand why. If they get into
trouble, they have to leave and then the housekeeper has to train a new girl.'

'Yes, I see that—but why not let her stay
until she has the baby? Afterwards, she could
work part of the time, couldn't she?'

'I dare say Mrs Brancaster is doing what she
thinks right. You see, Alice had been immoral
by her standards—and that is how most people see it.'

'Do you not think it unfair?'

'Well, yes, I do. However, one has to live by
the rules, Francesca. If it had happened to a girl
in my employ, I should have tried to help her—
but she would still have had to leave, because
of the example it sets to others.'

'I still think it's unfair,' Francesca said. 'I
liked Alice and I cried when she left.'

'Yes, I can see that it would upset you. I dare
say Mrs Brancaster did not like to do it, but
she might have lost her own job if she had ne-

glected her duty. Your grandfather would not have wished for a girl like that to continue in his service. It's the way of the world and we shall not change it.'

'Women can't change anything, can they? Men rule our lives. If we have a fortune, our father or guardian controls it until we marry and then our husband takes over and it belongs to him.'

'Not always…' Sarah frowned, because her uncle had tried to control her and failed. 'If a woman has a fortune and is strong enough and clever enough, she may control it herself.'

Francesca was silent, as if absorbing this knowledge.

Sarah hesitated, then, 'My father was not a poor man, Francesca, and what he had he secured to me in his will. It remains mine even if I marry.'

'Why do you work as a governess if you have some money of your own?'

'Because it suits me. I have done other things—but I wanted a change of scenery and…I came here on a whim, but when I met you and John I knew I wanted to stay.'

Sarah took a deep breath as she waited for the girl's reaction. She had told her as much as she dare and felt better for it. Francesca did not know the whole truth, but Sarah no longer felt so guilty over deceiving her.

Francesca looked at her curiously. 'You're not like any governess I've had before.' She tipped her head to one side. 'Do you have a secret, Sarah?'

'Yes, there is something—but I would rather you did not tell your uncle, because he might send me away if he knew.'

'Are you in trouble?'

'I am hiding from a man who is trying to trap me into marriage. I do not like him, but my family thinks it a good marriage. I came here to avoid him while I consider what I should do.'

Francesca's gaze narrowed. 'You're not truly Hester Goodrum, are you?'

'My name is Sarah Hardcastle,' Sarah said. 'Hester wanted to get married. I gave her a little money and exchanged places with her. Do you think me very dreadful to have deceived you?'

'No, I think you are amazing.' Francesca looked thoughtful. 'Lord Myers would send you packing if he knew—and Grandfather would not be pleased, but I want you to stay. You tell us the truth instead of making up lies to protect us from what we want to know.'

'I suppose I do have different ideas.' Sarah looked at her awkwardly. 'Do you feel compelled to tell your uncle? I know you ought, but if you do I must leave.'

'It will be our secret,' Francesca promised. 'I shall not tell John, because he would be sure to let it out. My uncle may be angry when he discovers the truth.'

'I have told myself that if I give you a proper education I am doing no harm.'

Francesca laughed. 'I do not care who you are, Sarah. I do not think you mean us any harm—and I want you to stay. You are my friend.'

'Yes, I should like to be that,' Sarah said. She glanced at the little silver watch pinned to her gown. The time was getting on. 'We'd better return or we shall be late for the games.'

'Yes.' Francesca's eyes sparkled with mischief. 'I shall enjoy keeping your secret, Sarah—it's fun.'

Sarah smiled. When Francesca had guessed so much she'd felt compelled to tell her the truth and was glad she need not lie to at least one member of the household—but was she setting a bad example by encouraging her pupil to keep secrets from her uncle?

Perhaps she ought to confess the whole to Lord Myers and leave the decision to him—yet the house was so beautiful and she'd already become fond of her pupils.

Surely she could not harm people she wanted only to help?

They returned to the house, speaking only occasionally. Francesca was deep in thought and Sarah had her own thoughts to keep her busy. Being a governess had seemed such a simple matter, but it was no such thing. Sarah had no training to guide her and she had used her own instincts, her own experience, to answer Francesca's natural questions—but had she exceeded her authority? Had she perhaps put ideas into the girl's head that her grandfather and other ladies might think wrong for a young lady of quality?

Sarah was independent because of her father's will, which had given her complete control of her fortune and his business empire. Had he willed it so that her uncle had become her guardian she did not think she could have borne her life, for she would have been hedged about by convention and would not have dared to voice her opinions as freely as she did. Was she harming Francesca's chances by teaching her to be as free in her thoughts?

The sound of laughter shattered her more serious thoughts. When they came upon Lord Myers, John and two of the footmen playing with an oval-shaped ball on the green, Sarah was intrigued, for she had not seen such a rough game before.

She watched as John caught the ball and then ran off with it, only to be pursued by his uncle, who tackled him and brought him down. John managed to pass the ball to one of the footmen, who took it and ran while the second footman tried to stop him. He was unable to and John gave a shout of joy as he threw himself down at a certain spot and touched the ground with the ball.

'A try. We scored a try,' he said. 'Well done, Jenkins. Well done.'

'Yes, good show.' Lord Myers applauded. He turned and saw the ladies, frowning for a moment before turning to John. 'I think we should play cricket now so that Miss Goodrum and Francesca can join us.'

John agreed and one of the footmen started preparing the wicket. Francesca joined Lord Myers's side and Sarah joined Jenkins and John. Apparently, Jenkins was as good at the game as at the earlier one and he was elected to bowl at Lord Myers.

Sarah had no idea what game they had been playing when she arrived with Francesca, but knew the game of cricket and was happy to field. She was forced to run after balls that went into the shrubbery several times until she suddenly saw it coming straight at her, put out a hand and caught it.

'Out. You're out, Uncle Rupert,' John crowed. 'Now it's Francesca's turn and then Mason's. We'll soon have you out, won't we, Sarah?'

'Yes, certainly,' Sarah agreed with a smile for his enthusiasm.

However, Francesca played well and scored five runs before Jenkins caught her. Mason took his turn and proved to be a clever batsman; it was some minutes before he became too adventurous and was run out for twenty-five.

A tray was brought out by one of the maids then and they all sat on blankets on the grass until John's team went in to bat. Sarah had enjoyed her glass of barley water and was on her feet again when Lord Myers came over to her.

'I should like to speak to you in the library before you go up, Miss Goodrum.' His expression was grim and Sarah's heart caught. He was angry, she was sure of it and could not for the life of her think what she had done.

Surely he had not discovered her true identity?

Chapter Five

Sarah followed behind the others as they all trooped into the house. The tea ceremony had been dispensed with for the day since they'd all enjoyed cool drinks on the lawn and no one was hungry. Sarah would have liked to escape to her room to tidy herself, but a look from Lord Myers sent her straight to the library. He followed her in and closed the door behind him. One look at his face made her catch her breath.

'What is this I hear about your lesson this morning, Miss Goodrum? Can it be right that you condoned the behaviour of a maid who was dismissed for immorality—and did you really give Francesca books that described the procreation of children?'

'We were talking about poetry and Francesca

happened to say that a man could let a woman down. I hadn't realised how innocent she was and I thought it better she should know the truth.'

'And John—is he old enough to hear it like that?'

'I did not explain anything in detail and he seemed to know more than Francesca. I gave her books on anatomy, but tried to explain about feelings and the consequences of being carried away by them.'

His gaze narrowed. 'What kind of books did you deem suitable for a young woman of sixteen?'

'They have pictures, which show the workings of both the male and female body, and explain about childbirth and...the rest of it.'

'And you think that suitable reading for a young lady of quality?'

'It is better she should know than go to her wedding night in ignorance, wouldn't you say? We talked further on our walk and I was careful to impress on her the consequences of having...intimate relations before one is married.'

'Good grief!' Lord Myers seemed stunned for a moment. He ran his fingers through his thick dark hair, his grey eyes wintry. 'I was told you were an unusual governess and you certainly are, Miss Goodrum.'

'Would you prefer I'd lied? Would you have

Francesca ignorant of the facts of life? She will know now precisely why she ought not to give in to the persuasion of rakish men—and what may happen if she does. She will also be more prepared for her wedding night.'

'You take my breath away.'

Sarah swallowed hard, her hands turned inwards, the palms sweating. 'Forgive me. I did what I thought was right. I know some ladies might think I was too direct...'

'A great many men would feel the same. Such revelations would undoubtedly have led to instant dismissal in most households.'

'I did not intend it to be part of the lesson, it just happened. I realise that convention decrees that these things remain hidden from a young woman—but I think it unfair that girls should marry without the faintest idea of what to expect. In some cases the shock may damage their marriage. Besides, most girls hear it from a servant rather than their mother. John had some garbled version from a stable lad and I thought it best to be open.'

'Yes, I see that...' Lord Myers was staring at her. The heat in his eyes seemed to burn her skin. 'Well, it is over now and perhaps no harm has been done. I would ask you not to indoctrinate your charges with your radical ideas too often, Miss Goodrum.'

'No, of course not—though I feel Francesca's mother would have told her the facts of life by now had she lived.'

'In a rather different way and not in front of her brother, I imagine.'

'Yes, perhaps that is true. John did not seem surprised or particularly interested. I imagine he's heard more in the stables than he heard from me.'

'And that is to be regretted,' Lord Myers said. 'The language of the grooms is something most boys learn, but it must be tempered with proper explanation so that he understands what it means to be a gentleman. He must learn where the dividing line comes between taking one's pleasure and guarding one's honour and that of a lady.'

'Yes, of course. It is a good thing that you came here, sir. He very much enjoyed himself this afternoon.'

'I have decided that in future I shall take over John's lessons. I do not disagree that Francesca should be prepared for life—and she will be aware of the consequences, as you say—but John needs a firm hand.'

'I am sorry you feel I have let him down, my lord.' Sarah's cheeks were stinging for she felt herself at fault, though in her opinion she'd done nothing to merit such censure.

'No harm has been done that a few lessons with me cannot put right. We shall continue to have games or other pastimes that we share, Miss Goodrum, but I no longer want John to join you in the mornings.'

'As you wish, sir.' Sarah stood stiffly, her hands in front of her. She felt his censure unfair and yet understood his point of view. John did need male guidance and would do better not to gain his knowledge of the world via the stables. 'May I go now? I should like to write some letters before I change for the evening.'

'Yes, you may go,' he said, then, as she walked to the door, 'Wait a moment, Sarah— I did not wish to censure you. I felt it my duty after what John told me.'

Sarah turned to look back at him. There was no hint of tears in her eyes, though she could feel them inside. 'You were doing your duty, sir. If I failed in mine, I am sorry.'

She went out and closed the door before he could answer, hearing him curse as she did so. She was feeling subdued as she walked up to her room. Her first day had seemed to go well, but clearly she had made mistakes and aroused Lord Myers's disapproval—and that hurt. It hurt more than she would have imagined.

What he would think if he knew of her deception she dared not think. No doubt he would believe his opinion of her as some kind of adventuress thoroughly vindicated.

At dinner that evening Sarah wore her same gown. She had no other evening gown suitable and would not have dared to venture downstairs in it if she had. She had already aroused doubts and suspicions in Lord Myers's mind. Next he would be thinking her a courtesan or some such thing. She did her best to seem natural and held her head high, answering any questions that came her way, but keeping her opinions to herself. Even when Lord Myers mentioned the Regent and Francesca asked if it was true that he had been married to Maria Fitzherbert, she refrained from joining the conversation until directly addressed.

'Well, I think it was very unfair of him if he did,' Francesca said when Lord Myers merely shrugged and said he didn't know. 'What do you think, Sarah?'

'In any other case I would say it was wrong and that she had a right to be upheld as his wife—but because of the law about royal marriages it may not have been a true one. I do not know the truth of the matter.'

'If he did not truly marry her, he tricked her into being his mistress.'

'Francesca.' Lord Myers glared at Sarah.

'This is not the right subject for the dinner table. Please refrain from discussing this in mixed company. You may speak to Miss Goodrum in private on the matter if you wish.'

Francesca blushed and Sarah threw Lord Myers an angry glance. He was taking a moral stance that was hardly necessary. Such things were often discussed openly in society, though rarely in mixed company and not before children or innocent girls. He was perhaps thinking of John, for he had decided to mentor him on matters of morality. Now Sarah saw her own fault in being too easy with Francesca and looked down at her plate.

As Francesca would have protested, she reached out to touch her hand. 'Later, my dear. Lord Myers is right on this occasion.'

He threw a speaking glance at her across the table. Francesca saw it and subsided into silence. She did not speak again until John was sent to bed and they were alone in the drawing room, waiting for Lord Myers to join them.

'Are you in trouble with Uncle Rupert because of what you told me about love this morning?'

'Perhaps I should have been more wary—waited to explain until we were alone. John is young and impressionable after all.'

'Nonsense! He knows far more than I do. We

talked about everything when we were alone, but there were things he wouldn't say. He said it wasn't fit for a girl's ears.'

'Lord Myers is afraid he may have heard things in the stable that may give him the wrong idea about such things. We are to have our lessons alone in future.'

'That's so unfair of him. It wasn't your fault. You are the only person who has ever treated me as a woman—the only one to tell either of us the truth.'

'A conventional governess would not have done so. She might have given you some information in private—and perhaps it is what I should have done. Well, it is not my decision to bar John from our lessons, but I am sorry if it upsets you. I believe in speaking my mind—but it is not always wise to do so in company, especially at the dinner table.'

'No, I see that—but it was just us, family...' Francesca stared at her. 'Are you crying?'

'No, of course not.' Sarah blinked away the wetness that had unaccountably come to her eyes. 'Do you truly think of me as your family?'

'You're the sister I never had.' Francesca smiled at her. 'She would have told me the things I needed to know—especially when she was married. It's silly the way they hide things from unmarried girls, isn't it? How can we make a sensible choice for a husband if we don't understand what it means to be married?'

'Oh, my dear,' Sarah said and was suddenly amused. 'You are supposed to enjoy your Season and have fun—and you would normally ask your mama what she felt about the gentleman you liked. She would give you her advice.'

'Will you be my chaperon when we go to London? Please, Sarah. I would rather it was you than someone I didn't know.'

'You hardly know me—though I feel as if I've known you always. I doubt if I would be thought suitable. You need someone of more consequence. Besides, I shall have to leave you before then.'

'You won't let Uncle Rupert drive you away?'

'You mustn't take against him because he corrected you at table, Francesca.'

'I shall hate him if he sends you away. I'm going to tell Grandfather that I want you as my chaperon when he comes down at Christmas.'

'We'll think about that later,' Sarah said, her throat tight with emotion. Francesca was becoming so special to her and the idea of being her chaperon appealed, but of course it was not possible. Sarah could not enter society as Miss Goodrum and, as Miss Hardcastle, she would not be acceptable to the girl's guardians. 'We have lots of time before then. I must teach you

so many things—and the first is to think before you speak. Whatever we may discuss in
private, and whatever your opinion of a situation or fact, it is sometimes better not to repeat
it to others, especially in company.'

'Oh, you do not need to tell me. I was so
mortified I could have died.' Francesca turned
to her and hugged her. 'You mustn't be hurt,
Sarah. If Rupert is mean to you, I'll tell John
to put something horrid in his bed.'

Sarah laughed. 'Now that you must never do,
dearest. Besides, it might result in the cane for
John and you would not want that. Lord Myers
takes his duty seriously and I think you must
both respect his wishes.'

'I was looking at those books you gave me.
Is that what really happens? It looks awful. I
can't see why anyone would want to do anything like that…'

'I think that feelings come into it,' Sarah said
with a smile, but then the door opened and she
shook her head. 'You might wish to go up now,
dearest, and I shall follow.'

Francesca nodded. She approached Lord
Myers and bobbed a curtsy. 'Goodnight, sir. I
am sorry if I offended you earlier.'

'Good grief, child. I was not offended, but
your reputation might suffer in company. I
wanted you to be aware.'

'Yes, Uncle Rupert. Sarah has explained that I may ask her anything in private, but not speak so openly in front of others.'

'Good. Run along now. I wish to speak to Miss Goodrum.'

Francesca threw a speaking look at Sarah and went out.

'Miss Goodrum—' Lord Myers stood looking at her uncertainly. 'Will you honour me with a game of chess this evening? You do play chess, I hope?'

'Yes, my lord. My father taught me. I played often with him.'

'I thought that might be the case. Will you oblige me?'

'If you wish.'

'I do wish. I also want to apologise for my display of bad manners earlier. I did not intend to squash the child—and I thank you for putting things right.'

'It was a misunderstanding all round, my lord. I do not think it will happen again.'

'I suppose I cannot prevail on you to call me Rupert in private?'

Sarah hesitated, then, 'I hardly think it wise, sir. If I could add uncle I would do so, as the others do, but I cannot—and so I feel that it would not be right.'

'Make it sir, then. I cannot stand to be my

lorded all the time. I would even prefer Captain Myers, as I was known in my army days.'

'Yes, sir. You were in the army?' Sarah asked politely, as she set out the beautiful ivory-and-ebony chessboard with delicate carved figures. 'I thought perhaps you might have been. My father always said it was easy to tell a military man by his bearing.'

'Indeed? I think I should have liked to know your father, Sarah.'

'Yes, you might. I think he might have liked you—he was very direct and to the point and honest.'

'Like you, I imagine?'

'I resemble my father in some ways. I cannot say all.'

Sarah was acutely aware of her lies. She was beginning to hate them and wished that she dare tell him the truth—explain why it had seemed such a good idea and why she wanted to stay here as Francesca's governess. Yet he would not understand. He would revile her for lying and worst of all he would dismiss her and install a new governess in her place.

Even though she had made mistakes on her first day, Sarah felt that she was helping Francesca. She had gained the girl's confidence and affection, too. It would hurt her if Sarah left—

and she might become sullen, taking against Lord Myers and the new governess.

Sarah was doing no harm. She would be careful in future to temper every opinion she gave with the counter-argument and explain why Francesca must conform to what society expected even though she might disagree privately, but she could not desert her.

She dismissed her qualms and brought her mind to the game. Lord Myers showed his mettle by his first few moves, but she was with him.

Sarah had learned from a chess master and she was well able to keep up her end. By the end of an hour she had beaten him twice and been beaten herself once when an early move on his part had sealed her fate almost from the beginning.

At the end of the third game, she stood up.

'I believe I should leave you now, sir. Goodnight.'

'Goodnight, Sarah,' he replied. He was on his feet, standing so close to her that she could scarcely breathe. Her heart was beating fast and she felt the heat start low in her abdomen and sweep through her. She was being drawn to him like a moth to a flame. In another moment she would be in his arms. He would kiss her and then…

She stepped back, breaking the fine thread that had bound them.

'I should go.'

'Perhaps you will let me try for revenge another evening.'

'Yes, of course, if you wish.'

With that she walked to the door and went out. He made no move to stop her or call her back, though she thought she heard a muffled groan as she closed the door behind her.

Alone in her room, Sarah closed the door, locked it and then stood with her back against it. She felt weak and knew that she had escaped by a hairsbreadth from a fate that was described as worse than death—another few seconds and he would have seduced her. She would have allowed it. She had wanted it, longed for his kiss—and what came after.

It was those feelings she'd warned Francesca of—feelings that would lead to her downfall. Even as Miss Sarah Hardcastle she would not have expected a marriage proposal from Lord Myers, unless he needed a fortune, of course. Somehow she did not see him as lacking wealth or the determination to make it if he had none. He was not the kind of man to need a Cit's daughter as a wife.

Sarah was well aware that as the daughter

of a mill owner she would not be thought suitable to marry into the best families—unless of course they happened to be desperate.

Sarah was trembling as she undressed and dived beneath the sheets. The awful thing was that she suspected she would enjoy being seduced by Lord Myers—and that would be stupid.

'Foolish, foolish, foolish!'

Yet the temptation to remain, to let him kiss her and do what he would on the rug before the fire had been strong. Why did he have this effect on her, something that no other man had before now?

She pounded her pillow. Before this, Sarah had resisted every advance, deflected every unwanted offer with ease—but something told her that if she stayed here she was in danger of succumbing to her wretched feelings. Even worse than being seduced was the fear that she might learn to care for him—and that must lead to terrible unhappiness.

'No, I shall not. I refuse to care about him,' she whispered and closed her eyes on the tears as they insisted on falling. 'I am not so silly as to care for a man who merely wants to seduce me.'

In future she would have to be constantly on her guard. Friendly but cool, even aloof.

She would be the perfect governess. In private, she would be open and friendly with Francesca, but whenever Lord Myers was around she would keep her distance.

God damn it! Rupert groaned as the door shut behind her, leaving him with the scent of her perfume in his nostrils and the want of her surging through his blood. What was it about Miss Hester Goodrum that had sent his senses haywire? He could hardly remember feeling such urgent lust before in his life. For a moment it had taken every last ounce of his strength to keep from dragging her into his arms, kissing her to within an inch of her life and carrying her to his bed.

His thoughts were outrageous and he knew it. If she was the governess she claimed to be, he would be doing her an extreme disservice and she did not deserve such treatment from him. Yet what if she were indeed an adventuress? There were things that did not sit well with her claim to be merely a governess—and why had she told Francesca to call her Sarah? Surely if her name was Hester a pet name would be Hetty or some such diminutive?

If she had been another man's mistress, then she was fair game and he would be justified in hunting her down until she agreed to be his. It was odd, but he did not wish that to be the case. Indeed, he feared that her appeal would be tarnished if he discovered that she was a schemer and a liar.

Why would she come here if she were not what she professed to be? The question bothered him, chasing round in his mind like a puppy after its tail. He could see no advantage to it—unless she hoped to seduce her employer, but she could have hardly hoped for that since the marquess was nearly three times her age and seldom visited his country house.

Was she hiding from someone or something? Had she been accused of theft or worse? Lurid thoughts chased through his mind—had she murdered her protector, stolen her employer's heirlooms or been snubbed by society?

A smile touched his mouth for he did not see Sarah as a fugitive from the law. Yet he would swear her name was not Hester Goodrum, nor had she been a governess until recently. So where was the real Hester and why had they changed places?

Yes, of course, it was what must have happened! Rupert felt certain of it, though he could see no reason for the masquerade. Sarah did not strike him as a society miss who would do something like this for a jest or a wager. No, she had a perfectly good reason for what she was doing.

If that turned out to be the case, she was a consummate liar and Rupert hated liars. His mouth thinned. In his experience women lied without thought for the harm they caused or the pain they inflicted.

He determined that he would discover the truth and unmask her and then—then he would show her no mercy. He would offer her an ultimatum: become his mistress or risk exposure and the scorn it would bring.

For a moment in his anger he dwelled on the prospect with pleasure, but then the picture faded and his expression hardened. He had never forced a woman into his bed and it would bring only a hollow victory. No, he would put the woman out of his head and, if he discovered she had indeed been lying to them, he would dismiss her.

Sarah Goodrum, or whatever her name was, would discover that she had made a mistake when she decided to try to fool him. By the time he'd finished with her she would wish she'd never been born.

It had rained during the night, which meant the grass would be wet if she chose to walk first thing. Sarah decided to forgo her exercise. Perhaps the afternoon would be warm and dry. In the meantime she would take an early breakfast and then spend some time in the library, preparing lessons for that day. She would try to be more conventional, and perhaps in the afternoon, if it were still damp, they could play the pianoforte. Francesca had told her she played, but needed help to achieve a higher standard. Since it was one of Sarah's chief pleasures and something she did well, she had hopes of achieving at least this much for her pupil.

She was the first in the breakfast room and had eaten when the door opened to admit Lord Myers. He looked at her coldly, his manner markedly reserved as he perused the chafing-dishes and then brought his plate to sit opposite her.

'Good morning, Miss Goodrum. I trust you slept well?'

'Yes, sir. I took my breakfast early since it was still wet out.' She pushed back her chair and stood, hesitating a moment. Why had he changed so much since the previous evening? He seemed a man of many moods.

'There is no need to leave on my account.' He frowned at her.

'I had finished, sir. If you will excuse me?'

'Yes, of course. You should prepare your lessons for the morning—a little more carefully today, if you please.'

'Yes, my lord.'

Tears stung behind her eyes, but she gave no sign as she lifted her head and swept from the room like a queen.

How dare he speak to her that way? For a moment anger rolled over the hurt, but then she remembered that he was here in place of her employer and had every right to address her as he chose. He could send her away if he wished.

Sarah bit her lower lip. She had no idea why he was angry with her. The previous evening she had sensed that he was on the verge of making love to her—so why had he changed so suddenly?

Obviously, he was a law unto himself. He was an aristocrat and had no interest in the feelings of a lowly governess—any more than he would in the daughter of a Cit, even a wealthy mill owner's daughter.

Sarah would be a fool to allow herself to care for a man like that—even if one of his sensual looks could make her feel weak at the knees and keep her sleepless in her bed.

She had made up her mind to keep her distance during a restless night and his manner this morning had made that easier. If they both kept their distance, except when in the children's presence, everything would be fine. She would conquer this temporary weakness and her heart would remain untouched.

Sarah would spend a few months in retreat from her own life and do what she could for Francesca—John, too, if he needed her, though he seemed to have taken to his mentor and hung on Lord Myers's every word. She would stay for as long as she could, but if life became unbearable she would leave.

Chapter Six

The rain had lasted for almost a week, making it impossible to hold the picnic John had wanted so badly. However, he spent most of his time either fencing, studying or riding with Lord Myers and seemed well pleased with the change. Francesca had told Sarah that he was learning to shoot.

'I hardly see him now,' she complained as they closed the pianoforte after an hour spent most enjoyably. 'I am so glad you are my friend, Sarah. I do not know what I should do if you were not here.'

'I dare say John will seek your company when he is ready. You must understand that this is the first time he has received the attention of a man like Lord Myers. He must feel pleased, excited and even flattered by it. After being neglected by his tutors he is suddenly of importance.'

'How understanding you are,' Francesca said and got up, wandering over to the window. 'Did you know that Uncle Rupert has decided to employ a dancing master for me? He is French and should be here any day now.'

'Oh...' Sarah bit her lower lip. Lord Myers had neglected to tell her, but then, she'd hardly seen him all week. At dinner he spoke to Francesca and John, but, other than asking if she were well and had what she needed, he had not directed a whole sentence at her for seven days. 'I had thought he might teach you himself.'

'He said he had considered it, but felt himself unable to convey the finer points. I think he finds that John takes up most of his time—and he has friends. You know he has dined out twice this week and he spent most of yesterday afternoon with them.'

'Yes, I dare say he wishes for some company of his own age, men he can converse with,' Sarah agreed. 'John was out with the groom all afternoon. I hear he is doing very well with his new pony.'

'Yes. He finds Blackie much more of a challenge than dear old Dobbie was, which was why Uncle Rupert purchased the pony for him.'

'Yes, that was thoughtful.'

Sarah could not fault Lord Myers for the way in which he was directing the youth's studies, giving him enough sports and activities to make the written work acceptable. She had paused outside the marquess's study on one occasion and heard Lord Myers reading aloud in Latin. Every now and then he'd stopped to ask John what he understood and to explain the story. His blend of authority and charm had carried John along and the boy seemed completely under his spell.

Francesca was respectful of the man she addressed as Uncle Rupert, even though he wasn't actually her uncle, but some sort of cousin.

'Rupert thought it better if I called him uncle. He says it is a matter of keeping up a respectable household that will give no one a chance to gossip about us. I told him that as long as I had you as a chaperon no one could possibly imagine there was anything improper in our domestic arrangements.'

Sarah resisted the temptation to ask what he'd replied. Since that night when they had played chess alone he had been reserved, even cold towards her, and she had followed his lead. It was better this way than allowing herself to imagine there might be something warm and exciting between them. If she had thought so a week ago, she did not think it now. She knew that it was the only way she could remain as Francesca's governess, but there was an ache in her heart that she could not quite banish.

Sarah stood up and joined her pupil by the window. The afternoon was pleasantly warm with just a slight breeze.

'I have some letters I should like to go first thing in the morning. I think I shall walk down to the Royal Oak and leave them. There might be something for me.'

'One of the footmen will take the letters in the morning and they bring back anything that has come for us.'

'Yes, I know, but I want these to go off— besides, I should have to rely on Lord Myers to frank them for me and I would prefer to pay some sixpences to send them myself. I was wondering if you would like to walk with me?'

'I think I would rather stay here and prac- tise my music, if you do not mind?' Francesca looked at her. 'You will be back in time for tea. Perhaps Uncle Rupert and John will join us today.'

'Yes, perhaps. I must go up and put on my bonnet. I shall not linger, but walk straight there and back.'

Sarah left her pupil sitting at the pianoforte and the sound of music followed her up the stairs. Francesca was still playing when she returned and left the house by a side door. She had the piece almost right, but there was one passage that she rushed every time. Sarah would show her how it should be played another day.

It was the first time she'd gone for a walk alone since it had rained. The air was fresh with the scents of early summer and the hedgerows were bright with flowers, wild roses twining amongst them and bringing the countryside alive with colour.

She had reached the village without incident and entered the inn, having noticed a horse with a white mark on its rump. She thought it might have belonged to Lord Myers, but wasn't sure. If he were here, she hoped they would not meet. It would be embarrassing if he thought she'd sought him out. As far as she'd known, he'd ridden over to a neighbour's house on some business.

She was met by the host's wife, who took her letters and asked her for four sixpences, to cover the cost of sending them post.

'It would be less if they waited for the mail coach, miss, but if you want them sent urgently it must be two shillings.'

'That is perfectly all right,' Sarah said and handed over her two shillings. 'Do you have any letters for Miss Hardcastle care of Miss Hester Goodrum?'

'Yes, as a matter of fact one arrived by post this afternoon.' The innkeeper's wife looked at her curiously. 'You're Miss Goodrum, governess to the children up at Cavendish Park, aren't you?'

'Yes, I am.' Sarah saw the curiosity in her eyes. 'Miss Hardcastle is...well, I am accepting letters for her.'

'Oh, well, I suppose it's all right, as it says "care of",' the woman said a little doubtfully. 'I normally like to be sure a letter is given to the right person.'

'I assure you I am the right person to receive this letter—and any others that are similarly addressed.'

'Is something wrong, Miss Goodrum?'

Sarah jumped and glanced round as Lord Myers spoke. 'No. I am just collecting some letters. Everything is as it should be.' She took the letter from the woman's reluctant hand as she seemed paralysed by Lord Myers's arrival and was staring at him, seemingly mesmerised.

Sarah slipped the letter, which was quite a thick packet, into her reticule, but she feared that Lord Myers might have caught sight of the wording of the address before she could do so.

'Is Francesca not with you?' he asked, walking to the inn door and opening it for her. He walked out into the yard, standing for a moment in the sunshine as she hesitated.

'Francesca wished to practise the music she is learning. I had some letters I wished to post.'

'Do you write many letters, Miss Goodrum?'

'Yes, several.'

'To your family? Or are you seeking another post?'

'I am not seeking another post at the moment. I have no reason to leave—have I?'

'Only you can know that, Miss Goodrum.'

Sarah hesitated, then, 'I understand you have engaged a dancing master for Francesca?'

'Actually, her grandfather did so himself. I wrote and said I thought it might be a good thing and he sent word that he had seen to it. I heard this morning and told Francesca. I believe he is French—Monsieur Andre Dupree, I think he is called.'

'Ah, I see. I had thought you might teach her yourself?'

'I decided it might be wiser to employ a dancing master—for various reasons. Besides, most of my time is taken up with tutoring John—and there is estate business.'

'You have been busy, I know.'

'Yes.' His gaze narrowed. 'I should be returning to the house. My business here is done—

and John should have had his riding lessons for the day.'

'Yes.' She hesitated, then, 'Francesca wondered if you would both join us for tea today. I think she misses her brother.'

'Yes, things have not quite gone to plan. We must have our picnic before the fine weather disappears again. Have you written the invitations?'

'They need only the day and date. I was waiting for your approval.'

'Then make them for this Friday. We must hope that the weather stays fine. I am told some of the strawberries will be ready for picking and that might amuse both the children and our guests.'

'It will not amuse Francesca to be called a child. She will soon be seventeen.'

'Not for a few months. I shall try to remember.' He inclined his head to her. 'I shall not keep you, Miss Goodrum—if that is your name...'

With that he walked away, leaving Sarah to stare after him in dismay. It was the first time he'd talked to her for a week, but she could not deceive herself; his manner was decidedly cool towards her. She was not sure if he was angry or whether he simply did not trust her.

Shrugging off her painful thoughts, she

walked on towards the house. She would read her letter later, alone in her room. Sarah had recognised the hand and knew it came from the agent who oversaw her mills. Since he had written extensively there might be a problem.

Sarah sighed. For the past few years she'd dealt with the problems as they arose, but it had been pleasant not to have to think of them for the past week. It might be nice to be married and leave business to her husband, but it would have to be the right man for the sake of all those who relied on her for their living. Sir Roger would squander her money and care nothing for her people. Until she found someone she could trust and like enough to marry, she would have to carry on—but her agents must manage without her for a while. She would not leave Francesca in the lurch unless she was forced.

What was she up to now? Rupert was thoughtful as he put his horse to a canter. His business that afternoon had concerned the governess and he wondered why he had not mentioned it to her. Something in her manner had been guilty and it had made him hold back the news he thought might be interesting for her. She had definitely hidden that letter and so quickly that he hardly caught sight of the lettering, but he was sure it had been addressed to someone care of Miss Goodrum.

He'd sensed a mystery from the start and now he was certain that she was hiding something. Could she be collecting letters for Francesca? Had the young girl formed an attachment before he arrived, one she now wished to hide from him? Rupert frowned. Francesca was surely too young to have a lover—would her governess be complicit in such a deceit?

Or was it simply that Miss Goodrum was not what she claimed to be, as he'd suspected almost from the start? Why had she lied about her identity?

The mystery deepened and he decided he had been right to keep his distance these past few days. To allow himself to like the governess rather more than was sensible would be to invite all manner of problems.

Whatever she was hiding was bound to be unsavoury. He felt disappointed to discover that she was almost certainly the adventuress he'd thought her at the start. She might seem innocent, delightful and charming, but she was undoubtedly playing a part for his sake—to deceive him, or to ensnare him?

The thoughts had gone round and round in his head as he had ridden rode home. Dismounting, he entered the house and immediately encountered John, who was full of his afternoon's outing. The youth's enthusiasm put the mystery of the letter from Rupert's thoughts. He told John to wash his hands and meet him in the drawing room for tea, taking the stairs two at a time in his haste not to be late.

Rupert must simply continue to keep the governess in her proper place for all their sakes. If she were truly innocent, his need to seduce her could only bring her to ruin—and if she were a courtesan it would lead to distress for Francesca.

Yet he lay restless in his bed each night, thinking of her in her chaste bed and burning with need that drove him mad. He wanted her as he'd wanted no other—and he could not put her out of his head.

Oh, damn the woman! He would not allow her beneath his skin. No woman had been allowed to ruffle his feelings in this way for years and he would not give this enchanting minx the satisfaction of knowing how she had affected him the night they'd played chess together.

'Oh, good,' Francesca exclaimed as she saw her brother and Rupert waiting for her in the drawing room. 'I'm so pleased you are to join us for tea. It isn't the same when you don't.'

'Blackie jumped the fence at Three Mile Bottom.' John's enthusiasm carried him away. 'You should come out with me one afternoon.'

'Yes, I should like that—but I'd like Sarah to come as well. I'm not sure we have a suitable horse for her.'

'As a matter of fact—' Rupert broke off as Sarah entered. She was wearing a plain, dark-grey gown, very suitable for a governess, but somehow managed to make it look as if a lady of quality was wearing it. 'I bought one this afternoon. So you will all be able to ride together.'

'Did you hear that, Sarah?' Francesca turned to her with a smile of delight. 'Uncle Rupert bought a horse you could ride. You will ride with us, won't you?'

'Oh… Yes, of course.' Sarah smiled. 'Sorry, my mind was elsewhere. Did you say the horse was bought for me to ride?' She looked at Rupert in surprise. 'That was extremely thoughtful of you, sir.'

'Francesca wanted you to be able to ride with her. She said you were accustomed to riding when at your home—is that true?'

'Yes, I ride whenever I have the time.' Sarah's cheeks were warm as she took her seat. 'Shall you ring for tea, Francesca?'

'Yes, of course.' Francesca did so and looked

at her enquiringly. 'Is something wrong, Sarah? You look worried.'

'I had a letter that was a little worrying, a family matter,' Sarah said. 'Forgive me if my mind wanders. It was something of a shock to me.'

'No one is ill, I hope?' Rupert asked, his gaze narrowed.

'Not exactly. There is a family problem, however. I hope to avoid it, but I may have to leave for a while should things develop.'

'Oh, no, I don't want you to go,' Francesca said instantly. 'Please don't—unless you have to, of course.'

'I have no intention of it,' Sarah replied and smiled at her. 'I think the problem may be dealt with by a series of letters—but should it not, then I might be away for a week or two.'

'Is there anything I may do to help?' Rupert asked. 'Any service I could perform for you?'

Sarah's eyes moved to his face and for a moment she seemed to hesitate, but then, as the door opened to admit the maids with the tea trays, she shook her head. He waited until after the maids had retreated and then persisted.

'We could speak later in private, if you wish?'

'You are…kind,' Sarah said and looked hesitant. 'I believe I can deal with the matter myself for the moment.'

Rupert accepted a cup from Francesca's hand and helped himself to rich fruitcake, which was always his favourite. He could see that the governess was more disturbed than she would say and his sense of frustration increased.

Was she in trouble or was her friend—the friend for whom she had received that letter? It had looked more like a packet and he was curious as to what was in it. He would be most interested in reading the contents of Sarah's package.

'Why don't you all go riding in the morning?' he suggested. 'I think we might forget lessons for once. Miss Goodrum should get to know her horse and yours will suffer if you do not exercise the poor beast more, Francesca.'

'Yes, let's all go riding in the morning,' John said, excited at the prospect. 'You will come too, Uncle Rupert?'

'Unfortunately, I have some things to attend to,' he replied. 'I may ride out and join you later, once it is finished.'

'It would be pleasant to ride again,' Sarah said and some of the anxiety seemed to leave her eyes. 'Although I do not have a habit with me, unfortunately.'

'I think there may be something in Mama's

trunks,' Francesca replied and smiled at her. 'You are not dissimilar in height and build and may make a few adjustments if they are needed.'

'If we could look for it before dinner, I could make the alterations this evening,' Sarah agreed. 'Riding is such good exercise and I have felt its lack of late.'

Rupert felt pleased that he'd been able to help her in some small way, even though there was guilt at the back of his mind. With all the children out of the way he would have the opportunity to enter the governess's room and make a brief search for that letter.

A part of his mind was horrified at the idea and yet the other was telling him that as her employer's representative he had every right to discover what she was hiding.

'It was so kind of you to purchase the horse for my use,' Sarah said when she came down the next morning. She was wearing a borrowed habit, which had belonged to Francesca's mother. Sarah had taken down the hem a little, but it was otherwise a reasonable fit. Although not fashionable or exactly Sarah's style, it looked well enough. 'It is a pity you cannot come with us. I think John was anxious to show you how much he has learned.'

Rupert looked into her clear eyes and felt his guilt deepen. It would be pleasant to ride with them and he almost gave in to temptation, but his suspicions needed to be answered.

'Yes, well, perhaps my business need not take long. Which way do you intend to ride?'

'Francesca said we might ride past the water meadows and come back through the village.'

'Very well, perhaps I shall join you later on your ride.'

'I do hope so,' she said, smiled again and went to join the others. He heard the sound of voices and laughter outside as the grooms helped them to mount and the party set out.

Walking upstairs, Rupert fought down his rising sense of guilt. He paused outside the governess's room, knocked and then entered. Looking round, he saw that it was very neat, the bed made and nothing out of place. Obviously, she was in the habit of keeping things tidy and did not make extra work for the maids.

He could see no sign of any papers. The desk that had been provided for her use was empty of letters or personal items, displaying only the inkwell and pen trays, also a pad for leaning one's paper on. His heart thudding and a sick feeling in his stomach, Rupert walked to the desk. He had never done such a despicable thing in his life. Feeling like the worst sort of rogue, he picked up the pad and saw that the soft surface had indentations, but though he studied them for a moment he could not pick out any words. He hesitated, then opened the long top drawer. It was empty. Each of the first two drawers on the side was similarly unused, but in the third he found a small wooden box, which was obviously used to store papers and letters. It was locked.

Rupert glanced round the room. Where would the key be hidden—or did she have it with her? He considered making a search and then the enormity of what he was doing swept over him.

This was despicable! Miss Goodrum was entitled to her privacy and he was not behaving as a gentleman ought. If he wanted her confidence, he must earn it. Replacing the box, he closed the desk drawer and left the room. As he reached the end of the hall, he saw a maid approaching. She looked at him curiously, no doubt wondering what he was doing so far from his own rooms.

He would change into his riding breeches, walk down to the stables and go in search of his pupils and their governess.

Sarah had been pleasantly surprised in the mare she was given. It was a spirited creature

and far superior to what she had expected might
be offered to a mere governess. Lord Myers
was clearly a good judge of horses and she was
going to enjoy the experience.

She had spent some hours thinking before
she was able to sleep the previous evening. Her
agent had sent her a package containing several business matters, most of which she had
managed to settle easily in a few words. The
letter was lying unfinished in her writing box,
because she had not been able to decide about
what to do on the other matter.

Sam had told her that he had received an
offer to purchase all her mills.

It comes from a solicitor, Miss Harding.
He has not revealed the buyer's name, but
says that his client is well able to purchase
all the mills and the price he is offering is
far better than anything you've been offered before. My only hesitation in urging
you to sell would be to do with his keeping his identity secret. There are certain
men—rivals of your father—who might
decide to either shut down the mills and
sell off the property to reduce competition
for their own trade or reduce wages and
increase working hours. Your father was
widely believed too generous and some of

the mill owners thought that he had made
it impossible for them to make the prof-
its they wished, because key workers demanded the same rates as your father paid.
However, I feel that while you have managed thus far you may find it hard to main-
tain the level of efficiency needed if you
marry and have a family, as your father
would have wished. Your husband might
not have the same feeling for the workers
as both you and your father have shown.
I await your decision as always,
Samuel Barnes

Sarah knew that the price offered was a good
one. Perhaps not the full worth of the mills,
but near enough to make it a viable proposi-
tion. It would be the easy way out for her, particularly since she had been wishing to make a
change for a while. Had she been content with
her life, she would not have felt the need to
change places with Hester Goodrum.

However, coming here had made her see how
pleasant a similar life might be. She would not
wish to simply hand over everything to someone else. Even if she married, she would wish
to be informed of all that was happening and
to be consulted about any changes in the way
things were run. It had come to her of late that

in the right circumstances she could happily amuse herself with a family and friends, leaving business to her husband for the main part. If she were involved in the decision-making and consulted before the workers were put on short time—or, indeed, more were taken on, if the mill prospered—she did not need to be involved in the day-to-day running of the place.

Her uncle had always insisted she should take a husband and leave her business to him, but Sarah had felt compelled to keep her hands on the reins. She no longer felt as if she wished to spend all her life coping with the problems of running her father's business empire and would be happy to hand much of it to another.

Yet she could not simply abandon her people and her principles to someone who might abuse them. Sarah was well aware that despite rumblings in Parliament, where the plight of mill workers and others in similar jobs had been debated, nothing of any consequence had been done to force the owners to treat their people decently. Women and even children worked in terrible conditions for long hours; they were given only a few minutes' break to relieve themselves or drink some water and their mealtimes were restricted to a quarter of an hour in many cases. If they complained they were sent home and would be blacked by the other employers so that they found it impossible to get another job. The men fared little better and any that dared to speak out against the conditions might have to travel miles to find work to keep their families from starving. Sarah had recently taken in a family who had been thrown out of their home and refused work. Sam had told her that once Mr Arkwright discovered what she'd done, he would be very angry.

'Matt Arkwright is a hard man, Miss Hardcastle. He fell out with your father over the wages he paid and they almost came to blows. He'll not take kindly to you giving succour to a man he's dismissed.'

'If he does not like it, he must learn to live with it.' Sarah had shrugged off her agent's warning, but the next day she'd received a visit from Mr Arkwright. He had spent an hour haranguing her and left after issuing threats.

'You're a haughty piece, Miss Hardcastle, but you'll come unstuck. You think your wealth entitles you to act like a lady and carry on with your head in the clouds, but one of these days you'll go too far.'

'I fail to see what business it is of yours whom I choose to employ, sir.'

'We mine owners stick together. If you give these troublemakers an inch, they'll take a yard. Before you know it, we'll have rioting and people will get hurt. You've been warned, Miss Hardcastle. Think on it!'

Sarah had put the unpleasant scene from her mind. She did not think the man she'd employed was a troublemaker and had no intention of letting a rival owner tell her how to run her affairs. However, she now wondered if it was Matt Arkwright who had offered for the mills. She'd almost made up her mind to reject the offer, but if it was Arkwright she would have made herself an enemy.

Yet to allow him to destroy all her father had set out to do was unthinkable.

'Isn't it lovely out?' Francesca asked, coming up beside her. 'How do you like your mare?'

'She is perfect. Very responsive,' Sarah said. 'John is ahead of us—shall we catch him up?'

'Yes.' Francesca did not immediately suit her actions to her words. 'Are you still upset? You won't have to leave us, will you?'

'No, I shan't leave you for a while,' Sarah said. 'Come on, let's try them out…'

She touched her heels lightly to the mare's flanks and set off in pursuit of John, who had ridden on with his groom at a faster pace. She would not let the problem of the mills upset her. Although this interlude could not last long, she was determined to make the most of it for as long as she could.

* * *

Rupert saw the group just ahead of him. He had set out after them, expecting that it might take some time to catch up, but obviously they had ambled along for much of the ride. They had separated out a little, John and the groom ahead and the two girls at the rear. He saw they were just about to set out in pursuit when something caught his eye. A man was watching them, and as Rupert watched he drew out a pistol and fired in their direction.

'Look out!' The warning made the rogue's arm jerk. He turned, stared at Rupert, then set off at a run, disappearing into the trees. 'Damn it!'

Rupert saw that the shot had caused one of the ladies to fall from her horse. He was tempted to pursue the rogue who had fired at them, but knew the ladies came first. Swearing to himself, he rode up to them, his feelings mixed as he saw it was Francesca on the ground. Relieved that Sarah was all right, he was off his horse and kneeling over Francesca in an instant.

'Are you all right? Did that rogue wing you?'

'No…' Francesca accepted his hand and stood up. 'The shot went wide of us, but my horse reared and I slid off. I feel such an idiot. I should have managed to hang on.'

'Not your fault,' Rupert said. 'Have you broken anything? Do you feel any pain?'

'No, just a little bruised. I think my pride is hurt more than anything else. I thought I was a good horsewoman.'

'So you are,' Sarah assured her. 'That poacher's shot spooked your horse, that's all. Anyone could have fallen off the way you did.'

'Sarah is right,' Rupert agreed. 'You mustn't blame yourself or your horse. Damned poacher! I would have gone after him, but I was concerned you might be hurt.'

'No, I'm all right. I thought Grandfather's keepers had scared off all the poachers.'

'Apparently not this one,' Rupert replied grimly. 'I'll have them double the watch. I know this isn't technically a part of the estate, but it's still private property. It belongs to Lord Henry James and he will have to be told. He will not want poachers on his estate.'

'Lord James is hardly ever here,' Francesca said. 'I think he spends most of his time in London. However, I heard that his nephew, Sir Roger Grey, had come down to oversee the property for him for a little while.'

'Sir Roger Grey?' Sarah asked, looking at her oddly.

'Yes, do you know him?' Rupert asked, gaze narrowing as he saw the expression in her eyes.

'Oh…yes, I may have met him once,' Sarah admitted, a flush in her cheeks. 'If Lord James is often away, I dare say he does not bother about protecting his game as he ought.'

'Well, perhaps he should. I must ride over and speak to his nephew about it. We cannot allow this kind of thing to continue. One of you might have been badly hurt,' Rupert replied and frowned. 'Are you able to ride, Francesca?'

'Yes, of course,' she said.

'Up you get, then,' Rupert said and dismounted. He gave her his hand and threw her up in the saddle, looking at her with approval. 'That's my good brave girl.'

'I've fallen before. Please do not worry about me,' Francesca said and looked at Sarah. 'Are you all right? I thought the shot was nearer you than me.'

'It passed quite close. I felt the wind on my cheek,' Sarah said and Rupert looked at her again.

'Has it shaken you?'

'No, not particularly, though it was not a pleasant experience. I am glad you arrived when you did, Lord Myers.'

'Indeed.' He looked at her hard and saw something in her eyes. She didn't think that shot had been an accident—and Rupert was damned sure it hadn't, though he was prepared to let

Francesca believe it. 'The rogue saw me and ran. His arm jerked and that may have made his aim go astray.'

'Was he aiming for a bird or a rabbit?' Francesca asked. 'There's plenty of game in these meadows, but I should've thought poachers preferred to set traps.'

'Some of them,' Rupert said. 'Shall we continue our ride? It is not likely to happen again. I think whoever it was will not do it again.'

'I'm sure he won't now that you are here,' Sarah said. 'It would be a shame to let him spoil our day and so we shan't.'

'Certainly not,' Francesca said. 'I've been looking forward to this and no poacher is going to put me off.'

John rode up to them and stared at his sister. 'Are you all right, Fran? Who do you think was firing at Miss Goodrum?'

'It was a poacher,' Sarah said. 'Just a foolish mistake.'

'No. I saw him,' John insisted. 'I looked that way. He took his pistol out and fired at you, Sarah. I know he did. Why would anyone want to kill you?'

'I am sure they wouldn't,' Sarah said and forced a smile, but Rupert saw that she looked shaken.

'It looked that way, John,' he said, 'but I

dare say it was just an accident. Please do not frighten the ladies. Come on, I want you to show me your pony's paces.'

John frowned, then inclined his head and obeyed his mentor. As the two of them set off, Francesca looked at Sarah.

'Is there anyone who would want to kill you?'

Sarah hesitated, then, 'I'm not sure. I would not have thought so—but if John saw him aim at me…'

'If there is anything, you should tell Uncle Rupert,' Francesca said. 'He likes you, Sarah. I am sure he would help you if you are in trouble.'

'Yes, perhaps. Forget it for now,' Sarah said. 'Let us catch up with the others. It will soon be time to return for nuncheon…'

Chapter Seven

Sarah was thoughtful as she parted from the others and went to her room to change before nuncheon. The shot had been very close to hitting her. The mare had shied, but she'd been able to control it and no one had noticed her difficulty because Francesca's horse had reared up and unseated her. It had been a most unpleasant incident and Sarah could not help thinking that the shot might have been meant for her. Yet who would want her dead?

Her uncle would inherit her estate as things stood, because she hadn't made a will. There was no one else she'd wanted to leave her fortune to and Uncle William had been kind after her father's death, even if he would have liked to tell her what to do. She did not believe for one moment that he would murder her for her money. So who else could it be—and why?

She had, of course, made some enemies since her father died. She'd refused several offers of marriage and a couple of offers to buy her property. That might cause some people to dislike her—but murder? As for Sir Roger…he hadn't taken kindly to being turned down, but she could not see how her death would benefit him.

Besides, how would any of her enemies know she was staying here—or where she would be that particular morning? The answer must be that they would not so it followed that the shot had been a mistake even if it had seemed to John that the poacher had fired with intent.

Sarah would be foolish to allow the incident to play on her mind. It was an unfortunate accident and unlikely to happen again.

She changed quickly out of her riding habit. No one had been hurt so they could go on as if nothing had happened.

Why would anyone want to kill Sarah? Rupert puzzled over it after having had a word with the groom.

'Did you see the poacher, Jed?'

'Yes, my lord. He seemed to act on impulse, if you ask me. Just fired quickly and then ran for it. I would've gone after him, but I thought I should stay with Master John.'

'Quite right. And I was concerned for Francesca. I fear the rogue got away too easily. It will not happen again. In future I want another groom to follow at a distance when the ladies go riding—and he is to be armed.'

'Do you think it was intentional, sir?'

'More like someone seeing his chance and acting impulsively. The question is, why would anyone want to harm either Francesca or Miss Goodrum?'

'We've never had anything like that here before, sir. Miss Francesca is an innocent— never been out in company much. Begging your pardon, sir, but none of us know much about Miss Goodrum. Not that I mean any offence, my lord.'

'None taken. One thing I am certain of, who-ever this rogue is he should not be allowed a second chance. I do not believe Miss Goodrum to have done anything that should make anyone want to kill her. She has excellent references.'

'Yes, sir. It was just a thought.'

It was indeed a thought, Rupert mused. He'd defended her to the groom, naturally, but it was perfectly true that they knew little enough about Miss Goodrum. She had been given an excel-lent reference, but—was she truly who she claimed to be? Could she have done something that had made someone want revenge—enough to pay an assassin to kill her? It would have to be something serious.

Rupert had drawn back from searching Sarah's room for the key to her writing box, but there was clearly a mystery and, after this morning's incident when Francesca had come so close to being injured, he needed to know the truth. He would ask to speak to her that afternoon and get to the bottom of this affair.

Sarah walked over to her desk. She had been mulling over the offer made her that morning, torn this way and that by indecision. Selling would be the easy way out, but she was not sure she wished to sell to someone who refused to identify himself. Perhaps if he were more honest she might consider it—and she would tell her agent that…

The drawer of her desk was not quite shut. Sarah stared at it and frowned. She was certain she'd shut it properly before she went out that morning. Had one of the maids been looking through her things? She pulled the drawer open and saw that her box was still there, but it had been taken out and replaced the wrong way round. She was quite certain it had been facing the other way when she'd left it.

Sarah checked it and found it was still locked. Whoever had been searching her things had balked at breaking the lock and would not have found the key in her room for she kept it with her at all times. The box contained money and her valuable pearls, as well as her papers, and she never let the key out of her sight, even at home.

Frowning, Sarah replaced the box as the gong sounded in the hall. It was time for nuncheon. She wondered whether she should speak to Mrs Brancaster, but, looking round her room she thought nothing else had been touched. Whoever had started the search must have drawn the line at going through her clothes. Besides, there was nothing of value for anyone to steal—other than her box and that had not been breached. Perhaps she had been mistaken. She might have placed the box differently that morning because she'd been anxious about her reply to Sam's letter.

Pushing the matter to the back of her mind, she went downstairs to the small dining parlour, where the others had already gathered.

'Forgive me if I've kept you waiting.'

'I've only just arrived,' Francesca said. 'I'm hungry. The ride out must have done me good.'

'Yes, you have colour in your cheeks. It was

pleasant to ride together. We must do so again when the weather is fine.'

'You should give your attention to the picnic now,' Rupert said. 'Once the invitations go out we are bound to have people calling to leave a card and someone ought to be here to receive them. It will be good for Francesca to greet our guests and give them refreshments. You will help her, Miss Goodrum?'

Sarah heard the question in his voice and was puzzled. 'Of course, sir. I shall be there to give Francesca any assistance she needs and to lend propriety to the occasion should a gentleman call.'

'Yes, that was what I meant, of course. I wondered if you might have business of your own elsewhere?'

How could he know that? Sarah hesitated, her spine prickling. Was it Lord Myers who had entered her room while she was out? She had known he did not quite trust her for a while now.

'If I do, I shall let you know in plenty of time, my lord. At the moment I think I am able to manage my affairs by letter.'

'Indeed?' His eyes seemed to probe into her mind, searching for answers that she had no wish to give. 'I wonder if I might speak to you before tea, Miss Goodrum. I do not wish to interfere with your plans for the afternoon, but I should like a few moments of your time in private.'

'Certainly, my lord.' Sarah gave him a frosty look and then moved to the sideboard to select her meal from the array of cold meats, cheeses, small boiled potatoes and green leaves picked fresh from the kitchen gardens.

She sat at the table and ate her meal, concentrating on her plate and trying to ignore the pounding of her heart. What could he possibly have to say to her this time?

Sarah had asked for basket chairs to be placed outside on the lawn and they took a pile of poetry books and a blanket in case the wind turned cooler. For the next hour or two they discussed the merits of the modern poets, comparing Coleridge, William Blake and Lord Byron, against the work of Shakespeare and Colonel Lovelace.

Finding themselves in almost complete agreement over the various romantic poets and their work, they laughed a great deal, their heads together as they pored over the slender volumes, some of which were worn with age and obviously loved.

Sarah was able to forget the impending interview with Lord Myers until she glanced at the time and realised they must go in and tidy their gowns for tea.

'I must speak with Lord Myers,' she said, gathering up the books. 'We shall continue this discussion another day. We must not neglect your music and of course you will begin dancing lessons as soon as the dancing master arrives.'

'I'm not sure how we shall fit it all in,' Francesca said, her pretty face alight with enthusiasm. 'The days seemed so long before you came, but now there are hardly enough hours to go round.'

Sarah laughed, but she agreed with her pupil. Her days had never been long enough for there was so much business for her to attend in the period following her father's death, but she had begun to grow tired of working on her ledgers all the time and of tiresome arguments with managers and foremen. If she listened to her head, she would sell her father's empire, but her heart would not comply. It would seem like a betrayal of his standards and the people he had employed, many of whom might lose their jobs if Mr Matthew Arkwright had his way. No, she could not destroy the trust her father's employees had placed in her—but perhaps she could find a suitable husband.

'Why does Uncle Rupert want to talk to you

in private?' Francesca asked as they walked up to the house. 'You haven't done anything wrong, have you?'

'I do not think so,' Sarah replied. 'I dare say it is to do with the picnic or some such thing.'

'Yes, perhaps,' Francesca said. 'My gown is very creased, I am going up to change.'

Sarah nodded and turned towards the library, where she expected to find Lord Myers. He was standing by one of the shelves, looking through the books. As if he sensed her entry, he turned with a frown on his face.

'I doubt if these books have ever been catalogued. There is no order to them at all.'

'No…' Sarah moved towards him. 'If I had time, I should like to organise them, but I am not sure…' She faltered as his gaze narrowed, seeming to disapprove. 'Have I done something to deserve your censure, my lord?'

'Have you? I thought I asked you not to "my lord" me all the time.' There was an irritated note in his voice as he snapped shut the book he was holding and replaced it on the shelves. 'What are you up to, Sarah—and why did you come here?'

'I don't understand you, sir,' she replied, but of course she did.

'John's groom saw that rogue fire this morning. He thinks you were the target, though the rogue fired in haste, as if tempted by a chance opportunity to frighten or wound you. Who wants to harm you? Have you done something to make someone hate you?'

Sarah hesitated, then, 'Yes, perhaps. I haven't stolen anything or cheated anyone, nor have I committed a crime—but I may have some enemies, though I cannot see what any of them could gain by killing me.'

'Perhaps it was just meant to be a warning of what could happen if the assassin really intended you dead.'

Sarah shuddered. 'I have considered that because I do not know why anyone should want me dead. I suppose someone might wish to scare me into doing something he wants...'

'Did you break it off with your protector? Is he trying to force you to return to him?'

'I should be insulted, my lord, if I did not understand your concern over this matter. I assure you I have not been any man's mistress. I have turned down offers of marriage...'

'Do you not think you should tell me the truth, Sarah? If there is someone out there who means you harm, I need to know. Francesca could also be at risk through association. If she were not so fond of you, I think I should ask you to leave.'

Sarah swallowed hard. She had always known

there was a chance she might be unmasked and to continue the lie now would be impossible. She had already revealed most of her story to Francesca and might as well confess the rest. Clasping her hands in front of her, she met his hard gaze.

'My name is Sarah Hardcastle. I changed places with Hester Goodrum, because she wanted to marry and I wanted a place to stay where I was unknown for a while.'

'You were never a governess, were you?'

'No. My father wasn't just the manager of a mine. He owned both mines and mills. When he died, leaving everything to me, I refused to hand over the management to my uncle and I have been overseeing my own affairs ever since. I have agents and managers, but I find much of my time is taken up with business matters. Because my father left me a fortune I have had to fight off men of all classes who think they are more entitled to run my affairs than I am. Some offer marriage in the hope of gaining my fortune that way—others try to bully me into selling my father's mills.'

'You are an heiress?' Rupert stared at her in amazement. 'Good grief. I've thought of almost everything else, but not that.'

'You thought me an adventuress or worse.' Sarah laughed softly, ridiculously relieved to have told him the truth. 'Is that why you searched my room this morning?'

She saw the awkwardness in his manner and knew she'd scored a hit. 'I began to search your room because of that letter... I saw you hide it when you noticed me.' Rupert frowned at her. 'Searching your room was not an honourable thing to do and I abandoned the idea. For that I ask you to forgive me—but do you think you have behaved in an honourable manner, Miss Hardcastle? You have lied to us and deceived us.'

'I know the deceit was wrong.' Sarah's cheeks flamed. 'At first it seemed to do no one any harm. I was well able to oversee Francesca's studies, as able as Miss Goodrum would have been, I think—but I have not been truthful with you, Lord Myers, though Francesca knows some of it.' She raised her head, looking into his face. 'Do you wish me to leave?'

'I ought to say yes. You know that, do you not?' He paused for so long that she was turning away when he stopped her. 'Who would that help?' he asked in a cold clipped voice. 'Francesca is fond of you and I believe you are helping her. I do not condone the deceit, but I see no point in distressing her and putting my uncle to the trouble of engaging a new governess. Are you able to remain here until Francesca goes to live with a chaperon?'

'Until Christmas?' Sarah hesitated, then, 'I might need to go home for a few days, but I could return—if you wished me to do so?'

'It is not a matter of my wishes. I am thinking of Francesca—and you.'

'Me?' Sarah was astonished. 'Why are you thinking of me?'

'You came here because you needed a break from your life, a chance to think and relax, did you not?'

'In part, yes.'

'Also to escape from fortune hunters and the like?'

'Yes. Sir Roger Grey did not take kindly to my refusal of his obliging offer. The fact that he is visiting his uncle's estate makes it awkward and may not be a coincidence. If he had discovered I was staying here…though I cannot see how he could….' She hesitated, then, 'I have recently received a generous offer to buy my father's business empire, but the buyer remains anonymous. If it is the man I think it may be, I should be reluctant to sell. He would close the less profitable mills, leaving both men and women without work or a home.'

'Would you wish to sell to a reputable buyer?'

'Perhaps. I am not sure…' Sarah hesitated.

'Since coming here I have discovered a different way of life. I have thought I might perhaps marry if I could find a gentleman who would agree to keep the mills running and to treat my workers decently. I should like to be part of a family like this, you see. I was an only child and my mother died when I was quite young. Father treated me as if I were his son.'

'That would account for your confidence.' Rupert nodded. 'Are you looking to buy yourself a husband—someone who needs a fortune to repair his ancestral estate, perhaps?'

For a moment her heart raced. She thought he might be going to offer his services and the thought both frightened and thrilled her.

'I thought something of mutual benefit… perhaps a widower with a young family,' she said in a voice no more than a whisper as his eyes continued to dwell on her. They seemed to sear her flesh and penetrate her inner being. Her whole body was tight with tension. 'I know that I am a mill owner's daughter. I received the education a gentleman's daughter might expect, but I do not come from gentle stock. I cannot look too high for a husband.'

'You have the manners of a lady of breeding. You should not put yourself down, Sarah—nor sell yourself short. Sir Roger may have been after your fortune, but I dare say there are plenty of gentlemen who would take you for yourself if you presented yourself in the right circles.'

'I do not have time to be a lady of leisure. Removing myself from my home and my family was a spur-of-the-moment thing and I imagine my uncle is angry with me for sending him a letter informing him that I shall be away for some months.'

'Would you not consider handing over the reins to your uncle?'

'I have sometimes wished that I might. He is a dear, but he has no head for business. My father always said it. Uncle William would probably sell to the highest bidder and think he was doing me a favour.' She frowned as the words left her mouth. 'Indeed, were I to die I have no doubt he would accept an offer for the mills, for he is my heir.'

'Then perhaps we have the answer to the question I posed earlier. It seems likely that, with you out of the way, your uncle would accept the offer you are considering.'

'Was considering. I shall most certainly turn it down. Anyone who would employ a rogue to frighten me into selling is certainly not fit to care for my workers.'

Rupert nodded, his eyes narrowed, expression thoughtful. 'I cannot supply your lack of a husband, Miss Hardcastle. However, I might settle with this rogue—if you tell me his name.'

'Mr Matt Arkwright of Newcastle,' Sarah said, looking at him uncertainly. 'He did not give his name, but I happen to know he was very interested in purchasing the mills. Would you wish to become involved in this business, sir?'

'I imagine I might bring pressure to bear on the man—make him back off and aware of the consequences if anything were to happen to a lady under my protection.'

Sarah felt a thrill of pleasure shoot through her at his words, then realised that he was speaking of Francesca. 'I doubt he would harm one of your charges. However, if I had been killed, my uncle would have been in a position to sell to him.'

'Perhaps you should make a will, tying your property up in a trust that may not be sold? In the meantime, I could look into these matters for you and see what can be done to protect you against similar attempts to relieve you of what is yours by right.'

'Is that possible?'

'A clever lawyer could make all sorts of legal trusts and conditions that would cause Arkwright or your uncle a devil of a time trying to sort them out. I imagine it might deter either of them from thinking of your estate again.'

'Uncle William would not be a party to my murder.'

'He may have mentioned that he thinks it wrong for you to be in sole charge, Miss Hardcastle. An obliging husband would, of course, be the best solution to your problem.'

'Yes…if I could find a man I could bear to marry who would be willing to make such a commitment.'

'I dare say we might find you one.'

'I beg your pardon? I do not understand you.'

'Francesca will enter society next year. It was planned that my sister would be her chaperon, but she has been set back by a difficult birth. I dare say she would be glad to be relieved of duties she might find onerous. If you and Francesca were to stay in my house in town for the Season, with an older lady to act as chaperon—we might find husbands for you both.'

Sarah gasped. He was being generous to consider such an idea, but she felt as if he'd poured a bucket of cold water over her.

'Why should you put yourself to so much trouble? Besides, I am not certain I could spend so much time away from my business affairs.'

'I am willing to do much to see that Francesca has the companion she trusts and loves—

and I would never stand by and see a woman abused.'

'I see…' Sarah licked her lips. 'I should like to oblige you, but I cannot spend too much time away from the mills or they may suffer.'

'If you had someone to oversee them for you, to make certain that this Arkwright—if he is the man behind the offer—was sent packing, and that you were well served by your agents, you might consider it.'

'I don't see—' Sarah broke off as she saw the gleam in his eyes. 'Are you suggesting…?'

'I will visit your agent and speak to him, make certain he has all the necessary instructions he needs from you. Until you take a husband I shall stand as your…*guardian* is not the word, but in place of a male relative. I believe that once it is known I have a hand on the reins you will not be bothered by the attentions of rogues. And I will speak to Arkwright, make him understand that the mills are not for sale.'

Sarah breathed deeply. His offer was so startling that she did not know how to answer him. 'Why should you do so much for me, sir?' she asked at last.

'Someone tried to harm you while you were in my care. As an employee here you are entitled to my protection. As a young woman alone apart from a foolish uncle, and at the mercy of unscrupulous rogues who want to take what you have for themselves, you are entitled to my help as a gentleman.'

'Oh…' For a moment she had thought that perhaps he cared for her, but if she'd hoped for it her hopes were dashed. He would offer his protection, but he was not offering her his heart or even a marriage of convenience. 'I am not sure I could ask so much of you, sir.'

'You have not asked.' Rupert smiled and her breath fled. Her knees felt as if they might buckle and she had to hang on to her senses tightly. He was so handsome and, when he chose, utterly charming—the perfect gentleman. She would not be a woman if she could remain untouched by that smile. 'I feel it my duty to help you. The only other alternative is to send you away and break Francesca's heart. I believe she is happier now than she has been for most of her life. I do not wish to see her unhappy.'

He was doing this for Francesca? Remembering his concern when Francesca had fallen from her horse, Sarah wondered if he felt something warmer than mere affection for his cousin, but then decided that he had shown no sign of it. His manner towards the young girl was that of a kindly uncle, nothing more.

'I should be reluctant to hurt Francesca,'

Sarah faltered, because she could not help thinking that much of his concern was for her. If she accepted, she would be breaking down the barrier between them. Was that wise? He had seemed to be intent on seduction at one point, but that was when he suspected her of being an adventuress. How did he feel now that he knew the truth? 'Yet I feel that I am asking too much of you. After all, you know so little of me—and I did deceive you by coming here under false pretences.'

'I think we should keep your true identity to ourselves for the moment. When we go to London, I shall reveal the truth to Francesca's grandfather and I am sure he will forgive you when he learns your story and knows that you have been good for his granddaughter.'

'If you are sure he will not think me a scheming adventuress. Perhaps I ought to leave as soon as a replacement could be found...'

'You will do me a favour by remaining here under this roof,' Rupert said. 'I gave my uncle my word I would mentor John and protect Francesca, but he knows I have business from time to time. I can attend to yours and my own with only a small detour.'

Sarah swallowed hard. 'I can only thank you for your consideration, sir. I think most gentlemen in your position would have simply dismissed me.'

'I am not most men,' Rupert said and there was mocking laughter in his eyes. She felt coldness at her nape. What made him look that way? Had a woman hurt him so badly that he could never trust another? 'Do not review your opinion of me, Sarah. I am still the rake you thought me, but I do have a code of honour that I respect—and that concerns young ladies in need of protection.'

'I am not so very young, but I understand your concern for Francesca—and I have become so fond of her. She is to me the sister I never had.'

'Yes, I thought that might be the case.' His smile was intriguing. 'I shall not leave until after the picnic—and now I think we really must join the others for tea.'

'Yes, of course. I can only thank you—'

'Oh, there may be something more you can do for me—but we shall discuss that at a later date. Do not look alarmed, I promise I shall not harm you. When I thought you an adventuress or a courtesan I might have taken advantage, but that is no longer the case. Come now, we shall start again. If I may call you Sarah—and you will address me as sir or Rupert in private. No more my lording me, if you please.'

'I shall try to remember.'

Sarah could not resist smiling. Her heart was beating very fast, for she could not dislike him even when he was cold and reserved. Something must have made him that way, for underneath she had now and then glimpsed a very different man. Sarah knew that she could easily fall in love with the man she'd seen on those rare occasions—but was he the real Rupert or was he the hard-eyed rake he claimed to be?

Only time and further acquaintance would tell.

She turned and left the room, preceding him to the drawing room where the others were gathered for tea.

'Ah, there you are,' Francesca said. 'Is everything all right? I was afraid you might have to leave us or something.'

'No, no, not at all,' Sarah replied. 'I had a small problem, but Lord Myers has promised to see to it for me.'

'I have some business of my own I must attend to,' Rupert said and gave the girl a warm look of affection. 'I shall do what I can for Miss…Sarah while I'm gone. It will not be until after our picnic and I know you will be quite happy here together while I've gone.'

'I wish I could come with you,' John said. 'I shan't know what to do when you're not here.'

'You have your riding lessons—and you may join Sarah and your sister for lessons and other pursuits until I return. I shall not be long and I shall give you some reading to catch up on while I'm gone—something you will enjoy. Do not look so sulky, boy. You must learn to conquer that habit for it will not wash when you go to public school. I promise you that you will enjoy the books I choose for you to study. And when I come back we shall ride together.'

John was mollified and accepted a muffin from the plate his sister offered him, biting into it and chewing as the melted butter ran down his chin.

Sarah looked round the elegant drawing room, feeling truly at peace. She was glad to have confided in Lord Myers and relieved that she would not have to deal with the objectionable Mr Arkwright herself. Sam would need a letter from her, introducing Lord Myers as a friend who would oversee things for a while, leaving her free to enjoy the next few months.

It was an excellent arrangement, though temporary. She could not expect Lord Myers to continue it for longer than necessary. Once they were in London for Francesca's Season, she would have to look around for a suitable husband. One who would be happy to run her affairs in the way she liked, and to give her a family.

The thought sent a tingle down her spine. A husband would expect the marriage to include intimate relations and she wanted children— so she would have to respect and like this man. Perhaps it would be easy to find such a person once she was mixing in society, but she'd mixed with gentlemen and men of her father's class before and found no one she could even contemplate marrying. Except...her eyes focused on Lord Myers's features and she felt a spasm of something she knew to be physical desire in her stomach.

Sarah would not object to a marriage of convenience with Rupert Myers, but he'd made it clear where the boundaries of their relationship ended.

He was prepared to offer her his protection, but love and marriage were very different things. Therefore, she would be a fool to let herself fall in love with him...and she would do well to dampen the physical feeling she'd had towards him on several occasions. Lord Myers might be a gentleman, but she was still not certain that he would not seduce her given the right opportunity.

Chapter Eight

The morning of the picnic was fine and warm, a perfect day for it. All the invitations had gone out and everyone had replied, accepting with pleasure, it seemed. Francesca was excited and John was beside himself. Several youths of his age had been invited and he was looking forward to the games he'd been promised.

Francesca and Sarah had been wrapping small gifts in secret for days. The games of running, jumping, throwing hoops over prizes and shooting arrows at a board would all be rewarded by sweetmeats and things like a silver penknife, a silver pencil and other similar trinkets, including a riding whip with a beautifully engraved silver handle, which Rupert had donated to their little hoard.

'I think this is an excellent idea,' he'd said to Sarah when giving her the gift. 'It was time this place came to life again. I'm sure you will have callers while I'm gone—and when I return we'll give a reception of some kind. I might ask a few friends of mine down, men I can trust not to try seducing Francesca before she has her Season.' He hesitated, then, 'What do you think of the dancing master? I've scarcely seen him, but he seems pleasant enough.'

'Yes, he is charming,' Sarah replied, keeping her reservations to herself. 'He has given Francesca one lesson thus far, but I think she enjoyed it. I played for them, of course, so was unable to watch all of the dancing, but I think she has a natural grace.'

'He is French, of course, and young.' Rupert frowned. 'I am trusting you to make certain he does not try to take advantage of her. She will never have met anyone like this Monsieur Dupree and may foolishly think herself in love with him. Make sure he does not get ideas above his station, if you please.'

'Most young girls have a crush on their dancing master,' Sarah said and smiled. 'He is a very handsome young man, but I think Francesca is looking forward to her Season too much to be foolish over him.'

'Well, I rely on you to keep an eye on her while I've gone.'

Sarah had promised she would. With the excitement of the picnic and the promise of her Season to come, she thought Francesca's heart was safe enough for the moment and nothing the girl had said concerning the dancing master had given her any cause for concern. Lord Myers would naturally feel more concern because he was very protective over Francesca and did not want her breaking her heart over a man her family would never allow her to marry.

Monsieur Dupree seemed to be a very honest open young man, who had proved a hit with John from the start, showing himself willing to join a game of rounders or cricket. He had also taken on himself the task of tidying the library shelves.

'It is a task after my own heart,' he told Sarah when she found him rearranging a shelf early one morning. 'I have too little to do, you see. As charming as it is to teach the adorable *mademoiselle,* I wish to earn my salary—no?'

Sarah nodded, inspecting the way he was arranging the books in better order. 'This is a task I have wanted to do. If you could put all the poetry, plays and works of fiction together, I should be grateful—and I am sure Lord Myers would be, too.'

'If I 'ave your approval, Miss Sarah, I am the 'appiest of men.'

The look in his eyes had given Sarah some qualms. She could not be certain for it was early days yet, but she rather thought he might be flirting with her. Lord Myers had feared he might try to seduce Francesca, but Sarah suspected she might be the object of the Frenchman's amorous intentions. She hoped not, for she would have to deter him and that made for an uncomfortable atmosphere in the house.

However, for the moment he made no advances, though he was swift to open a door, pull out a chair or compliment her. Sarah thanked him while maintaining a cool but friendly manner.

On the day of the picnic she could not help but be glad of his help, for he voluntarily took on the management of the games for the children, leaving Sarah and Francesca with little to do but present the prizes.

Lord Rupert had greeted all the guests, introducing them to Sarah and to Francesca using just Christian names. She noticed that he allowed people to think of her as Francesca's companion rather than a normal governess, who would naturally have remained in the background.

'I am delighted to see Francesca looking so happy,' Lady Rowton said to Sarah when they stood watching some of the sports. 'At Christmas when Merrivale was here she seemed a little dispirited. You have been good for her, Miss...I did not quite catch your name?'

'Sarah Hardcastle,' Sarah said without thinking, then realised what she'd done. 'Please, call me Sarah. Everyone does.'

'How delightfully informal. I shall do so in the spirit of the occasion, my dear. It is a pleasure to see the girl happy—and her brother. You have worked a little miracle.'

Sarah thanked her. Since she'd given her own name there was no point in hiding it and she decided to give the housekeeper a curtailed version of her story that evening. It was best if everyone understood she was in the house as a friend rather than an employed governess.

All of their neighbours seemed friendly people, including Squire Browning and his lady, Mr Honiton and his sister Gillian, the Monks family of three lively children and Mr Monks's brother James, also his wife Susan. At least thirty of the family's acquaintances had accepted invitations and Sarah had difficulty in recalling all the names, but Mr James Monks had made himself known to her.

'I say, you're rather pretty,' he said as he joined her when she was applauding John and one of his nephews in the egg-and-spoon race.

'This is quite jolly. How long have you been staying with the Merrivales?'

'Only a few weeks,' Sarah replied, amused to find herself being quizzed through an eye-glass. The young man was quite a fop, a tulip of fashion if she were not mistaken. 'I am glad you are enjoying yourself, sir.'

'One needs a spot of entertainment in the country, what? I find it dull after the town, don't you know.'

'Oh, I think there is so much to do in the country. Do you not like walking and riding, sir?'

'Well, I dare say that is well enough...' His attention was drawn to Francesca as she pre-sented the prize for the race her brother had lost by falling over just before the line. 'Growing up, ain't she? I imagine the old marquess in-tends leaving her a bit in his will, what?'

'I'm afraid I have no idea,' Sarah said. Some-thing about the man made her take him in in-stant dislike. 'Francesca will have her Season, but I have no idea of her prospects, sir. I think she will marry well whether she has a fortune or not.'

'Oh, I say. Only an idle question, you know.'

He wandered away, clearly annoyed with her for taking him up on the remark. As she watched, he approached Francesca and said something, which made the girl smile. She was frowning and did not notice Rupert approach.

'Was he annoying you just now?'

Sarah started and glanced at him. 'He was speculating on whether or not the marquess intended to leave Francesca a fortune.'

'Was he indeed?' Rupert glowered in the direction of the young fop. 'Impudent pup! I dare say he has run through the fortune his grandfather left him and is hanging out for a rich wife. I'd heard he was rusticating because his creditors were dunning him. Watch him if he comes calling while I'm away.'

'I would hope Francesca would have more sense than to be taken in by someone like him.'

'I'm not so sure. She seems to be enjoying his company.'

Sarah saw that the girl had taken his arm and was going in search of a drink. The maids had just brought out trays of iced lemon barley and orange juice for the younger members of the party. For the older guests there was champagne and a cool white wine.

'I think Francesca will be courted by many gentlemen,' Sarah said. 'She is lovely of face and nature. Once she comes out I think she will be very popular with the gentlemen. I have spoken to her about these things and I think she has enough sense not to let anyone seduce her.'

'Well, that is all we can hope for.' Rupert's eyes came back to Sarah. 'Are you enjoying yourself? Lady Rowton described you as Miss Hardcastle—have you told anyone else yet?'

'I shall explain to Mrs Brancaster tonight and hope that she will forgive me.'

'I am sure she will. I dare say she will understand if you explain you were in need of a place to hide. It may be best if she believes I have been aware of the truth all the time.'

'Yes.' Sarah looked at him uncertainly. 'Have you forgiven me for lying to you?'

His brows rose and his smile was absent. 'The jury is out, Sarah. I shall reserve judgement until I see how you conduct yourself in future.'

She caught her lower lip between her teeth, feeling unaccountably near to tears. 'I am sorry to have lost your good opinion—if I ever had it?'

'I am teasing you,' he said and smiled, sending her heart rocketing. 'Not that I condone lying, for I generally abhor it—but I believe I understand why you did what you did.'

'Thank you.' Her throat caught. When he smiled like that it was enough to break her heart—but she must never forget that he could never wish to marry a woman of her class. At one time he had considered seducing her, but that was when he believed her an adventuress. Since she'd confided the truth in him, he had treated her as he would any other lady, showing her politeness, but keeping a certain distance between them.

It was all she could expect, of course. Sarah suspected that her own heart was not untouched and she knew that her heart raced whenever he smiled down at her. However, he had given her no reason to think he might feel anything more for her than the natural concern of a gentleman for a woman in trouble.

Why did he guard his heart so well? Sarah wondered about the woman who had hurt him. She must be very lovely—and a lady, of course. Sarah was neither of those things. Why should he ever look at her?

He had thought of seduction, but he was a self-confessed rake and she could not think a light affair with a governess would have meant anything to him.

Her breath in her throat, she fought her own desire to rest her head against those broad shoulders.

'Will you be gone long, sir?'

'I'm not sure—at least a week, I imagine, possibly a little more.'

'John will miss you—and Francesca.'

'I think John has already found a good substitute in Monsieur Dupree.'

Sarah followed his gaze. 'He has certainly been a great help today. Some dancing masters would consider games with the children beneath them, but Monsieur Dupree has proved his worth.'

'Do you like him? Do you trust him?'

'Yes, to both questions.' Sarah glanced up questioningly. 'Do you doubt him for any reason?'

'None—except experience. When my sister was young her dancing master attempted to run off with her. She was foolishly infatuated with him and would have eloped had I not discovered his little plan. I paid him to disappear and he took the money.'

'Your sister must have been in some distress?'

'For a time, I believe, but she soon recovered once she became the toast of the town. She fell in love with a decent man and is very happy— so do not think me a monster for sending her would-be lover away.'

'I think you may rest easy in your mind. Monsieur Dupree has shown no interest in seducing Francesca. In fact, he seems—' She broke off and shook her head.

'What were you about to say?' His eyes narrowed. 'Please do not lie to me, Sarah. If you know something, tell me.'

'I was about to say he has shown more inclination to flirt with me—but that sounds conceited.'

'I trust you gave him no encouragement?'

'No, of course not. Why on earth should I?'

'He would not make you a suitable husband, Sarah. You must look higher than a dancing master, even if he is handsome.'

He sounded a little put out, which made her smile, but when she looked at him she saw no sign of jealousy, just annoyance.

She put her chin up at him. 'I have no intention of it—and please do not lecture the poor man. He has merely been charming. I should not have mentioned it.'

He nodded, but his frown did not lessen. 'You should think carefully before you make your choice. I know your preference is for a widower with a family. I have been giving the matter some thought and when I return I may be able to introduce you to certain gentlemen of merit. You would do well to choose wisely and not let yourself be charmed by a dancing master.'

'Thank you.' Sarah's smile felt fixed. She was grateful for his help, of course she was— but how could she consider any candidate he might produce as a suitable husband when she was beginning to think… But she was being so foolish! Lord Myers was not for her. Even if his smile could make her pulses go wild, it was merely the foolishness of a lonely woman. Once she met other gentlemen she would soon discover that Lord Myers meant nothing to her.

'Excuse me, I must see that the children all have enough to eat and drink. Shall we see you at dinner this evening, Lord Myers?'

'Yes, of course.' His gaze narrowed. 'What have I said now, Sarah? I do not mean to dictate to you—but you did say that you needed help with your problems?'

'Yes, I do and I'm grateful. You have said nothing to upset me, sir—nothing at all.'

It was her fault for allowing her imagination to provide her with pictures of the kind of marriage she would most enjoy—because his was unaccountably the face she saw every time she considered the idea.

Dressing that evening, Rupert frowned at himself in the mirror. Why had he made the offer to find a suitable husband for Sarah? Had his pride been hurt because she seemed to favour the dancing master? It was really none of his business whom she chose to marry for she could never mean anything to him—or could she?

Rupert pondered the thought. He had considered himself uninterested in marriage, knowing that he must marry one day for the purpose of getting an heir, but he'd deliberately shut the idea from his mind. The right woman would present herself to his notice one day in the future and then… But perhaps he need look no further. Sarah had aroused feelings of hot lust in him and something more. If he wanted a wife to be a companion in his advancing years and to give him a family, why not her as well as any other?

He frowned at himself in the mirror. No, it was impossible. Sarah deserved more than he could give her. She ought to have love and the kind of happiness that comes from such a marriage—and yet she was considering a marriage of convenience.

He'd promised to help her find a husband and he must keep his word, bring some of his friends down so that she could meet them and perhaps find a man she wished to marry. A part of him persisted in thinking that it might suit him to marry her, but there was still a barrier in his mind—still a part of him that was wary of taking the irrevocable step of asking any woman to be his wife.

A handful of their neighbours had stayed to dine that evening. Lady Rowton was one,

Squire Browning, his wife and Mr Honiton and his sister, also the Reverend Hoskins. Sarah found herself placed between the vicar and the squire, who was a little hard of hearing and tended to boom at her.

Sarah had answered all the questions directed at her, but was conscious of watching Rupert for much of the evening. He had been the perfect host, keeping everyone amused and making sure that it all went smoothly. She had noticed that he paid attention to all the ladies, but particularly to Lady Rowton. The lady was more than thirty, but still youthful in her looks and attractive, her smile warm whenever she had replied to something Rupert said to her.

'Did you notice Rupert flirting with Lady Rowton?' Francesca whispered as they went into the drawing room later. 'I think they had an affair a year or two ago. It was just after her husband died—and I heard Grandfather telling someone that Lord Myers was consoling her.'

'You mustn't repeat overheard gossip, dearest,' Sarah said.

'Very well.' Francesca's eyes sparkled. 'Then I shan't tell you what Monsieur Dupree said about you.'

'Please do not, and do not tease,' Sarah said, but she was laughing. She had noticed the dancing master looking at her several times during the evening, even though he'd been seated next to Miss Honiton.

Monsieur Dupree had no notion of her being an heiress. He imagined her a friend of the family, not quite a governess, but not the heiress to a fortune. That must mean he liked her for herself alone. The idea was novel and pleasing. It made Sarah smile to think that a young and handsome man found her attractive for her own sake and, when she discovered him staring at her, she smiled.

Glancing then at Lord Myers, she saw him scowling and wondered what had caused him to look so annoyed. Surely not because she'd smiled at the dancing master? Sarah might be flattered by the young man's admiration, but her heart was completely untouched. He was not at all the kind of husband she would ever consider—though she did quite enjoy being flirted with across the table.

When the ladies were assembled and tea was served, Francesca was asked if she would play for the company.

'Only if Sarah plays a duet with me,' she said, blushing prettily.

'Yes, of course,' Sarah agreed and took a seat beside her on the stool.

'Allow me to turn your music, *mesdemoi-*

selles,' Monsieur Dupree said, coming up to them with alacrity. 'I will sing later if Mademoiselle Sarah will play for me.'

Sarah could not do less than agree. She and Francesca played a lively melody, then the girl got up and left the entertainment to Sarah. After some discussion, it was decided that Monsieur Dupree would sing 'Greensleeves' in English and in French.

He proved to have a delightful voice and they were asked for three encores. He sang two further songs in French and then a love song in English.

At the end of this melody Sarah rose from the pianoforte and walked away, leaving Monsieur Dupree to take over. His playing was as proficient as his singing and she was about to say goodnight to Francesca when Rupert came up to her.

'His song was for you,' he said. 'I think you have made another conquest, Sarah.'

'Another? I assure you none of my other admirers have wanted me for myself.'

'Can you be sure of that? Might you have misjudged some of them?'

Sarah wrinkled her brow. 'Perhaps. I thought it was all Father's money, but some of them…' She shook her head and sighed. 'I had no interest in any of them, even if—'

'I've told you before, you should not sell yourself short.'

'I have no intention of doing so. I like Monsieur Dupree, but I have no intention of listening to an offer from him—of any kind.'

'That's very much better. I like to see my Sarah standing proud.'

His Sarah! A tingle went down her spine and her stomach clenched. What could he mean—his Sarah? For a moment a feeling of joy spread through her. If he cared for her... But, no, his attention had wandered. He was watching Francesca, who had gone to join the dancing master at the pianoforte. The two of them were now playing together and seemed to be amusing themselves with the lively piece.

Sarah squashed the nonsensical hope. Lord Myers was a gentleman and it had merely been a figure of speech. When he looked at her again it was merely to raise a quizzical eyebrow.

He was still treating her as Francesca's equal, a young woman of some consequence. Sarah almost regretted telling him the truth. He had shown more interest in her when he'd believed her an adventuress.

Alone in her room, Sarah undressed and sat before the mirror, wearing a soft robe. She hadn't been able to part from all her clothes when she left her trunks behind and had brought her own under- and night-things, because no one was going to see her when she was alone in her room.

Sitting before the mirror, she brushed her hair so that it fell on her shoulders, shining and straight with just a little curl at the ends. She wasn't truly tired and was regretting that she hadn't thought to bring a book up with her. It would be easy enough to walk down to the library, but she could not bother to dress again and did not think it appropriate to wander at night in her night robes.

She was just about to retire when she heard the tap at the door, stopped and walked to it, her hand on the catch as she said, 'Yes, who is it?'

'Rupert. May I speak to you for a moment, please?'

Sarah's heart pounded as she opened the door. What could he mean by coming to her room? She felt her pulses race as she saw him standing there, still dressed for the evening. Suddenly, she felt an overwhelming longing for him to take her in his arms and kiss her. It would undoubtedly lead to him seducing her, but at that moment she almost felt it worthwhile.

'You are ready for bed. Forgive me for disturbing you—but I am leaving very early in the morning. You were going to give me a letter to your agent. I suppose with the picnic and then our guests for the evening you forgot?'

'I have it ready. It was my intention to give it to you in the morning.' Leaving her door ajar, Sarah walked to her desk, pulled open the bottom drawer and took out her writing box. She took the key from the pocket of her robe and opened the box, extracting the slim paper sealed with wax. As she turned, she saw that he had followed her in and closed the door and her breath caught in her throat. 'Lord Myers… should you have done that?'

'Probably not,' he said. 'You look so lovely, Sarah. You make me want to do this…' Before she knew what he was about, he reached out and drew her into his arms, lowering his head to kiss her on the mouth. It was a sweet soft kiss that made her pulses race, but she stepped back, putting her fingers to her lips.

'You must not. You really must not, sir.'

'Rupert. Please, call me Rupert.'

'You should go at once. This is impossible.'

'Is it really so impossible, Sarah?'

'You know it is. It must be…in the circumstances.'

Did he think she was prepared to have an affair with him? What was he thinking of? Did he imagine that she would become his mistress out of gratitude? The thought was painful and she pushed it to a tiny corner of her mind.

'Have you been drinking, Rupert?' She could taste the brandy on his lips.

'Yes, just a little,' he said and then laughed ruefully. 'Too much. The way you look and the wine…a powerful combination, my dear. Forgive me. I am merely human—and you are very desirable. You do not realise the effect that cool exterior with just a hint of the fire below can have on a man. Thank you for the letter and your trust. Goodnight and sleep well.'

'Goodnight, Rupert.'

Sarah closed the door behind him, pressing fingers that trembled slightly to her mouth. His kiss had been so sweet—so tempting. She had wanted it to go on…to be so much more than a kiss. A hunger so swift and so powerful swept over her that she cried out as if in pain. She had never felt like this before in her life, never wanted anything so badly that it hurt. Her whole being longed to call him back, to take him by the hand and lead him to her bed.

No, she would not be foolish. Rupert had admitted that it was merely the wine and the sight of her in her nightclothes. He was a confirmed rake and accustomed to taking a mistress whenever he chose. She must not condemn him for a mere slip of manners. He had not tried to force himself on her and had apologised for his lapse.

Sarah's problem was not that he had insulted her by kissing her, but that she had wanted more. Earlier she had been regretting that he kept a distance between them. Her heart had leaped at his touch, but her good sense had told her she could not conduct an affair with him while they were both staying under the same roof as Francesca. It would be most improper and might lead to a scandal that could reflect badly on the young woman.

Would she have had an affair with him if it hadn't been for Francesca's reputation? Sarah thought about it as she slid into bed and pulled up the covers. Her lips still tingled, and at the thought of the caresses that might have been, the rest of her body felt suffused with heat. She was desperately attracted to him. His absence these next few days would cause her grief, but his presence might be even more distressing.

Sarah had promised to stay with Francesca until she'd had her Season in town. In return, Lord Myers was sorting out her problems. She could not renege on her bargain even if she wanted to—so she was just going to have to keep a tight rein on her emotions.

Alone in his own room, Rupert threw himself down on the bed, lying staring at the ceiling. What had possessed him to kiss her that way? She'd looked so delectable in her night attire that he'd been seized with a sudden need. Had she not drawn away from him, he might have carried her to the bed and made passionate love to her, thereby sealing both their fates.

He'd flirted with Lady Rowton that evening in an effort to put Sarah out of his mind, but she had taken root there and was beginning to haunt him day and night.

Surely he wasn't thinking of marrying her? Taking her as his mistress was not an option now that they had become friends and he knew she was a respectable young woman.

It was marriage or nothing. Was he ready to cast off his past and take that step? Was he ready to trust again?

As well that he was going away on her business and his own. He needed time to get things into perspective and decide where his future lay.

Chapter Nine

'Monsieur Dupree is so funny,' Francesca said as they picked roses for the house that morning, clipping the long stems and taking care not to prick themselves as they placed the buds carefully in their baskets. 'But he's sweet, too—and he likes you so much, Sarah.'

'I agree that he is charming. I hope you are not infatuated, dearest?'

Francesca laughed delightedly. 'Oh, he doesn't want to seduce me. Andre has far too much sense. He knows that he must make his living and any such nonsense would result in his being dismissed without a reference. He might never work again. No, you are the one he wants to seduce, Sarah. He says you are a rose without compare.'

'Well, he is French,' Sarah said and her friend

went into another peal of laughter. 'Besides, I told you. I need a widower—a nice sensible English gentleman who will take care of my business.'

'I still cannot believe how rich you are,' Francesca said and inhaled the perfume of a dark red rose. 'It is such a romantic story—you coming here to escape a persistent fortune hunter. I was so lucky that you changed places with Miss Goodrum. If you hadn't, we might never have met.'

'I should have regretted that,' Sarah said and looked at her with affection, feeling glad she had decided to confide her whole story in the girl. 'I think these past weeks have been some of the happiest of my life.'

The one thing to mar her content was the way she felt about Lord Myers. A part of her wanted to give in to the need he aroused in her, but she knew that she would be a fool to give her body—and perhaps her heart—to a rake.

'Do you think we have enough roses?'

'Yes, quite enough, because it's nice to have fresh ones often. Shall we go and arrange them…?' She paused as they turned the corner to the front of the house. 'It seems we have visitors….' Two gentlemen had just dismounted and grooms were leading their horses away.

'I wonder who it can be?' Francesca said

and her eyes sparkled. They had received visits from most of their neighbours in the past week and Francesca was enjoying herself, because several gentlemen had been paying her compliments. 'Oh, I do believe it is Mr Monks.'

Sarah smothered a sigh, because Francesca looked so pleased. The young man had visited three times already and seemed intent on fixing his interest with Francesca, though as yet Sarah was not sure how she felt.

'There's someone with him…I think it's Sir Roger. He must have come down for a visit.'

Sarah's throat caught as she looked at the second gentleman and knew him. It was the very man she'd come here to avoid. Could he know she was here or was it a coincidence?

The gentlemen had become aware of them and turned to wait for them to reach the steps leading up to the portico. James Monks had eyes only for Francesca, but Sir Roger was staring at Sarah, his gaze narrowed and intent. Sarah felt certain he'd known she was here all the time.

'Ah, Miss Hardcastle, Miss Francesca,' James Monks said and bowed. 'I was sure you would not mind my bringing Sir Roger with me? He was most anxious to present himself when he knew you were staying with the Merrivale family, Miss Hardcastle.'

'Mr Monks...Sir Roger.' Sarah gave both gentlemen an equally cool nod. She had not told Francesca the name of her persistent admirer and so the girl was completely unaware as she greeted their guests with a warm smile and invited them to stay to nuncheon.

'Will you not come in, Sir Roger—James? You must stay to eat with us. It will be a simple meal, but we shall be happy to share it with you, shall we not, Sarah?'

Sarah could only agree to Francesca's request, though her stomach was tying itself in knots as Sir Roger inclined his head, his gaze narrowed and wary.

'Miss Hardcastle—Sarah, how pleasant to see you again, and you, Miss Francesca.'

'I trust you are well, sir?'

'Not as well as I might have been had a certain person smiled on me more,' Sir Roger said in a low voice as the others went ahead into the house. 'Forgive me if this visit makes you uncomfortable. Should I go away at once? Or may I hope that you will allow me to renew my offer? I know the ladies like to change their minds.'

'Not this one,' Sarah said and gave him a straight look. 'Forgive me, sir, but I shall be blunt. I do not wish for another offer from you and my answer remains the same.'

'You are hard, Sarah. My feelings have been hurt by your coldness. I find it difficult to enjoy life as I was wont to do—I must languish in your shadow since you will have none of me.'

Sarah felt a rising impatience. How many times must she tell this man that she had no interest in becoming his wife? If she had been at home, she might have been rude, but she was a guest here and could not insult Francesca's guest. The girl had invited him to eat with them and Sarah would simply have to endure his company as best she could.

'If we are to remain friends, sir, I would ask you not to flatter me with insincere compliments.'

'Surely you do not accuse me of insincerity?' Sir Roger looked indignant and for a moment she saw anger in his eyes, which was quickly hidden behind a false smile. 'I assure you, my feelings have always been completely sincere.'

Sarah refused to answer. It was impossible when he seemed determined to ignore her refusal. All she could do was to remain cool and indifferent, to hope that he would eventually tire of being rebuffed.

John was in the front parlour with the dancing master. They had taken a book of plays from the library and Monsieur Dupree was declaiming aloud from one of Shakespeare's works as they entered, which made Sarah smile inwardly as the words sounded very different in a French accent.

'I must give these roses to one of the maids to put in water,' she said, excusing herself. 'I shall return in a moment.'

She wished that she might take the time to arrange the flowers herself, but she could not leave Francesca to cope with the visitors alone and returned quickly, to find them all laughing and discussing the book of plays. Apparently, the gentlemen fancied themselves as actors and it seemed they were amusing Francesca by vying for her attention.

'We should put on a play in the gardens,' Francesca said. 'We could all act out parts and entertain our neighbours.'

'What a wonderful idea,' James Monks said and sent her a look of foppish adoration. 'You would be adorable as the fairy queen, Francesca.'

'Are you reading *A Midsummer Night's Dream?*' Sarah asked. 'It is one of my favourites—so amusing. I like it when she falls in love with Bottom…'

'You must play the queen,' Francesca urged. 'I should not like to take the leading part, but will take on the role of one of her attendants.'

'I shall be Bottom,' Sir Roger said. ''Tis vastly amusing, I vow.'

'No, no, I could not. Besides, the play is far too long and we should never learn all the words.'

'We could play just the scene where Titania awakes to find herself bewitched,' Francesca said. 'I think it is so funny because she loves Bottom despite the fact that he has been turned into a donkey.'

'*Mais non,* it is a tragedy,' Monsieur Dupree objected. 'The *pauvre* lady is bewitched as a punishment by her so-cruel husband.'

His words were greeted by heated exchanges and the next few minutes passed pleasantly enough, as all the aspects of the play were discussed and analysed. Sarah was pleased to see that Francesca held her own, having read the play with her, and relieved that by the time they had all been called to nuncheon and eaten their meal in a spirit of festivity, the idea of actually performing the play had been forgotten.

By the time the gentlemen took their leave, Sarah had relaxed sufficiently to forget to be on her guard and it was something of a shock when Sir Roger held her hand too long and then raised it to his lips.

'I shall visit you again soon, Sarah.'

'Francesca is always pleased to see her guests.'

The look he gave her was supposed to be ardent, but to Sarah it merely seemed menacing. Even if Monsieur Dupree liked her for herself, she was convinced that Sir Roger wanted something from her.

She shivered and wished that Lord Myers was here rather than on what might prove a wild goose chase. If Sir Roger wanted the mills, she believed that he might be willing to hire a rogue to either frighten her into signing or…might he actually want her dead?

If Sarah were dead, her uncle would sell to the highest bidder.

She was relieved when both gentlemen turned away and she returned to the house. About to go in search of Francesca, who had gone to look for a book she wanted, Sarah was surprised when Monsieur Dupree waylaid her in the hall.

'A moment of your time, *non?*'

'Was there something I can do for you, *monsieur?*'

'It is I who may perhaps do something for you, *mademoiselle.*' The Frenchman's dark eyes dwelled on her face with something like adoration. 'I think you did not like the so-charming Sir Roger? He distresses you, *non?*'

'I would not say I was distressed, *mon-*

sieur—merely wary. I should not like to be left alone with that gentleman.'

'No, of a certainty,' he replied and made a face of disgust. 'If the so-charming Sir Roger attempts to force his attentions on you, Mademoiselle Sarah, you may call on Andre Dupree. With the pistol I am—how you say?—a dead shot.' He made a shooting motion. 'I will kill him if he harms you.'

Sarah resisted the temptation to laugh, because, looking at his expression, she could see that he was in earnest.

'You are very kind to offer your protection, *monsieur*—but I hardly think we need come to such measures. Sir Roger is a nuisance, but I think I am able to fend off his advances.'

'If he harms you, he will answer to me.' Andre took a step towards her, quite clearly intending to make his devotion to Sarah's cause even plainer, but before he could speak the knocker sounded and in the next moment the footman had opened the door to Lord Myers.

'You are back, my lord.' Sarah turned to him, a smile of welcome on her lips. She felt relief surge within her and something more. How much she wished she could run to his arms and give him a welcome-home kiss.

'Yes, Sarah, I have returned.' Rupert's brows arched. 'Have I been missed?'

'You must always be missed—' Sarah would have said more, but at that moment John came flying into the hall and threw himself at Rupert, giving him an exuberant hug. 'I saw you from the window. You've been gone such an age.'

'Nine days, I think.' Rupert laughed and disentangled himself. 'Steady on, old chap. Surely things are not so bad?'

'Oh, I've had loads of lessons and I like being with Fran, Sarah and Monsieur Dupree—but no one is like you. I've missed my fencing lessons.'

'Well, you shall have one tomorrow,' Rupert promised. 'I might have a gift for you in my trunk—but if you continue to ruin my coat I shall consider whether to give it to you.'

'You wouldn't.' John saw he was smiling and laughed, but stood back. 'I'll keep you to your word about the fencing.' He turned to the dancing master. 'Will you give me another French lesson, *monsieur?* It sounds so much better when you speak the language.'

'Oui, mon petit,' the Frenchman said. 'Come, we shall go to the library and find a book of French plays.'

Rupert glanced at Sarah. 'I see our dancing master has many talents. I think he has relieved me of some of my duties.'

'But not all. John is willing to accept a substitute when you are not here, but of course we all miss you. Francesca was only asking this morning when you would return.'

'Your affairs took me a little longer than I had anticipated, but I am able to set your mind at rest concerning Mr Arkwright. It was not he that made you an offer. He has bought more mills and now has all he requires.'

'So it was not he that made it? You are certain?'

'Oh, I think you may be sure of it. He was reluctant to speak to me at first, but I persuaded him to my way of thinking. I made it clear that you have placed your affairs in my hands and that—should anything untoward happen to you—your estate would be subject to many trusts and clauses that would make it difficult to buy. He told me in no uncertain terms that he could not give a brass monkey's…'

'Then I may forget him. How good of you to take so much trouble over my affairs,' Sarah said. 'I am not sure how I may thank you.'

'Do not trouble yourself over it. If I needed a reward, I would ask.' His gaze intensified. 'You still look troubled—has something happened while I was gone?'

'Sir Roger visited in the company of James Monks this morning. He seems to imagine that if he persists in his pursuit it is only a matter of time before I cave in.'

'I shall speak to the man—and, if need be, give him a thrashing.'

'No, you must not. If I am unable to make him see I shall never give into his blandishments, I might ask you to warn him—but no violence.' Sarah smiled. 'Monsieur Dupree has already offered to shoot him for me if he attempts to seduce me.'

'Indeed? And what business is it of his? You are not considering him as a husband, I hope?'

'No, of course not. He is a pleasant young man—but perhaps a little young for me. Not much more than two and twenty I would imagine.'

'And you are so long in the tooth, of course—four and twenty? Five and twenty?'

'I was five and twenty on my last birthday,' Sarah replied, a little smile on her lips. Her pulses raced and she felt a surge of joy. Oh, she had missed this banter so much. It was wonderful to have him home, even if his expression was already a little stormy. 'No, I dare say I am no great age—but some people think a woman is on the shelf if she is much past twenty.'

'Stuff and nonsense,' Rupert said. 'Young girls can be delightful, of course, but I prefer a woman of sense.'

Sarah glanced away quickly. The heat in his eyes suggested he wished to take up where they had left off the night before he went away. She was torn by a swift violent longing, a burning desire to be in his arms and to know the sweetness of his kisses. Sarah was ready to become a woman in his arms, to learn why her body sang every time he was near. How they had haunted her dreams since his departure.

She knew she must tell him of her suspicions concerning Sir Roger, but now was not the time. All she could think of for the moment was the look in his eyes and what his lips would taste of if they touched hers.

'You must excuse me,' Rupert said. 'I am stained from the journey. I must change and then speak to my uncle's agent before tea. I shall leave you to continue with whatever pleasures you have planned for this afternoon.'

'I think we may take a turn round the gardens as it is so warm. I shall take a book of plays, which Francesca has gone to fetch…and here she is now. I am sure she will be so pleased to see you.'

'Rupert… It is so good to have you home,' she said and then blushed. 'We've missed you, haven't we, Sarah?' Sarah nodded, noticing the blush and slight hesitancy. John had rushed to embrace his mentor, but Francesca merely dipped a little curtsy and smiled. She was growing up, Sarah thought.

'You look well, Francesca,' Rupert said, going to greet her. He leaned forwards and kissed her cheek. 'I am pleased to tell you that I have invited some friends for this weekend. I believe you will find companions that will bring excitement and pleasure to your life. I have a gift for you, as well as John—I will give it to you this evening. Now, if you will both excuse me...'

Rupert glanced at Sarah before walking away. She was confused by the signal he was giving her. Before he left he had shown her plainly that he meant to keep his distance, but now...having seen her home and realised that she was not a lady despite her education and wealth...did he now feel it was permissible to seduce her?

What could he be thinking of? It was quite out of the question, even if her body did clamour for his and her nights were disturbed by the feverish longings he'd aroused in her.

She could not but think that he was a dangerous flirt, a rake who could not help exercising his powerful charm on the ladies, even if he were not serious about pursuing them.

A part of her mind told Sarah that he was no such thing—that he was decent and honest and misunderstood—but she knew that he had had several mistresses, because Mrs Brancaster had warned her of the fact.

She had visited the housekeeper in her parlour one afternoon, taking a dish of tea with her when Francesca had been practising at the pianoforte. Mrs Brancaster had given her a particular look and she wondered if the staff had noticed something about Rupert's manner towards her. They must think it odd that she continued in the house since she was not a governess and no longer in the marquess's employ.

'Such a pleasant gentleman,' the housekeeper had said as she passed a cup. 'Good-looking and in possession of a handsome fortune, so they say—but it will be a clever woman that catches that particular fish. I've heard he's broken a score of hearts in his time.'

'Well, I dare say he's like most gentlemen,' Sarah said, outwardly calm. 'He has enjoyed being single and may settle once he's married. Do they not say that reformed rakes make the best husbands?'

'I've heard it said, miss,' Mrs Brancaster said, pursing her lips. 'But as I said, it will take a clever mind to trap that one—and he would never marry out of his class. His family is very proud. I suppose if he were desperate for money—but from what I hear of it, he has done very well for himself since he left the army.'

'I expect he will fall in love one day, Mrs

Brancaster. Who knows—perhaps he has done so already.'

'He's more likely to marry for property and rank than love,' the housekeeper said darkly. 'You mark my words, his sort always do.'

Sarah had not argued, for her mind told her it was the truth—though sometimes her heart whispered a completely different story.

Sarah was surprised when she went up to her room and discovered that her trunk had been taken up without her being aware of it. She'd sent most of her things home in this trunk, but when she opened it, she discovered that it had been repacked, probably by her maid. Indeed, she found a short note from Tilly, asking if she should join her mistress at Cavendish Park.

Sarah considered and then decided against it. Francesca was aware of her true standing, but she had not told the housekeeper or the maids that she was an heiress, only that she had come here to escape from an importunate suitor, and thought it best to keep things as they were. After the trip to London, she would never return here and no one need know about her masquerade.

Looking at some of the gowns that Tilly had packed for her, Sarah was tempted by one in particular. It was a yellow silk that she'd never worn. She hadn't taken it with her on her business journey, but it was lovely and would look very well for an informal evening. However, since Rupert had invited guests to stay she would save it for a special occasion.

Sarah's own gowns were all simply cut, but the quality lay in the fit and the material. Most of them were far too elegant for a governess and would occasion comment if she were to wear them here.

When they left for London, she would send for her maid to join her and ask for some of her best evening gowns to be sent to her—though it was the chance of a lifetime to buy herself a new wardrobe. Most of her gowns had been made in Newcastle, by a wonderful French seamstress, who had somehow found herself in the northern city and established her business there. However, it would be pleasant to have a new stylish wardrobe made in London.

She dressed for the evening in her usual gown and was just putting the finishing touches to her *toilette* when someone knocked at the door. With one last glance in the mirror, she went to answer it, feeling a shock as she saw it was Rupert.

'Forgive me, I wanted to give you this in private,' he said and handed her a parcel. 'I've brought gifts for Francesca and John, which I

shall give them before dinner—but I wanted
you to have yours first.'

'A gift for me?' Sarah was surprised. It was
most unconventional for a man to offer someone like her a gift. 'Really, you ought not—I'm
not sure that I can accept....' But she wanted
to and her heart skipped a beat.

'It is merely a token of my appreciation. Perhaps not what I should have liked to give you,
but a simple gift like this should not bring censure on you for accepting it.'

'Perhaps...' Sarah breathed deeply. 'Thank
you, I shall accept it in the spirit it was given.'

'Then I am in your debt. I shall leave you to
come down in your own time. I must see John
and Francesca.'

Sarah nodded and retreated into her room,
closing the door behind her. When she could
breathe properly again, she untied the string
holding the brown paper in place. Inside the
package was a small prayer book in white
leather chased with silver and set with what
looked like a diamond clasp. Not a small gift
by any means, but not an intimate gift—not the
kind of gift a man might give to his mistress.

Of course, Sarah wasn't his mistress yet.
Now what had put that thought into her head?
It was never going to happen!

She ran her fingers over the smooth leather,

thinking how much she would like to use this when they went to church on Sundays. It was a thoughtful gift and just the kind of thing she liked—the kind of gift her father had often given her for birthdays and Christmas. Mr Hardcastle had not often given impromptu gifts and Sarah wondered why Lord Myers had chosen to do so; he'd only been away a few days, even if they had seemed like a lifetime to Sarah.

'Look what Rupert bought for me,' Francesca said, glowing with pleasure as she showed Sarah the pretty fan she'd been given as her gift. The sticks were pierced ivory with gold chasing and painted with French pastoral scenes. 'Is it not lovely?'

'Yes, very pretty,' Sarah agreed, pleased to see the girl so delighted with a simple gift.

His gift could hardly have been more appreciated, for it was something the girl had lacked. She spent most of the evening fanning her cheeks and peeking over the top at them, as if she were practising how to flirt.

Sarah found her innocent pleasure most attractive and a little amusing and, her eyes seeking Rupert's, she saw the glisten of laughter there, as if he shared her thoughts. Then his eyes met hers and his expression changed, becoming so intense that it burned her. He half raised his glass to her and then turned away to speak to John.

Sarah looked down at her plate. Just what was in his mind? She was finding it difficult to judge because the signals were mixed. Rupert seemed so gallant, so kind and considerate at one moment and the next he was the charming rake, intent on making a conquest.

And if she did not stop thinking such foolish things and pay attention to what was being said, they would all wonder what was the matter with her.

John had been given a pair of York tan riding gloves and a sturdy whip made of good leather, but without embellishment. He had worn his gloves to table, but a nod from his mentor made him remove them in order to eat his dinner.

Looking about her, Sarah thought she had never been so content. She'd always regretted the lack of a sister or brother and this was the family she would always have wished for had she been given a choice. The only thing that could make things better was if Rupert actually cared for her…but that was dangerous territory and she pushed it from her mind as the talk turned to a discussion of their guests.

It appeared that they were to have four ladies and six gentlemen, all of whom were Rupert's particular friends, and, Sarah was certain, handpicked for their reliability.

At least with guests in the house, Rupert was unlikely to start an affair with his charge's companion.

Chapter Ten

Mrs Brancaster had had the maids polishing and cleaning like fury ever since Rupert's return. It was obvious that she was delighted at the prospect of having guests and fussed over every detail.

'It's always awkward when the house has no mistress,' she told Sarah in confidence when they were sharing a dish of tea. 'I know what the master likes so it's easy to prepare the menus for Christmas, but it is a long time since we had ladies to stay in the summer. They will want ices and a lobster mousse and an iced soup, besides all manner of sweet trifles….'

'I am sure you will get everything just right,' Sarah said and smiled.

'Would you mind taking a look at what I'd

planned—just to give me an idea whether I'm doing right or not?'

'Yes, of course, if you wish, though you always give us a varied menu.'

Mrs Brancaster had seemed pleased with her interest, especially when Sarah approved all the menus, but added one or two fancy puddings for the ladies. She wasn't sure whether or not she'd imagined it, but of late the housekeeper had seemed more respectful...as if she had recognised that Sarah was more than just Francesca's companion. She was aware that Sarah had money, but of course she had no idea that she was a wealthy heiress.

'I think you've planned everything perfectly,' she said and returned the neatly written menus.

'I'm glad of your advice, miss, for I think you understand the running of a big house and we've lacked a mistress for a long time. A lady's touch makes all the difference.'

'I am used to the direction of a large house, though nothing as splendid or important as this,' Sarah told her. 'I am respectable, Mrs Brancaster, but I was not born a lady.'

'You're as much a lady as any I've met,' the housekeeper said. 'I know it isn't right, but if I'm to call you Sarah—would you call me Dorothy, in private like?'

'I should be delighted to,' Sarah told her.

'Honestly, I've no wish to be put on a pedestal simply because Father left me some money. I am a very ordinary person.'

'Respect is what you're due, miss, and respect is what you'll get—or I'll want to know the reason why. I was honoured when you told me your story. It's understandable you should run away for a while if that man was making himself unpleasant.'

Sarah had not identified the man who had pursued her so relentlessly, giving the housekeeper just the bare bones of her story. She could not cast aspersions on a man's character, even though Sir Roger made her squirm every time he visited the house and did his best to ingratiate himself in her favour.

'Well, you may ask me for help whenever you need it.'

'I was wondering what we should do about the flowers, miss? You'll need more than usual, for the ladies' bedrooms and all the parlours.'

'Yes, we shall. Leave it to me. That is something I can do with pleasure.'

Sarah had spoken to the gardeners herself, requesting more flowers than normal for the house, and on the morning the guests were to arrive she was up early so that she could have them properly arranged. Rupert came into the front downstairs parlour while she was putting the last touches to a large vase she had placed on a table by the window.

'Very pretty,' he approved. 'I've certainly noticed a difference of late. It must be your influence, Sarah.'

'Oh, no, I do very little,' she said, her gaze going over him. She hoped that she was managing to hide the hot sweep of longing that had surged through her. He was so very attractive in those tight-fitting riding breeches. 'Did you take your horse for a gallop?'

'Yes. I like to ride early, before most people are about. I think you have not been riding much of late?'

'We went out twice while you were away,' Sarah replied. 'There doesn't seem to be time for the moment. Mrs Brancaster has been so busy that I've tried to help where I could.'

'It isn't your job to care for the house. We have plenty of maids for that, I think.'

'Yes, of course. I didn't mean it that way...' Sarah blushed as his gaze narrowed. Impossible to explain that a house that was to receive guests for the first time in an age needed a lot of attention. The maids had been working hard and Sarah had merely advised on what furniture should be moved to more advantageous positions, chosen silver and porcelain, inspected linen and checked that the guestrooms were all as they ought to be. Mrs Brancaster was efficient, but she liked her work to be noted and approved, and Sarah had been playing the part of the mistress of the house for the past four days in the flurry to prepare everything to the highest possible standard.

'This is your home, Sarah, for as long as you choose to stay,' Rupert said, giving her a brooding look that made her toes tingle. 'You are my guest and you must join the company while they are here. I do not want you to hover like a spectre at the feast.'

'I'm sure I should do no such thing!'

He smiled at her spark of defiance. 'I meant that I wanted you to enjoy our guests and feel a part of things.'

'Yes, my lord. I shall of course enjoy having guests.'

'Back to that, are we?' His eyes gleamed. 'One of these days I'm going to make you so sorry for this, Sarah. Why do you find it so impossible to say my name?'

Because she needed to keep her distance, lest she fall into a heap at his feet? Her knees were decidedly unreliable and she felt a need to put her arms about him, kiss that wonderfully soft yet firm mouth and run her fingers through his dark hair. What else she might wish to do was completely out of the question for a respectable unmarried lady and brought a hot flush to her cheeks. She fought the need, forcing herself to speak coolly and ignore the heat coursing through her entire body.

'Forgive me, Rupert. I do find it difficult sometimes.' Especially when he looked at her with dark eyes that seemed to burn into her soul. His breeches moulded to powerful thighs, his shoulders were broad and seemed almost to strain the seams of his immaculate coat— just right for a woman to lean on in times of trouble....

Was she mad? Sarah was suddenly amused by her wandering thoughts. She had never dreamed that she, Sarah Hardcastle, would ever meet a man she would lust after to such an extent that her wits were scattered every time he came close.

'Just what is going on in that beautiful head?' Rupert's voice had dropped, become intimate and husky. Sarah tingled with anticipation as he moved closer. He was going to kiss her and she would simply melt into a puddle. 'I could almost think—'

'My lord, a carriage has drawn up in the courtyard.' One of the footmen entered the room and Rupert moved away with a muffled snarl of frustration.

'Thank you, Hodges. I shall come at once. We shall continue this interesting conversation at another time, Sarah.'

'Yes, sir.' Sarah dropped her gaze, her cheeks warm, but her heart was pounding. Had she given herself away? She rather thought she might have. The question was: would he take advantage? 'I must find Francesca. She will want to meet your guests.'

She hurried after him from the parlour, hearing him greeting someone called Freddie as she ran quickly up the stairs. Francesca was just emerging from her bedchamber. As Sarah had anticipated, she looked nervous at the prospect of meeting people she did not know.

'What shall I say to them?' she asked, her eyes on Sarah's face. 'I'm not sure what I ought to do....'

'Just be yourself, Francesca,' Sarah said. 'People will not expect you to be witty or clever, so there is no need to try to think of something interesting to say. Just greet everyone—as you would the friends you know—and tell them you are pleased to have them here, welcome them to Cavendish. When everyone has settled in we shall meet and conversations will begin. Make your contribution if you have something to say—but always think before you say anything controversial.'

'I haven't forgotten what Rupert said to me at dinner that night.' Francesca smiled and reached for her hand. 'I'm so glad you're here, Sarah. I should have been terrified if I'd been alone.'

'Everyone will love you, as I do, dearest.'

Francesca nodded and linked arms with her. 'I feel much better now.'

'Good. Remember this is an experience to enjoy, not one to dread. Just because these people have come down from London, it doesn't mean they will be different from your neighbours. I am sure they will all be delighted to meet you.'

The shadows had lifted from Francesca's face. She looked beautiful and happy, and Sarah's own mood lightened. For the next few days she would forget her problems and do her best to see that all the guests were content.

'I am not sure I understand your position here.' Lady Foxton looked down her long nose at Sarah. 'You are Francesca's companion— but you are also the daughter of a wealthy mill owner. Is that correct?'

'Yes, ma'am.' Sarah's head went up slightly as she met the look of disapproval in the older woman's eyes. Lady Foxton had a lovely daughter of a similar age to Francesca and the two had become friends immediately. The girl was open and charming, radiating friendliness to everyone she met, but her mother was another matter. 'I came here to be with Francesca—and I have helped her with her studies.'

'What are you—a governess or a companion?'

'Sarah is a friend,' Rupert said, coming up to them. 'Are you quite comfortable there, Lady Foxton? Would you permit me to show you the long gallery before dinner?'

'How delightful,' the lady cooed, bestowing a warm smile on him. She got up as he offered his arm and walked away without another glance in Sarah's direction.

Sarah was unruffled by the lady's interrogation. It was not the first time she'd come up against barely concealed hostility when mixing in society. Lady Foxton was one of the haughtiest she'd met, but others had been even ruder, if not to her face then behind her back. She was well aware that while the gentlemen seemed ready to accept her for what she was and even to admire her, some ladies found her company not to their taste. As a young girl staying at the home of one of her friends from school, Sarah had come up against prejudice and she no longer allowed it to disturb her. She had friends enough amongst the lower echelons of society and the daughters of rich merchants. To imagine she would ever be universally welcome in the drawing rooms of London would be to deceive herself—and Sarah was not her father's daughter for nothing.

'I say, was that old trout giving you the third degree?' Sir Freddie Holloway came up to her. A man of about Rupert's age, he was not exactly handsome, but he had a nice smile and Sarah liked him. 'Take no notice of her, Miss Hardcastle—she's buried three husbands and they say they were all glad to go.'

'Oh, no,' Sarah said and laughed. 'You really must not, you know. I don't mind at all. I'm not Lady Foxton's equal and I would not presume to think it.'

'A damn sight better, if you ask me, m'dear,' he said. He sipped his wine. 'One thing about Merrivale, he keeps a good cellar. Pity he couldn't be here, but I suppose the place has too many memories.'

'Yes, I dare say. Francesca and John have missed his company, but it is better now that they have Lord Myers.'

'Myers is a good fellow. Bit of a dasher with the ladies, don't you know. He manages to find the sweetest little fillies…but I ought not to say. Reformed character, he tells me.'

'I dare say Lord Myers is no different from

most gentlemen,' Sarah said and smiled, though her heart caught with pain.

'Has more luck than most,' Freddie said. 'I remember when we were both after the same charmer—an opera dancer, she was. Thought I was in with a chance, but as soon as he looked her way...' He rolled his eyes and laughed. 'Wouldn't say this to Francesca, of course, but you're a lady of sense. She's a beauty, ain't she?' He sighed and looked across the room at the two young girls laughing together. 'I'd make a stab at fixing my interest with her—but I need an heiress. Pockets to let, don't you know. Suppose you wouldn't be interested in taking pity on me, Miss Hardcastle?'

'I believe you are teasing, Sir Freddie.'

Sarah wondered if Rupert had invited him for her benefit. He was a personable man and she liked him. She thought they might become friends in time—but would she be able to trust him with the management of her empire? He seemed the perfect fop, a man of fashion without a serious thought in his head—but of course she did not know him well enough to judge.

'Of course, m'dear. What else is there for a man to do? Life is boring enough as it is—not when in delightful company, of course.'

'Do you have no ambition, sir?' Sarah looked at him in amusement. He was pleasant company, but such an attitude would drive her mad in a week. She was accustomed to hard work and would expect it of the man she married.

'Ambition?' He raised his brows in mock horror. 'Terrible word that, Miss Hardcastle. I had it once, I think, but somehow it just drifted away like mist on a summer morn. Should I take up poetry, do you think? I dare say it would serve me as well as that Byron fellow.'

'I imagine Lord Byron works hard at his poems. They are very clever, you know.'

'Another avenue closed.' Sir Freddie laughed. 'Yes, dear lady. I know I am incorrigible. Excuse me, I must talk to Morrison. He has a filly I'm interested in—of the equine variety.' He winked at her and strolled off.

Sarah's gaze passed over the assembled company. Mr Norris was only a year or two older than Francesca and seemed pleasant. Lord Phillips was a little older than Rupert and of a serious disposition; Captain Francis was a dashing fellow and talked endlessly of the *regiment*. Mr Stevens and Sir Andrew were both in their early twenties and looked handsome, pleasant young men—the kind that might become suitors for Francesca. The other two ladies were Mrs Carter and her daughter Helena. It was Helena who came to Sarah and took a seat beside her next.

'Lord Myers told me that he was thinking of giving a small dance while we're here—nothing grand, just an impromptu affair. He said he was going to send out invitations to his neighbours. I prefer the balls in London, because country affairs can be so boring, do you not think so? There are never enough personable men to go round.'

Sarah hesitated. She knew exactly what the young girl meant, for quite often at home the assemblies were very thin of presentable gentlemen, most being older and married or the kind that trod on your feet and exuded sweaty odours—and there were usually more unmarried girls than eligible gentlemen.

'We do have some presentable neighbours,' Sarah said with a twinkle in her eye. 'Besides, some of our guests are rather attractive, Miss Carter.'

'Yes, I know—but Mama says I must look higher than a mere knight and she would not consider a plain Mr anything, even if he is rich.' She sighed deeply. 'This looking for a husband is so frustrating, is it not? I suppose you do not bother over such things? You can afford to be independent and not worry about catching a husband.'

'No, I do not bother over such trifles,' Sarah agreed, managing not to laugh at the girl's clumsiness in describing her as an old maid and past such things—which perhaps she was. Even Sir Freddie had treated her as he might a favourite aunt or an older lady with whom it was safe to flirt. 'I am much too old to worry about marriage.'

'Oh…' Helena flushed. 'I did not mean it to sound like that—but I heard Mama say you were rich and could buy yourself a husband if you chose.' Her colour deepened, as if she realised she had plunged deeper into the morass.

'Please do not worry,' Sarah said kindly. 'I am not in the least offended.'

'I did not intend—'

'Sir Roger Grey and Mr James Monks….'

'Oh…' Helena flushed as the names were announced. 'I did not know that Sir Roger was staying in the country.'

The painful expression in her eyes told Sarah that the gentleman had made an impression on her, though she could not be sure whether it was favourable or otherwise.

'Helena, come here, my dear,' Mrs Carter called and the girl rose obediently and went to her mama.

Sarah saw that Rupert had returned with Lady Foxton. Immediately, he made every other man in the room look less impressive. There was something so very masculine about him…

so powerful. His long legs looked strong and muscular in his tight-fitting breeches, his shoulders broad without being massive, and his countenance noble—like a beautiful marble statue from ancient Rome, only vital and very much alive.

'Sarah.' Sir Roger bowed his head to her. 'We did not realise you had guests staying. I trust we do not intrude?'

'How could you, sir? I am sure Lord Myers must welcome all his uncle's neighbours.'

'May I sit beside you for a moment?' He fluffed out his coat-tails and sat without waiting for her answer. 'You look very well, Sarah. That gown becomes you.'

Sarah knew that he'd been puzzled by the plain gown she'd worn when he called at the house for the first time since her arrival. She was now wearing one of her own.

'Thank you, sir. You are most kind,' Sarah said. 'I believe that was the gong for nuncheon. I am sure you will be welcome to stay.'

'Oh, no, we shall not intrude further,' Sir Roger said. 'I am returning home in a few days—when may I call on you? I should like to speak with you in private.'

'I fail to see what you can have to say to me, sir. I have told you before that you are wasting your time.'

'A matter has been drawn to my attention. I think you would be wise to hear what I have to say—unless you wish to be ostracised by all your new friends?' The look in his eyes was so menacing!

Sarah went cold all over. 'What on earth can you mean?'

'I see you are listening now. A pity this is neither the time nor the place. I shall call in the morning at about ten. Please be prepared to see me. I should be loath to threaten you, Sarah.'

With that he got up and walked away, leaving her to stare after him in dismay. As she joined the general exodus to the dining room, Sarah's thoughts were in a whirl. Whatever could he have meant? Surely he was not referring to her masquerade as a governess. While that might make some of the guests frown, it was hardly likely to ruin her.

He was bluffing. She had done nothing of which she ought to be ashamed and she would not allow him to intimidate her.

'Is something wrong?' Rupert asked when he found her alone in the small parlour later that day. 'Why are you not with the others?'

'I wanted a moment to be quiet. I shall join them for tea.'

'Did Lady Foxton upset you? Her bark is

worse than her bite, Sarah. She will become accustomed to you in time.'

'Will she?' Sarah frowned. 'I wasn't upset by what she said. I've met ladies of her kind before and they do not bother me particularly.'

'Something has distressed you—was it Sir Roger?'

'It isn't important. Shall we join the others for tea?'

'He has disturbed you. Please tell me. If he has made himself unpleasant I'll thrash him for you.'

'No, please do not. He did make a threat, but I shall not regard it.'

'What kind of a threat?

'He said that a matter had come to his attention—one that, if revealed, would mean that my new friends, as he called them, would no longer wish to know me.'

'That is nonsense! You haven't done anything improper or illegal, have you?'

She lifted her head. 'You shouldn't need to ask. I told you the truth about myself. You must know I did.'

'Yes...' He nodded. 'He must have something up his sleeve. Leave him to me, Sarah. I shall sort the rogue out for you.'

'No, I will deal with it. I have done nothing wrong so he can have no reason for his blackmail.'

'You think he hopes to blackmail you into accepting his offer?'

'He might. I have made it clear I shall not accept him.' She shook her head. 'Please do not trouble yourself, Rupert. He can do nothing to harm me.'

'He's a sly rogue,' Rupert replied and looked thoughtful. 'Forget him for now, Sarah. Whatever he has to say to you, we'll sort him between us.'

'Yes, of course,' she agreed, but a cold shiver ran down her spine.

What could Sir Roger know that might make her an outcast from society?

Sarah spent a restless night, tossing on her pillows. She had painted a smile on her face the previous evening, but felt as if a shadow hung over her. The look in Sir Roger's eyes had been menacing and triumphant. Clearly, he believed he had found a way to coerce her into doing what he wanted—what could it be?

Surely there was nothing in her past that he could learn to her disadvantage? She had tried to dismiss her fears as nonsense, as Rupert clearly felt them to be. Her father was the owner of several mills and her mother had been the daughter of a clergyman. Sarah Richards was the granddaughter of a baronet, of good birth if no fortune. Sarah had been named for her and she remembered her mother as a quiet gentle lady who had always been respectable and had taught her daughter to be the same.

How could Sir Roger know something that would make the people gathered in this house turn against her?

Of course he could not. It was an empty threat intended to force her into accepting his offer. He would quite possibly invent a lie, but she must simply deny it and hope that others believed her—particularly Rupert.

With that in mind, she turned over and finally fell into a restless sleep in which she dreamed that she was on an island in the mist and all alone.

Sarah dressed in a plain but stylish grey gown. She went downstairs to the kitchen and told Mrs Brancaster that Sir Roger might call that morning.

'I shall be in the back parlour if he does,' she said. 'I believe he wants to speak with me in private on some matter—if you will kindly have him shown there.'

'Yes, of course.' The housekeeper looked

at her oddly, but made no comment as to the wisdom of her decision.

Standing looking out at the garden, Sarah heard the footsteps and turned as someone entered. Sir Roger had dressed smartly, obviously intending to impress.

'Ah, Sarah,' he said and gave her the false smile she disliked so much. 'I am delighted you granted me this interview. You know, of course, that I wish to renew my offer of marriage. You are the woman I adore and it would make me the happiest of men if you were to become my wife.'

'Forgive me, sir. I have told you before that I shall never marry you.' Sarah looked at him coldly. 'If that is all you have to say, I shall leave you.'

'You would be well advised to stay,' he said and moved to block her path. 'I had hoped you might be sensible—but as you force me to tell you, I have no choice....' He paused for effect as Sarah dug her nails into her palms. Why did he look so pleased with himself?

'Nothing you can say will harm me. I have good friends...'

'Lord Myers, I presume?' Sir Roger sneered. 'How long do you imagine he will harbour you in his house when he discovers you are an impostor?'

'What do you mean?'

'You believe yourself to be the daughter of Sarah Richards and Hardcastle, do you not?'

'Yes, I am.' Sarah's mouth was suddenly dry, her heart racing. 'Please be plain, sir. I do not know what you mean.'

'Have you really no idea, Sarah? Did you never wonder why you were the only child of the marriage?' He looked horribly confident and sure as he added, 'Your mother could not give Hardcastle children. He went to a prostitute and lay with her, kept her in seclusion and gave her money to stay away from other men. When she gave birth to you, he took you home with him and his wife accepted you as her own. You have no claim to gentle blood at all—you are, in fact, the daughter of a woman of low birth who made her living on her back.'

Sarah gasped and stepped back, feeling as if he had thrown cold water over her. 'No, it is not true,' she gasped. 'You are lying. Father would have told me…my mother loved me…'

'Your father never told anyone, but someone knew his secret. Your true mother came looking for you before she died. You might wish to know that she died of the whore's disease and your father refused to let her see you even though he knew she was dying.'

'No…' Sarah put her hands to her face. 'You are a wicked, evil man to say such things. My father would not have been so cruel.'

'If you do not believe me, ask your uncle. He told me the truth—which is why he has agreed that you should marry me without delay. Who else would want you now?'

'You are lying. This is just a wicked tale to discredit me and force me to sell my father's business. I suppose that offer came from you?'

'I would buy the mills if I could, but I want you to marry me, Sarah.'

'Even though you say my mother was a whore?' Sarah's eyes flashed with temper.

'I don't care whose daughter you are. I am willing to overlook your birth. You have the money and that's all I'm interested in. If you want to know, I shall be ruined if you don't marry me. My creditors have hung on because they thought I had prospects, but if they learn you have other ideas…'

'Your money problems are not my concern,' Sarah said coldly. 'This is the final time I shall tell you. If you persist, I shall speak to Lord Myers. Please leave and do not return. I have no wish to speak to you ever again.'

Sir Roger glared at her, disbelief in his eyes.

He had been so certain she would crumble when he revealed her terrible secret.

'You'll pay for this, Miss High and Mighty Hardcastle,' he said and lurched towards her in a fury. 'I shall give you twenty-four hours to reconsider and then I'll start spreading the tale. If you imagine your friends will wish to know you, then you are mistaken. Think about it carefully before you ruin yourself for good—and don't think your fine friends will save you. If they should manage to avert a scandal, I'll kill you. One way or the other I'll have my revenge on you.'

Sarah stood absolutely still as he stalked out of the room. His threat to kill her had not sunk in as yet. She was numb, but the pain had started deep inside her. Her mother was not her mother, even though she'd always loved her as if they were related by blood. Her father had gone to a prostitute to get himself an heir....

'How could you?' Sarah whispered as her throat began to close. 'How could you die without telling me the truth?'

Hot tears burned behind her eyes. She struggled to hold them back but her throat was closing and she felt so much pain that it was all she could do to stay on her feet.

'Mama...' Sarah brushed away the tears that squeezed from the corner of her eye and ran down her cheek. She felt sweeping loneliness as she realised that her whole life had been based on a lie.

Sarah had always known that she could not hope to mix in the upper echelons of society, but her mother was of gentle birth and that had been sufficient. It did not matter that her father was a rough northern man with an abrasive tongue and a sharp business brain. He'd been honest and kind to her, giving her all the love she could want—except that it had all been a lie.

How could he have left her to discover the terrible truth for herself? He must have been certain his secret was safe, believed that no one knew she was not his wife's daughter.

The knowledge that her mother was not truly her birth mother was so painful that Sarah hardly knew how to hold her tears inside. Yet she knew she must go on, she must put on a brave face and pretend that everything was as it should be. There were a few more hours before Sir Roger would carry out his threat.

Chapter Eleven

What was she to do? Sarah's problem lingered on her mind as she consulted with Mrs Brancaster on the menus, changed flowers and then waited for the guests to come down. Some of the gentlemen and most of the ladies did not rise until just before noon and were down in time for nuncheon. Until that time Sarah was free to attend her chores, to walk in the gardens if she chose, or, had she wished, to go riding. However, she knew that Rupert had ordered she was to be accompanied by two grooms whenever she rode out, whether or not in the company of Francesca. To put them to so much trouble just for her pleasure seemed wrong. Besides, walking was a favourite pastime and she decided on a walk to the lake.

The fresh air cleared her head a little. She was still Miss Sarah Hardcastle, still wealthy and she still had friends—but for how long once the spiteful Sir Roger had carried out his threat? Some might not care a fig for his revelations, but the kind of society hostesses that would welcome Francesca would not wish to know Sarah once the rumours began to circulate.

She was determined not to allow him to frighten her into submission. Nothing would make her agree to his proposal now. If it were only she who would suffer, she would remain where she was and accept the consequences— but could she inflict her shame on Francesca? The girl was so looking forward to her come out and to Sarah being her chaperon, but if the scandal became common knowledge that would be at an end. No one would invite the daughter of a low-born whore to their social evenings— at least none of the important hostesses—and that meant Francesca would be tarnished by Sarah's shame. Also, the very fact that she had bad blood in her would cast doubts on how she had conducted herself while living under the marquess's roof. It only needed someone to say she had come there under a false name and she would be finished.

Her throat was tight with pain and she could scarcely control her desire to weep. To leave the girl she had come to love—and Lord Rupert—would slay her. The way he had looked at her the previous day...she'd hoped that he truly cared for her. Yet Sir Roger had said he'd shut Arkwright up—so did he know the truth?

No, she shook her head. Had he known he would have requested her to leave. He would have been aware of the scandal it would cause if her secret became known.

Sarah could not hold back her tears. They trickled silently down her cheeks as she stood by the lake, watching the swans swim gracefully across the still waters. Normally the sight would have been a pleasure, but all she could think was that she was seeing it for the last time. She would have to leave...and she could not tell anyone why.

Brushing away her tears, Sarah raised her head. She would leave a letter for Francesca, assuring her of her love and apologising for having to leave. She would tell Rupert that she had discovered something that made it impossible for her to take up his kind offer to stay with them in London.

Having made up her mind, she turned as she heard a voice hail her. She saw it was Monsieur Dupree and forced a smile as she walked to meet him.

'Forgive me, my so-dear *mademoiselle*—'

Andre began just as the shot rang out. Sarah felt it strike her left shoulder, gave a cry of distress and fell to the ground in a heap.

'*Mademoiselle*... Mademoiselle Sarah...' The Frenchman sounded distraught as he bent over her to discover the extent of the damage. She was barely conscious as he exclaimed and clucked over her, but then, as he gathered her into his arms and began to stride away in the direction of the house, she fainted.

'What happened?' Rupert demanded. He had seen them from the house and went out immediately to meet them. 'Good grief! She has been shot.'

'She was by the lake,' Andre said. 'I had seen her walking there and she seemed distressed. I was told she had a visitor this morning—that so-dreadful Sir Roger. I do not why she wept for he is nothing but a scoundrel.'

'He has been trying to force her to marry him, which was why she came here as a governess.'

'He is the one who so upset my Sarah?' The Frenchman's eyes flashed with anger. 'I, with my bare hands, will kill him.'

'I would have been there before you, but I need to know who did this to her.' He held out his arms. 'Give her to me, Dupree. You've carried her far enough. Alert Mrs Brancaster that we need someone to fetch the doctor and help Sarah undress.'

'*Oui,* my lord. This I shall do at once.'

Rupert frowned as he carried Sarah into the house. She moaned slightly and he thanked God she was still alive. Pain assailed him as he realised he might have lost her—lost her before he'd even had time to be sure of his intentions for the future or to tell her of his feelings.

Who could have done such a wicked thing? Had Sir Roger taken a spiteful revenge on her for refusing him—or was her uncle playing a double game? He was, after all, her heir, though Sarah could change things if she made a new will.

He felt the frustration and anger burn inside him as he looked down at her pale face. If ever he discovered who had done this wicked thing, he would thrash him to an inch of his life—and he would see the culprit hanged. A fraction of an inch closer to her heart and Sarah would have died. The thought shook him to the core. What would he have done if she had been killed? The pain of it was almost overwhelming as he realised that he would find her loss unbearable. She had intrigued him from the start, but much warmer feelings had been gradually growing within him.

God damn it, he was in love with her. He'd found her amusing, contrary and at times irritating, but this feeling had been growing inside him for a while now. It wasn't just lust he felt for her, but something much deeper—something he'd never expected that he would feel. Indeed, until this moment he had doubted that the romantic love of the poets truly existed, but now he knew exactly how those tortured knights felt when their love was lost to them.

Rupert's wariness had made him hold back from giving more of himself than he had. Having been burned and scorned by Madeline as a young man, he had held a part of himself aloof, never giving his heart, always keeping a part of himself in reserve. He'd enjoyed pleasant relationships with his various mistresses, but, he acknowledged now, none of them had meant even a tiny part of what he felt for Sarah.

She must not die! He would seek out the rogue who had done this to her, but for the moment the answers must wait. He had given orders that she was to be accompanied by grooms if she rode out beyond the estate, but he had not dreamed she might be in danger here. The keepers must be doubled, but that would do later. All that mattered for the moment was that she should be made as comfortable as possible—and that she should not die of her wound.

Rupert knew only too well how painful these wounds were and how easily they turned septic, resulting in blood poisoning or a fever that killed. He'd seen too many strong men succumb to fevers after being tended by the surgeons.

Pray God she did not die. He would never forgive himself. He should have protected her better! The wild thoughts churned endlessly in his mind as he strode towards the staircase.

'My lord…' Mrs Brancaster had been alerted and came running at him as he reached the bottom of the stairs. 'Oh, poor Sarah. Who could have wanted to harm her? She's such a lovely lady.'

'Yes, she is,' he agreed grimly. 'Rest assured that when I discover the culprit he will be punished. If I do not kill him myself, I shall see him hang.'

'He certainly deserves it, sir.' Mrs Brancaster hesitated. 'Do you think it was that man…Sir Roger? He called to see her this morning and one of the footmen said they had words. Jennings did not hear what was said, but he heard raised voices and he thought she sounded upset for he was in two minds to go in, and then Sir Roger came out with a face as black as thunder and pushed past him in a right temper. Sarah went straight up to her room and looked as if she was crying.'

'Indeed. If that is the case it may explain why she was out at the lake alone, when I'd told her…' Rupert shook her head. 'It does not matter. Draw back the sheets, Mrs Brancaster. We need someone to undress her and sit with her until the doctor comes. I would stay myself— but I have guests to see to.'

'Yes, of course, sir. Besides, that would not be fitting.'

'You are perfectly right, Mrs Brancaster. If I may, I shall call to see how she goes on after the doctor has been. You will make sure that someone stays with her all the time—at least until we are certain she is out of danger.'

'Yes, of course, sir. I'll come in as much as I can myself. I don't mind telling you I've become quite fond of the lady. When she first came I wasn't sure—but of course she is a lady, not a governess.'

'Thank you.'

Rupert placed Sarah gently amongst the soft linen sheets, stood looking at her for a moment and then turned away. His eyes were dark and angry as he left the room. He wanted to inflict vengeance on the devil who had hurt her. He wanted it to be him who had been shot in her place, to take away the pain he knew she must suffer. If he had only himself to think of he would not have stirred from her side, but it would be impossible in the circumstances. Besides, he must tell Francesca and John, both of whom would be distressed.

'Sarah has been shot?' Francesca looked at him in dismay. 'Then that shot *was* meant for her when we were out riding. She dismissed the idea as nonsense, but John said he saw the man take aim directly at her.'

'Yes, I know. He could not describe the man's appearance, unfortunately, except to say he wore the clothes a gamekeeper or poacher might wear—a large grey coat over dark breeches, a muffler about his neck, which hid his chin, and a black hat pulled down over his eyes. The description is accurate, I think, but of little use in finding the rogue.'

'How is she?' Francesca asked. 'Is she in terrible pain?'

'I imagine she will be when she recovers her senses. The doctor has been sent for and one of the maids is caring for her until then. Mrs Brancaster will send for me if I am needed.'

'May I visit her, please?'

'I think you should wait until the doctor has been, Francesca. She is being looked after and will be better once her wound is tended and she has been given something to help the pain—either laudanum or some brandy, I think.'

'Poor Sarah. I do not like to think of her in pain. She has been as a sister to me, Uncle Rupert—I cannot tell you the difference she made to our lives here.'

'Sarah has her own charm,' Rupert agreed and frowned. 'We should all miss her if she left us.'

'She wouldn't leave us!'

'She might wish to go away somewhere once she feels better—perhaps to France or Italy where she could recover in peace and quiet.'

'It is peaceful at Cavendish. I need Sarah here with me,' Francesca protested.

'Yet her life may be in danger if she stays here. She may have to travel for her own safety.'

'If she does, I shall go with her.' Francesca set her mouth stubbornly. 'I have no wish for a London Season if Sarah cannot be with me.'

'She would feel guilty for taking you away from it, Francesca. I am not sure what she will wish to do. She has been shot at twice now and in a place where she had every reason to feel safe. I cannot think what might have happened had Monsieur Dupree not chanced to be walking by the lake.'

'He did not happen to be there. He followed her,' Francesca said. 'I think he is in love with Sarah. He told me he would give his life for her.'

'I see.' Rupert frowned, for he had not realised the dancing master's intentions were so serious. Had Sarah encouraged him to think of her? He felt a sharp slash of jealousy, but quashed it. His feelings were not important. Only Sarah mattered now. 'Shall you tell John about her injury or would you prefer I did?'

'I'll tell him. I suppose you will have to inform the guests.'

'Yes, I imagine they have the right to know, if only to warn them a dangerous man is in the vicinity.'

'You don't think he will shoot anyone else?'

'I think not, but I shall be asking the keepers to patrol the grounds frequently just in case.'

Francesca shuddered. 'It is so horrid, just as we're having such a lovely time. Poor Sarah. Who could want to harm her?'

'I do not know—unless it was Sir Roger?'

Francesca's brows rose. 'Why would he do such a thing? I thought he liked her.'

'He wants to marry her for her money and she does not wish to oblige him. I gather he has been quite unpleasant on more than one occasion. She told you why she came here—did she not tell you about him?'

'Not his name, though I did notice she seemed to avoid Sir Roger if she could. To think I asked him to stay to nuncheon! Sarah should have warned me.'

'I dare say she thought he would accept her answer in time—and we cannot know who did this to her. We can surmise, but we have no proof.'

'Well, I shall tell Mrs Brancaster that I do not wish him admitted again.'

'That would be the height of rudeness and might harm you. We have no proof of his guilt. However, should he come again make sure you are never alone with him—and make sure someone is with Sarah. I shall speak to the man myself if he dares to show his face here.'

'I think I shall just pop up and see if the doctor has arrived. I shall not go in if he is with her, of course.'

'You must not forget your guests,' Rupert reminded her. 'Sarah will be properly cared for and you may visit her when you can.'

'Yes, I understand. She would tell me the same, but...' Francesca's face creased. 'I should be so upset if anything... If she should die...'

'She will not die,' Rupert said, his expression grim. His fists balled at his sides. Sarah's death was unthinkable. He could not bear to speak of it, even to the girl who loved her. 'I shall not allow it. She is to be attended at all times and the doctor will be sent for if she shows the slightest sign of taking a turn for the worse.'

'You care about her, too, don't you?' Francesca

said. 'I'm glad. I thought once you didn't like her, but I was wrong. You do not show your feelings openly—but you care.'

'And you, miss, see far too much—or imagine that you do,' Rupert said and smiled. 'Run along and try not to worry overly. I am sure she will recover. Sarah is far too strong to die over a little thing like this.'

Francesca nodded and left him, walking quickly from the room. His expression hardened after she left. He wished he was as confident as he'd made out to Francesca.

If Sarah should die or become a permanent invalid because of this, he would kill the man who shot her if it took him the rest of his life to find the devil! And to hell with the law. What would his life be to him if she were dead? When the rogue was caught he would wish he had never been born!

Sarah moaned and opened her eyes. The room was lit by one small candle and she was aware of someone sitting by her bed in the semi-darkness.

'Mother…' she whimpered. 'Mother…' She could feel the dampness on her cheeks and was aware of both the pain in her left shoulder and her heart. 'I was walking and…'

'It's all right, Sarah, I am here,' Francesca

said and came to the bed. 'Rupert told me I should leave your nursing to the maids, but I sent Agnes to bed and said I would sit with you for an hour. She was falling asleep when I came in and I didn't trust her to look after you. Mrs Brancaster will be here soon. Are you in terrible pain?'

'My shoulder hurts,' Sarah said. 'You should go to bed, Francesca. Rupert was right. There are plenty of maids to nurse me. It is not fitting that you should wait on me.'

'Would you like a drink? Or some of the mixture the doctor left for you?' Francesca placed a hand on her forehead. 'You do not seem to have taken a fever. I think that is what has been worrying them all. The doctor said it was just the laudanum that made you sleep so long, but everyone has been so anxious. All our guests have been asking after you—especially Sir Freddie and Lord Phillips.'

'How very kind,' Sarah said and reached for her hand. 'How long is it since I was shot?'

'Yesterday morning. You fainted and then the doctor gave you a strong dose of the medicine—and you have been given more since so that you did not feel too much pain.'

'Has anything happened? Have you heard anything?'

'Rupert has the keepers out looking for strangers. Monsieur Dupree found you and the description he gave of your attacker was the same as John's, when he described the rogue who fired at us when we were out riding. This time he met with more success. Rupert is furious. He has taken on more keepers and has them patrolling the grounds at all hours.'

'Oh, no, what a nuisance for him,' Sarah said, pushing herself up against the pillows. The movement was tentative, because her shoulder hurt rather a lot and she did not wish to make it worse, but the room seemed stuffy and her mouth was dry. 'Do you think I could have some water, please?'

'Of course.' Francesca went over to the washstand and poured some of the cold water into a glass, bringing it to her. 'Would you like me to hold it for you, dearest?'

'I think I can manage.' Sarah took the glass, sipped and swallowed a few times and then handed it back, groaning a little as she felt the ache start up again.

'You are in pain. Shall I get you something to ease it?'

'If you mean laudanum, no, thank you. I would rather put up with this than become addicted to that stuff. I know Mama was taking too much towards the end…' Sarah caught her breath as a far worse pain struck her. 'Francesca…' She reached out to touch the girl's hand. 'If you should hear something about me—something unpleasant—you will not hate me. Believe me, I did not know. I should never have come here had I known the truth, if it is the truth….' She shook her head. 'I'm not rambling. There is something I must tell you all, but I think I should tell Rupert first. Depending on his advice…I may have to leave you…'

'Rupert said something…' Francesca faltered. 'I don't want you to leave me, Sarah. Rupert said you might have to travel abroad for a while for your own sake. Would you not let me accompany you? I don't care about a silly Season. I dare say we should meet lots of gentlemen I might like.'

'Oh, my love—did he truly say that to you?' Sarah felt a pain stab at her heart. So Sir Roger had already carried out his threat to betray her terrible secret to the world. It meant that all her plans for the spring would have to be forgotten. At home, Sarah would not care that people thought ill of her, but she could not have her shame blight Francesca's future. That would be selfish and unkind—though leaving her would be like losing the sister she'd never had. 'What else did he say?'

'He said he would thrash the devil that had hurt you if he caught him and…he said that I must be polite to Sir Roger despite what he did and he would deal with the matter. I don't even want to speak to him.' Francesca's expression was indignant. 'I hate him for hurting you.'

Any doubt that Sir Roger had begun to spread the word of her lowly birth was crushed. Francesca had dismissed it, of course, as Sarah had known she would; the affection between them was too strong. She was not quite sure what was in Rupert's mind—oh, he had asked her to call him that, but that was before he knew her secret.

What would he make of her now? He could not allow the plans for Sarah to be Francesca's chaperon to go ahead in town the following spring. He had a duty to the girl and so did Sarah. Francesca must be protected from scandal at all costs.

'I think I shall sleep now,' Sarah said, though it was far from the truth. 'Go to bed and rest, Francesca. I do not need to be watched now. I am out of danger.'

'I am so glad. I should have been devastated had you come to harm. I do truly love you, Sarah.'

'I love you, too, as if you were my sister. If I must leave you, it will be with a heavy heart— but I shall always write to you, until you tell me to stop, and perhaps we may meet again one day.'

'Yes, of course we shall. You are my friend. We shall be together sometime when this stupid business is over.'

'Yes. Kiss me, dearest, and then leave me to sleep.'

Francesca bent and kissed her cheek, then went softly from the room. Sarah lay back against her pillows, the tears running unheeded down her cheeks. She was hardly aware of them.

It hurt so much to know that her darling mama was not her true mother. She had loved her so much, been so happy and secure in the knowledge that she was Sarah Hardcastle's daughter, proud to carry her name. Now she knew that it was not true. The shocking revelation was hard enough for her to bear, but it must not be allowed to reflect on Francesca— or on Rupert.

He was a man and might take the news in his stride. He might find a way to hush the scandal up and deflect the mud that would inevitably be thrown at them, but Sarah could imagine the whispers.

'I did wonder at her living there with him...a confirmed rake...with no proper chaperon.'

'Well, my dear, you know how these things are. She is no better than her mother...blood will out.'

Everyone would think she'd been Lord Myers's mistress while sharing a roof with Francesca. She'd come there under false pretences and if that got out her fate would be sealed. If she dared to visit London with the girl, she would be shunned, ostracised by the proud hostesses who ruled society. Francesca's chances would be ruined. She might find a man who would love her enough to marry her, but her Season would be overshadowed by the scandal.

No, try as she might, Sarah could see no way she could carry out her promise. Indeed, the longer she stayed here, the worse it would be. If she could raise the energy she would dress, pack a small bag and leave now. Her things could be sent on later. She tried putting her legs over the side of the bed and immediately felt dizzy. Her departure must wait for another day. If Sir Roger had spread his lies, the damage was already done. She would go as soon as she was able to dress herself. In the meantime, she would write to her uncle and ask him to confirm or deny the truth of her birth, but she had little hope that the story was a lie. Why should anyone invent such a pitiful tale?

Lying back against her pillows, Sarah tried to make sense of what she had been told. Her father was a hard man in business, but she had always thought him decent. Would he really have paid a whore to have his child and then refused to allow her to see her child when she was dying?

That poor woman! What must she have suffered? For the first time Sarah thought properly about the woman who had given her birth. Even if she were a whore, forced to make her living on her back, that did not make her a bad person. Sarah had no means of knowing her story. Suddenly, she knew that it was important to her to know the truth. Her birth mother's blood flowed in Sarah's veins and even though society might reject her because of it, her mother had loved her enough to want to see her when she knew she was dying.

If only she had not died. Sarah would have sought her out, found a home for her and got to know the poor lady. Tears trickled down her cheeks again. She dashed them away. She was turning into a watering pot. One thing remained constant. She was her father's daughter and strong enough to overcome this hurt and the scandal. If Sir Roger imagined she would spend the rest of her life in hibernation, he was wrong. Her friends at home would not desert her simply because she was not her mother's daughter—but whatever happened she must know the truth.

* * *

Sarah was feeling much better the next morning. She managed to wash herself without help and to brush her hair, but was still a little unsteady on her feet. However, the maids had been very kind, bringing her books as well as all manner of treats that Mrs Brancaster had prepared for her.

'It is so kind of Mrs Brancaster to spoil me this way. Thank her for it, Agnes. I know she is very busy with the guests.'

'We're all concerned for you, miss. Lord Myers is looking for the wicked villain wot done this—and I wouldn't like to be in his shoes when they catches him.'

'I was wondering whether Lord Myers had time to see me,' Sarah said, holding her sigh inside. She'd had no reason to expect him to visit her room, but she missed him—which was very silly. In a couple of days she would be on her way home and he would forget her as the unusual governess he had for a short time been tempted to seduce.

'I don't know, miss. I could pass the message on, but he's been out riding most days—what with searching for that rogue and entertaining the guests. I should think he's too busy. 'Sides, it wouldn't be proper, miss. Him being a single gentleman and you a lady and not married. He did carry you up here, mind. Told us all that we had to look after you or he'd want to know the reason why.'

'Well, that was kind of him.' Sarah's heart eased a little, but she still longed to see Rupert, just for a moment. Surely he could not imagine her reputation mattered now? She had none left to speak of. He had not bothered to visit her and that must mean he did not wish to speak to her alone—perhaps he was afraid she would weep all over him and beg him to help her. 'Thank you, Agnes. I have all I need.'

But she didn't, of course. She wanted to be her mother's daughter and she wanted to be loved, passionately without reserve.

Sarah faced the truth. She loved a man who was far beyond her in station. He might have considered having an affair with her when he thought her a respectable governess, but now he was not even interested in making her his mistress.

She refused to cry. Sarah was feeling much better. In the morning she would get up and go downstairs. She would request that a post-chaise be sent for and then she would come back to her room, pack a bag, write a letter of farewell to Rupert and another to Francesca and perhaps also one to John. Then she would leave Cavendish Park.

Chapter Twelve

'My lord, a moment if you will…' Mrs Brancaster stopped Rupert as he came in from another wasted ride. For days sightings of strangers had been coming in and he'd investigated them all, but so far there was no sign of the rogue that had shot Sarah. He was beginning to think the fellow had left the district, as he would be well advised to do. He was but a pawn in the game anyway; the problem was—who had paid him to kill Sarah? Rupert would give a fortune to know.

'Yes…' He was aware that he sounded impatient. 'What may I do for you?'

'Miss Hardcastle wondered if you could spare her a few moments, sir?'

Rupert frowned. He had visited Sarah's room

twice when she'd first been ill, but had made himself leave her to the care of the servants for the sake of her reputation. Lady Rowton had a vicious tongue and the merest hint of scandal would have given her some ammunition to use against Sarah. He'd already heard her wondering aloud why someone would wish to shoot Miss Hardcastle and her tone had implied criticism of Sarah. Mindful of the damage a woman like that could do, he'd curbed his feelings and contented himself with almost hourly updates on her condition. Fortunately, the woman was due to leave the next day. After that he would be able to let down his guard a little—and he'd made a decision to call off the hunt for the rogue and set a couple of Bow Street Runners on the case. It would mean a trip to London, but he had other business and on his return Sarah would be well enough for him to discuss the business that was burning at the back of his mind.

'You will please ask Miss Hardcastle to forgive me,' he said. 'Convey my sincere apologies, please. Tell her I am delighted she is so much better and say that my duties as a host have kept me from visiting her. I shall make it a priority tomorrow.'

'Yes, my lord—only she did seem anxious to talk to you.'

Rupert hesitated. Ought he to cast convention to the winds and follow his inclinations? No, that would be foolish. Such a thoughtless act on his part might result in Sarah being compromised. He would not wish her to be forced to accept him as a husband simply because she would otherwise lose her good name.

'I dare say another few hours will not matter. You did have the roses I asked for sent to her room?'

'Yes, my lord. She said they were beautiful.'

Rupert nodded. 'Please excuse me. I have planned an excursion for our visitors' last day. We are to take a picnic and visit the Abbey ruins this afternoon. I really must change or I shall keep everyone waiting.'

It had been such a long day. Francesca had popped in for a while during the morning. She'd told Sarah that Rupert was out riding.

'He goes out most mornings,' she said. 'This afternoon we're going to the ruins of an Abbey. It's about ten miles from here and they say it's haunted.' She laughed. 'I do so wish you could come with us.'

'I am sorry to have missed the treat. I dare say I shall feel better soon.'

'I just think things are more fun when you're there.'

'Are you not enjoying your guests? Is there no one amongst them that you feel attracted to?'

'I like Miss Rowton, though not her mama very much. I like Mr James Monks, but he hasn't visited for a couple of days. I believe Sir Roger has gone home—good riddance to him. I suppose I like Sir Freddie as much as anyone. He makes me laugh.'

'Yes, he is amusing,' Sarah agreed. 'I liked him. He was kind enough to send me a new novel he purchased by Mrs Burney.'

'Yes, he told me he thought you might like it.' Francesca's cheeks flushed. 'I can't quite de-cide...but, no, I shouldn't say. He hasn't shown any preference; indeed, I think he likes you more than me.'

'Are we speaking of Sir Freddie or Mr Monks?'

'Sir Freddie. I like him very well, Sarah—but Mr Monks is so flattering. He says I'm beau-tiful and that his heart stops when he sees me. He compared me to a rose in a poem.'

'Did he, indeed? I wonder if it was one of Mr Shakespeare's sonnets?'

'Well, I did think he might have borrowed pieces of it from someone else.' Francesca gig-gled. 'Some gentlemen say foolish things just to amuse one, do they not?'

'They do indeed.' Sarah's brow wrinkled.

'Are your feelings for either of the gentlemen likely to be serious?'

'I'm not sure. They might be for one...' Francesca shook her head. 'No, I am foolish. It is much too soon. I should not imagine myself in love with anyone. Love takes time to grow, does it not?'

'Yes, perhaps,' Sarah said, though she was not sure of the truth. Perhaps sometimes love came suddenly like a blinding light.

'I suppose I must go down and mingle,' Francesca said and kissed her cheek. 'I shall tell you all about it when I return.'

Sarah had smiled and nodded. She'd hoped for a visit from Rupert, but supposed that he was with his guests. Unfortunately, Mrs Brancaster came up later to tell her that he had sent a message to say he was too busy and would see her the next day.

'Yes, of course, it does not matter,' she said, swallowing her disappointment. She was the last thing on his mind, of course. 'Tomorrow I'll be fine.'

Rising, she went over to her desk and wrote the letters she needed to write. She was much better now and the sooner she began to make her preparations, the better.

To Rupert she wrote a brief note.

Dear Sir, I know you are aware of what happened or, if you are not yet, you soon will be. Sir Roger has threatened to ruin me with a scandal I knew nothing of until he informed me of it. I had hoped I might save you this scandal. Had I been able to travel I should have left before this, but I trust you will find my short notice acceptable. I realise now what a terrible thing I did by coming here as Hester Goodrum and I beg you to forgive me. I am sure you will easily replace me with someone far more suitable.

Yours truly, Sarah Hardcastle

The letter to Francesca was much harder.

My dearest friend. I cannot regret meeting you for I have come to love you as my sister and I hope with all my heart that you will forgive me for leaving you this way. I do so hope that you will understand that it is for your sake. I shall bring scandal on you if I stay and my hopes of being there at your come out in London are useless. Should I carry on, as I know you would wish, I should ruin you, my dearest one. For your sake I shall not see you in public again, though it is my hope that we may one day meet privately and, if you will honour me by accepting my letters, I shall write to you. Leaving you breaks my heart. Forgive me for causing you pain.

Your sincere and loving friend, Sarah Hardcastle

Satisfied that she could do no better, she wrote a brief note to John and enclosed five guineas for him as spending money when he went to his college at Christmas.

Her letters written, Sarah packed a small bag. She placed a few of her more personal items in it and left the rest to be sent on to her home. Mrs Brancaster would see to her trunks for her and she would take her leave of her in the morning, quite early.

Even the small amount of movement involved in packing a bag had aggravated her shoulder and made her feel tired. She decided to lie down and was soon sleeping.

Sarah was awakened by the sound of loud voices and footsteps outside her room. The next moment the door was flung open and Lord Myers entered, looking wild and angry. She pushed herself up against the pillows and met his furious gaze, wondering what on earth had caused him to burst in on her this way.

'My lord—is something the matter?'

'Where is she?' he demanded. 'I know she tells you everything. Is that what you wanted to tell me this morning? Why the hell did you not say it was urgent?'

'Because it was not,' Sarah said and frowned. 'Are you speaking of Francesca? What is wrong?'

'She has run off with that Monks fellow—eloped. I blame you for encouraging her.'

'No, she has not run away with anyone,' Sarah said, ignoring his last remark. 'Please tell me exactly what happened?'

'You sound very sure.' He glared at her. 'She told us she was going for a little walk to the other side of the ruins. Miss Rowton went with her. She says that they were looking at a particularly fine wild rose, which had grown through the fallen stones. Francesca had wandered a little apart from her when Mr Monks came up to her. They spoke urgently. Francesca hesitated and then went off with him. They got into a chaise and drove off at speed. Now tell me she has not run away.'

'I have no idea where she went, but I imagine she was tricked,' Sarah said. 'Francesca spoke about her feelings this morning and I am quite certain she would not have chosen to run away—with Mr Monks at least.'

'What do you mean?'

'I think she loves someone else. She is not sure that he cares for her and Monks has been flattering her, but she would not have gone off with him.'

'Who does she imagine herself in love with?'

'I'm not sure I should say.'

'I need to know. This is important—it isn't that scoundrel Sir Roger?'

'Good gracious, no. She dislikes him. You must not breathe a word—but I rather think she hoped for an offer from Sir Freddie.'

'Good grief.' Rupert looked stunned. 'I had no idea. He's perfectly suitable if he would offer for her—but why did she go with Monks? Miss Rowton said she was not abducted.'

'Do you not think she may have been tricked?'

'Tricked…' Rupert's expression grew darker. 'He made her think something was wrong… good grief! Do you suppose he told her you had been taken for the worse? She would have gone with him then without a thought for herself.'

'Oh, no, I do hope it was not that.' Sarah was stricken. 'Yes, I believe you may be right. How wicked he is—but why would he do such a thing?'

'Monks is deep in debt. Sir Freddie warned me of it the other day, felt I should be on my guard. No doubt the scoundrel knew his chances of getting her to marry him were nil so he decided to snatch her, but did so by a trick rather than risk her screaming and bringing me down on him.'

'You must find her, Rupert,' Sarah said, jumping up from the bed. 'If you are quick all may not be lost. If you wish, I will pretend to be ill and you can say that she came here to me—but you must go now, without delay.'

'I have already lost time. I thought you would know.'

'Believe that she has not gone willingly.'

'I'll kill him,' Rupert growled. 'If he touches her, I'll tear him limb from limb.'

'Go quickly, please. I shall remain in my room in case we need the excuse, but I shall be anxious.'

Rupert turned, saw the letters she'd written on the desk and picked up the one addressed to him. He turned to her, accusation in his eyes.

'What is this?' Without waiting for an answer he broke the seal and scanned it. 'Damn you, Sarah! Were you planning to leave without a word? What scandal is Grey supposed to have revealed to me?'

'He has not done so?' For a moment relief flooded through her, but she knew it was a mere respite. If Sir Roger had not yet spoken, he was waiting for the right moment.

'He has threatened to ruin me by revealing

a scandal I knew nothing of—something from my mother's past,' she said, unable to meet his eyes. 'Please, do not bother with this now. Francesca needs you. I give you my word I shall not go until she is safe back where she belongs. I am not worthy of your notice. Francesca is all that matters here.'

'For the moment that is true,' he said. 'But if you break your word I shall hunt you down and you will be sorry. Have the decency to tell me when you are ready to leave and I shall arrange for you to be taken wherever you wish to go.'

'Yes, thank you. I could not bear to leave now while Francesca is in such danger. I pray you are in time.'

'Amen to that,' he said and was gone. She heard him shouting at one of the footmen and she went to the window in time to see him leave the house. As she watched, another gentleman went out to him. They spoke for a moment and then went off toward the stables together.

Sir Freddie must have offered his help. Sarah felt a choking sensation in her throat. It seemed as if that kind gentleman cared enough to join in the search. She could only hope that the two of them would be able to catch up with Mr Monks and stop him carrying out his wicked plan to force Francesca to marry him because she was compromised.

All her thoughts now were for the girl she loved, the scandal that had threatened her forgotten as she felt fear for Francesca.

She regretted the impulse that had made her write the letters. Crossing to the desk, she tore Francesca's into little shreds. The situation was changed. Francesca would need her now and her own reputation might be stained beyond redemption.

Rupert would not allow her to marry that odious rogue, would he? She knew that marriages had been forced on an unwilling girl for less, but surely he would not condemn her to a marriage that could never give her happiness?

She supposed that Mr Monks believed Francesca would inherit a small fortune from her grandfather and that might well be the case. He had other relatives, of course, but John and Francesca were the children of his only daughter and must surely be his favourites. It was the reason she had been abducted of course.

Sarah was anxious for the girl she loved. Rupert's fury on discovering her letter would have had her shaking in her shoes at another time, but for now she could only worry about Francesca. Where had Monks taken her—and what was she doing now? She must have been so frightened when she discovered that she'd been abducted....

* * *

'I demand that you take me home,' Francesca said, raising her head in a way she imagined Sarah would approve. She had been told about men like this and if he thought she was going to weep all over him and beg him to marry her, he was wrong. 'You lied to me. I thought I liked you. I might even had agreed to marry you, had you asked—but to tell me Sarah was dying and then to drive off with me to goodness knows where is outrageous! I shall not marry you now if you keep me here for a month.'

James Monks glared at her. 'Damn you, Fran, I thought you would find it amusing to be abducted. Sir Roger put me up to it. He was thinking of abducting Miss Hardcastle, but then he asked her instead and what she said…well, he gave up. Told me she wasn't worth the effort and he would find another heiress. He mentioned you and I told him he'd have you over my dead body. Why won't you let me take you to Gretna? I know you'd like me if you gave me a chance.'

Francesca stared at him. He was almost begging her. She'd been frightened at first, but now she saw he was weak. He wouldn't dare to harm her because of what her relatives might do to him.

'Abduction is a hanging offence, you know.'

He stared at her, his eyes popping. 'It was an elopement. You know it was, Francesca. You didn't really believe Miss Hardcastle was dying. She's been fine for days....'

'You frightened me and I shan't forgive you for that,' Francesca said. 'I love Sarah—she means a lot to me and I really did think something might have happened to her. Now, please, take me home.'

'I can't,' he said, sounding desperate. 'I have to keep you here until someone comes. Your family will send someone to look for you— and we shall be forced to marry to save your reputation. I'll be good to you, Fran. I promise.'

'Do not call me Fran,' Francesca said. 'My name is Francesca. Indeed, I would prefer to be called by my father's name, if you please—because our friendship is at an end. I do not wish to speak to you again and I shall never marry you. You may keep me here for a month, but it makes no difference. I don't like you and I will not be your wife.'

'I could force you,' he said and his tone was suddenly ugly. 'I could seduce you. You would be ruined. I dare say you would marry me soon enough then.'

'I care nothing for my reputation. I would rather never enter society again and live in obscurity with a man I love rather than marry a rogue like you, sir.'

'I suppose that's what she taught you,' Monks said, scowling. 'Sir Roger tried to blackmail her into taking him, but she faced him down, told him to go to the devil. I thought you would give in....' He sat down, putting his head into hands, then lifted it to stare at her in desperation. 'I shall be ruined if you do not marry me. They will throw me into the debtors' prison and throw the key away.'

'I am sorry for you. If you had spoken to Lord Myers, he might have arranged a loan for you, perhaps.'

'Couldn't do that...one gentleman to another.' He stood up and raked his fingers through his hair, his cheeks flushed. 'What the hell do I do now?'

'I suggest you take me home,' Francesca replied haughtily. 'If you do that immediately, I shall tell everyone I was needed urgently at home, but we had an accident and the chaise overturned. We shall pretend that you were unconscious and I had to wait until you recovered....'

'Would you do that?' He looked at her hopefully. 'I've made a mess of this, haven't I? It is all Sir Roger's fault for putting the idea into my head.'

'What did he say to Sarah? What did he think she had done that he could blackmail her over?'

'I have no idea.' Monks shrugged gloomily. 'He was in a temper and went off without finishing his tale—just said she was a stubborn wench and he would get even somehow.'

'Then he must have been the one who shot her.'

'It might have been him, but I thought he'd left the district.'

'Take me home. I have to tell Rupert—and the sooner we get back the better. You'd better wrap your cravat about your head if you don't want my friends to kill you. Rupert wouldn't have made me marry you, you know. He would just challenge you to a duel and send me abroad with Sarah until the scandal died down.'

'In that case we'd better leave now,' he said. 'I don't suppose you could forgive me and…? No, I didn't think so. I can only say I'm sorry.'

It was almost dusk. Sarah was standing at her bedroom window when she saw the chaise draw up outside. Her heart started to race and she leaned forwards as she saw the man get down and help the girl out of the carriage.

'Francesca! Thank God—oh, thank God,' she whispered and went quickly out of the room.

She had reached the top of the stairs when

Francesca burst in. She looked up, screamed Sarah's name and raced up the stairs to her. Sarah opened her arms to receive her.

'I thought you were worse,' she sobbed against her neck. 'I thought you were dying.'

'What happened, dearest? As you see I am fine now, even though I had a little headache this morning. Mr Monks exaggerated the situation—is that what happened, my love?'

Francesca looked at her, took a deep breath and nodded. 'Yes,' she said in a voice that carried to the people gathering in the hall below. 'I asked to be brought here to you quickly. Mr Monks was kind enough to oblige. We went at such a pace that the chaise overturned. He was thrown and hit his head and lay unconscious for more than two hours. By the time someone came and helped us, half the day had gone. That is why we are so late….'

'You have had a terrible experience. Mr Monks is at fault for driving so carelessly. Are you hurt, dearest? Is there anything else you should tell me—in private, if you wish?'

'Nothing at all. Mr Monks was good enough to bring me back, though he has a terrible headache.'

'Where is he now?'

'I left him outside. I could not wait to see if you were well.'

'As you see, I am back to normal. Come into my room, dearest. I shall send for some tea and Mrs Brancaster will bring you some sandwiches.'

Francesca opened her mouth and shut it again. 'Thank you,' she said meekly. She turned to look at the people in the hall. 'I am sorry if anyone was worried. It was all a mistake.'

Sarah could feel the girl trembling as she drew her inside her room. She led her to the bed, sat her down, then looked at her. 'Now tell me the truth, my love.'

'He told me you were dying and abducted me. He thought Uncle Rupert would make me marry him for the sake of my reputation. I told him I would rather be ruined and I would go abroad with you—and if this causes a scandal I shall. You wouldn't desert me for a little scandal, would you?'

'No…' Sarah looked at her and, seeing the girl's determined pride, she laughed. 'No, my dearest, that would be foolish. We shall neither of us let the gossips hurt us. I am not going to run away as if I've done something terrible and neither are you. We shall carry on as we are and those who do not wish to know us may do the other thing.'

'You haven't done anything wrong, have you?'

'I learned something recently—something

that I did not know when I came here. My mother was not the lady of gentle birth who loved me and married my father. She loved me as her own until the day she died, but she was not my birth mother.'

'That is sad, but it just shows how kind she was to take you in. Who was your mother?'

'I am told she was a prostitute my father paid to have his child,' Sarah replied. 'I am told she died of a disease women of her profession sometimes get in later life….'

'Oh, how awful for her—and for you to be told that,' Francesca said and hugged her. 'I was told Sir Roger threatened to blackmail you, but you faced him down. He gave Mr Monks the idea, you see. How horrible some men can be.'

'Yes, they can,' Sarah agreed. 'But others are very different. Both Sir Freddie and Rupert have gone to search for you. Rupert swears he will kill Mr Monks, but when we tell him there is no scandal he might be prepared just to land him a facer… I believe that is the word gentlemen use for knocking someone down.'

'Yes, it is.' Francesca giggled. 'I've heard them say it when they think one is not listening. He deserves it—but he did bring me back. He could have refused. He could have forced me…'

'Had you been another sort of woman he

might have,' Sarah said and smiled. 'He thought you a silly girl, but you're not. You are a young woman and perfectly able to stand up to a rogue like him.'

'Yes, I am,' Francesca said and smiled. 'I wasn't until you came. I should probably have run off with him for real—but you taught me about truth and honesty and thinking before doing something silly.'

'Oh, my love, you make me want to cry,' Sarah said and blinked hard. 'I am so very glad you are back and unharmed.'

'So am I. In future I shall think carefully before I get into a gentleman's chaise alone.'

'Had he been a proper gentleman it would not have happened—there lies the difference. You might travel anywhere with Sir Freddie and he would not lift a finger to harm you.'

'If only he liked me enough to…' Francesca sighed. 'You did say he was helping to search for me?'

'Yes, he is. I'm not sure when they will be back. I think we should ring for our refreshments and then I'll ask Mrs Brancaster to tuck you up in bed, my love.'

'I ate some sandwiches at the inn he took me to. I am not hungry.'

'I couldn't eat a thing all day for worrying,'

Sarah said and smiled. 'We'll have a light supper and you will be all the better for it. Do not argue, Francesca—in this case I know best.'

Francesca laughed. 'You win. Are we truly going to London together?'

'Yes, if Lord Myers agrees. I must, of course, tell him the truth—though I think Sir Roger may have done so already.'

'No, I don't think so. Mr Monks said he left in a temper without telling him the rest of it. So if he didn't tell him, I doubt he told anyone. I think he realised that it was a waste of time. Who would care when we all love you so much?'

'Dearest Francesca…' Sarah was thoughtful. 'I wonder why Rupert did not come to see me? I thought it was because he knew that I was the child of…' She caught her breath because it still hurt so much.

'It was because he was concerned that he might compromise you, of course,' Francesca said. 'He did visit twice late at night, because I saw him leave when I came to sit with you. Agnes said he gave her a guinea not to mention it to anyone.'

'Oh…' Sarah's heart lifted a little. 'It was good of him to be concerned for me.'

'He likes you. I've told you before.'

'Perhaps…' Sarah shook her head. 'It isn't

important. For the moment I want you to eat your supper and be tucked up safe in your bed—and then we can all sleep soundly.'

Chapter Thirteen

Sarah was in her dressing robe and on the point of going to bed when she heard footsteps outside her door. Someone knocked and she rose from her stool, going to open it. Rupert stood there, his hair windblown and his look frustrated rather than angry.

'Is it true that she got that scoundrel to bring her home?'

'Yes, perfectly true.' Sarah hesitated, then stood back. 'You had better come in—oh, do not look so worried. We must discuss this in private if you want to save Francesca's reputation.'

Rupert followed her in. He nodded as she locked the door. 'You do not wish to be disturbed—tell me the worst. Did he violate her?'

'Not at all. He did lie to her and make off with her, but only to an inn some twenty miles or so distant. It was his plan to keep her there until you arrived to force him to marry her.'

'He was far off there. She would have been a widow before she was a bride.'

'Fortunately, Francesca managed to keep her head. She told him that she would not marry him whatever he did and that you would kill him unless he brought her home. It seems he did not have the courage to force her, and after begging her to marry him without success, he brought her home and left again as swiftly as he could.'

'I'll thrash him when I catch up with him.'

'Not if you care for Francesca's good name. He brought her home because I was suddenly taken ill and their chaise met with an accident. He was thrown and rendered unconscious and it was some hours before he recovered enough to bring her home. That is her story and, if you do nothing to convince the gossips it is a lie, I think we shall brush through well enough. Besides, if Sir Freddie cares enough I believe her future is settled.'

'Do you indeed? Are you her guardian now?'

Sarah flinched at the sarcasm in his tone. 'No, I am not—and if you feel I have overstepped the mark I can…' Her words died away, for she could not simply leave. She had promised Francesca she would stay.

His gaze narrowed, nostrils flared as if in temper. 'Going to run off and leave us again, are you?'

'Perhaps if you would calm down a little I might explain why I felt it necessary to leave.'

'It had better be good.' He glared at her and then sat down in her chair. 'I'm listening.'

Sarah told him the tale Sir Roger had told her in his effort to blackmail her, leaving no sordid detail to his imagination. Then she paused and looked at him.

'I thought that I might ruin Francesca's chances. She has begged me to stay with her until and during her Season. I have, of course, told her the chance we take, but she says she does not care. You must be the judge of the situation, Lord Myers. I am prepared to risk it, but if you feel Francesca may suffer too much I shall withdraw.'

'And do what? Run away and hide?'

'No, not at all. I am determined that Sir Roger shall not win. I shall go home for a time—and then I may take a house in London for the Season.'

'Francesca would want to know you. No…' He frowned and Sarah's heart sank—he meant to forbid her. 'I have a better solution. You will become engaged and then in time you will marry me.'

Sarah gasped, feeling the colour drain from her face. It was the last thing she'd expected. Her heart leaped with joy, but the feeling was quickly followed by one of doubt. She would be a fool to think that his proposal meant that he loved her. Yet he was prepared to do so much to save her from public scorn—why?

'But you can't… I do not see why you should make such a sacrifice for my sake.'

'Who said it was for your sake?' His eyebrows rose imperiously and her heart sank. His offer had nothing to do with love or affection, but was intended to deflect more scandal from Francesca. The pain struck deep into her heart. 'I have reached the age where I need an heir, Sarah. You cannot be unaware that I find you attractive. I have already taken steps to protect you from unscrupulous men who might wish to force you to sell your mills—which in the minds of most people adds up to an interest on my part. It will solve everything neatly, do you not think?'

'Perhaps…yes, I mean, no.' Sarah's mind was reeling from the shock and she hardly knew what she said. If he'd spoken of love, she would have been so happy, for then a marriage between them would have been all she could wish for. 'Do you really want to marry the daughter of a low-born whore?'

Her mind was in a whirl. Sometimes she'd felt he was interested in her as a woman he would like to make his mistress, but she'd sensed that he held a part of himself in reserve. She'd wondered if perhaps he'd suffered some reverse or heartbreak in the past. Was that why he was willing to make a marriage of convenience to save them all from scandal? Had he been so hurt that it was impossible for him to love? The thought pained her and made her want to take the hurt from him, because whatever he felt she loved him with all her heart—so much that she did not think she could bear to lose him.

'You are a woman of sense, Sarah. I think we should do well together—and it will suit me to marry. This tale of Sir Roger's—do you mean to simply accept it as the truth? For my part I think him a liar and a knave. Had it not been for his prompting Monks would never have thought of abducting Francesca.'

'You think he might be lying? He said my uncle told him. I have written and hope to hear the truth from his hand.' She caught her breath, her heart taking a dizzying somersault as she thought what it might be like to marry Rupert. She knew it would bring her happiness to be his wife and bear his children, even if she could never truly have his love.

'I do not care if it is the truth,' Rupert said flatly. 'I've met whores who were more of a lady than some who call themselves by the name.' His gaze narrowed. 'Would it be so very hard to be my wife and bear my children, Sarah?'

'No…of course not,' she said, her breath expelling nervously. She must not betray herself for he would not want a clinging vine. She must remain the cool Miss Hardcastle despite the clamouring of her heart. 'You know I need a husband I can trust and—and I like you very well. Are you sure you wish to? I am stubborn and can be quite difficult at times, I'm told.'

'I imagine you can.' He laughed softly in his throat. 'I dare say I can manage you if I try. I should not want a woman who gave me all my own way. I need an equal, Sarah, and I believe you would match me in many ways.'

'What of Francesca? You know I must see her safe and happy…'

'Sir Freddie told me he has hopes of her. No doubt he will pet her and spoil her—and I dare say she will twist him round her little finger. That kind of relationship would not do for me. I want a woman of sense I can talk to about business as well as pleasure.'

Sarah was silent. What he was offering her

was not love, but affection, passion, at least for a time, and companionship. Well, she'd known that he did not particularly like or admire young women of his own class. Perhaps he had learned to distrust them for reasons of his own. Because of his past hurts, he'd decided that a woman of Sarah's class might prove more trustworthy. He liked her, even desired her, but his emotions were not deeply involved. He would be her husband, give her children and a home and protect her from men like Sir Roger. She supposed it was enough. If she refused, she did not think she would have the chance of happiness again.

'I thank you for your very kind offer…Rupert,' she said and a shy smile hovered on her lips. 'If you are perfectly content with the idea, I shall accept with pleasure.'

'At these times one is supposed to declare undying love, but I shall not bore you with that nonsense,' Rupert said, a mocking twist to his mouth. 'We'll announce it in the morning. Then I'll leave you for a while…' He laughed as she looked startled. 'I am not prepared to let the rogue who shot at you get away with his crime, Sarah. You might have died—and that means he must pay. Also, I intend to have it out with Sir Roger—make him apologise—and then I shall set private agents on to discovering the truth of your conception. If your mother truly was a whore, something caused her to be that way. I think you would like to know her story—and if you have another family somewhere. My agents are already working on your behalf and I dare say the mystery is halfway to being solved before we ask.'

'You would do that for me?'

'Once we are married, you will discover just how much I am prepared to do for the lady who honours me by becoming my wife.'

Sarah nodded, her throat too tight to speak for a moment. He was such a fine honourable gentleman. 'If what you discover is too terrible…'

He touched his fingers to her lips and then hesitated before bending to kiss her lips. It was a very soft, sweet kiss, but it left her feeling weak at the knees.

'You will not say foolish things. I am a man, not a boy, Sarah. I know what I want, believe me.'

'Yes…I have thought you wanted me…' She could feel the heat in her cheeks as she met his eyes. 'Your…kind feelings were returned.'

He flicked her cheek with his fingertips. 'I rather thought they might be or I should not have spoken. We shall do very well together. Now I should leave. If someone sees me coming from your room, you will have to put up with odd looks from the ladies and the occasional wink from the men. We shall announce our engagement tomorrow.'

'Very well, Rupert,' she said, her heart racing despite her controlled speech and steady manner. 'As you wish.'

'We must arrange something for Francesca while we are away on our wedding trip, which need only be a few days to buy you a wardrobe in Paris. Perhaps Merrivale will come down— or Sir Freddie may take her off to stay with his mother.'

'We must also think of John.'

'He seems to like Dupree. He may take over as his tutor until he leaves for school—and of course the boy can live with us until he leaves home. I am sure you would always welcome him during the holidays.'

'You seem to have worked everything out. What if I had refused?'

'Then I should have been devastated,' he said and gave her a mocking smile. 'Fortunately, I was able to persuade you it was for your own good.'

Sarah's expression altered, took fire. 'You sound like my father when I did something that pleased him.'

'Ah, I have struck a spark.' His eyes gleamed. 'Good. I like it when you fight back, Sarah. It would be a mistake to let me have my own way all the time.'

'I have no intention of it.'

'I am very pleased to hear it, and now, my dearest Sarah, I must leave you—or I shall be tempted to sweep you up into my arms and carry you to that tempting bed...'

Sarah gasped. Before she could recover her breath, he had opened the door, let himself out and closed it behind him. She locked it immediately and heard him laugh.

He was an arrogant rogue and altogether too sure of himself. His plans were so neat that she thought he must have been plotting them for a while.

Yet he might have his pick of the young ladies looking for husbands. He was handsome, rich in his own right and charming—why should he choose her?

He wanted an heir and he wasn't interested in a girl straight out of the schoolroom. He clearly had an aversion to women of his class. Rupert clearly felt a marriage of convenience to a woman he could trust would suit him well— and Sarah would be a fool to regret her bargain. He'd given her so much already and she could only think that being his wife would bring its own rewards. He might break her heart one day, but that was a chance worth taking.

Smiling to herself, Sarah removed her robe and slipped into bed. Before long she was sound asleep.

Rupert savoured his brandy and reflected on the future. He had gained part of his objective, but there was more to achieve. Sarah seemed content to accept his plans and he had much to do, much to sort out before he could relax and reveal all of them to the woman he intended to be his wife.

Had he truly considered making her his mistress? Only for a short time at the start; it had not taken him long to see her true worth or the potential of a match between them. Sarah might not like the idea of selling her father's property at the start, but if the right buyer could be found it would be the best solution. Her fortune could be joined with his and used for the benefit of them all. As yet he had not spoken to Merrivale about Cavendish Park. It would one day be John's inheritance, of course, but that was a long way off and the marquess was far from able to care for it, as it ought to be cared for. If Rupert did not take permanent charge it would dwindle into nothing by the time the lad was grown.

Of course he would need Sarah's agreement to his plan, but he thought she might be willing to listen. He would bring the subject up once their engagement was public knowledge and she had become used to the idea.

Sipping his brandy, he lay back against the pillows and smiled. Yes, it was all going his way, but he had to sort out this business of whoever had taken a shot at Sarah—and settle with Sir Roger. Not a pleasant business, but it had to be done. Either the rogue would take his punishment like a man—or he would have to be killed in a duel.

Either way, he must protect the woman he loved.

Sarah dressed and went down to breakfast. Some of the gentlemen were at table and rose with alacrity as she entered, making her welcome and enquiring after her health with such sincerity that she was overwhelmed by their kindness.

'We were all so sorry to learn of your setback,' Lord Phillips said. 'Such an upset—with Miss Francesca being involved in an accident. I dare say you found that distressing?'

'Yes, I did,' Sarah agreed and smiled at him. 'However, she was just a little shaken by her experience and will, I am sure, be herself today.'

'I was mightily relieved to hear it,' Sir Freddie said. 'If no one minds I've decided to stay on for a couple of days…talk to Rupert when I see him. I believe he went riding early this morning, had some important business, I understand.'

'Did he?' Sarah's cheeks were warm, as she wondered whether Rupert had said anything to his guests about their engagement, but as neither gentleman mentioned it she thought perhaps he intended it later. 'When do you leave, Lord Phillips? Or have you decided to stay on, too?'

'I wish that I might, Miss Hardcastle.' The look he gave her was so warm and admiring that Sarah's heart jolted. She had thought he might like her quite well at the start and he had sent messages of goodwill and flowers while she was ill. 'Had it not been such a difficult time—but you have been ill. I must keep another engagement, but I hope we shall meet again soon—should you visit London or perhaps Bath.'

'I do not think there is any intention of it as yet,' Sarah replied. 'We are here until Christmas, I believe—but we shall certainly be in London next year.'

'Then I may call on you before Christmas,' Lord Phillips replied, looking oddly shy. 'Sometimes one wishes one did not have so many engagements.'

He was a gentleman and it restored Sarah's pride to know that any feelings he might have had for her were not motivated by her wealth. He liked her for herself.

Sarah smiled and murmured something appropriate. She was not sure if he was hinting that he would like to make her an offer if the circumstances were more auspicious. Clearly, he felt she was not well enough to deal with a matter of that nature now.

Rupert had not let such notions weigh with him. He'd made his intentions very clear and, perhaps in something of an emotional state, she'd accepted his offer. A night of rest and reflection had not changed her mind, though she was aware that her position was not ideal.

She would be a fool to demand too much. Her ideas of loving and being loved were perhaps the dreams a young girl might cherish, but did not apply to a woman who was past five and twenty. No, she must accept passion and companionship and not look for romantic love.

Lord Phillips rose to his feet, having finished his breakfast. He bowed his head to Sarah and said he hoped they would meet again soon, took his leave of Sir Freddie and went out. She heard his voice addressing someone and thought he was asking for his trunk to be brought down.

'Now we are alone, Miss Hardcastle...' Sir

Freddie looked at her a little uncertainly across the breakfast table. He cleared his throat. 'I was thinking… I mean, I should very much like to speak to Miss Francesca this morning. Do you think she is well enough to see me?'

'Yes, I am very sure she will be,' Sarah said and smiled at him. 'Indeed, I think your failure to do so might be more distressing than anything else that has happened to her.'

He looked struck, then his eyes lit up. 'Do you say so? By Jove! Then there's hope for me?'

'You must ask Francesca,' Sarah replied with a smile. 'But I think everything may be as we should all wish.'

'You are an angel. She told me how wonderful you were…' He got to his feet. 'I think I'll go up and change. Want to look my best, you know.'

'I'll speak to Francesca. Shall we say half-past the hour of ten in the small back parlour?'

'Thank you. Thank you…' He bowed to her and hurried off and Sarah heard him speak to someone in the hall. The next moment the door of the breakfast parlour opened and Rupert entered. He had been riding and, as she looked at him, she saw a small cut at the side of his mouth. It had stopped bleeding, but swollen a little.

'Rupert...' She got to her feet and went to him. 'Are you all right? Did you have a fall?'

'No, I called on James Monks. We had a fight. I think you could say that he came off worst. It was my intention to thrash him and I did—but he threw a lucky punch.'

'I cannot pretend to be sorry that you gave him a good hiding,' Sarah said. 'But I think your lip may be sore for a while.'

'It was better than calling him out—besides, that honour is reserved for gentlemen and he does not deserve the name. I do not imagine he will bother you or Francesca again.'

'No, I should imagine not,' Sarah said and laughed. 'Well, since you are no worse, I shall go up and speak to Francesca. Sir Freddie intends to speak to her this morning.'

'Yes, he told me. I warned him that Merrivale will not think of allowing the marriage before she's had a Season—but there's no reason they shouldn't have an understanding, is there?'

'None, as far as I am concerned. The marquess would not forbid her—would he?'

'Oh, I think Sir Freddie is eminently suitable. He actually knows Merrivale quite well. I imagine there can be no objection. He will have to be told and I expect he will come down. The engagement might be announced at Christmas.'

'I think that should make them both content.

She is still young in years, though as sensible as girls much older.'

'Your influence, I imagine?' His eyebrows rose.

'Oh, in part, I dare say. She has a lovely nature and might have been taken advantage of by that rogue had I not been here.'

'Then I dare say Merrivale will forgive the small deception.'

'I suppose he must know?'

'He will need to be informed, but I shall vouch for you, Sarah.' Rupert's tone was teasing. 'Do not look so anxious, my love. I shall tell him of our engagement when I write—and that reminds me, I must give you a ring. You will, of course, have your pick of the family heirlooms when we are married, but I am not sure of your preference—emeralds, rubies or sapphires for your ring? Or do you prefer plain diamonds?'

'I've never worn rings, though I have Mama's,' Sarah said with a frown. 'I think something fairly simple would suit me—perhaps diamonds in the shape of a daisy. I think it is possible to purchase such a ring, is it not?'

'Perfectly possible. I shall send to my jeweller in London. In the meantime, perhaps you would care to wear this?' He took a small box from his pocket, in which, when it was opened, nestled a plain gold band set with one rather fine diamond. 'This was my mother's wedding ring. She stopped wearing it before she died, because her finger became too thin. You must have your own rings—but for the moment...'

There was a question in his voice. Sarah held out her hand and let him slip it on to the third finger of her left hand, where it fit perfectly.

'It is so beautiful. Do you think we might use it as our wedding ring?'

'If you wish.' He looked pleased. 'Wear it for now and I will buy you a ring of your own when I am in town.'

'Are you leaving us?' Her heart sank for she had hoped that they would have a period of quiet time when they could get to know one another better.

'Only for as long as it takes, Sarah.' Rupert smiled and it was a caress, making her heart leap. 'I have to settle certain matters. Someone almost killed you. We've searched for the villain, but I believe he must have left the district. I need to know who is behind this business.'

'I thought Sir Roger...'

'Yes, I think it likely he tried to take his revenge on you for refusing him.'

'I have always disliked him, but I did not think he would go that far. How could he benefit from my death?'

'I have no idea. It is one of the matters I mean to investigate.'

'When must you leave?'

'I shall not go until I know the outcome between Francesca and Sir Freddie. If that goes as we think, I shall ask him to remain here until I return—and, as I said, I think Merrivale will come down.'

'We shall have company, but—you don't think I am still in danger?'

'I hope that the danger is past, but I intend to make certain if I can. It would distress me greatly if you were to be shot at again. I find it outrageous that a lady in my care should be treated so shamefully.'

Sarah thanked him. His words at one moment seemed to indicate his care for her and at another his outrage that any woman should be subjected to such treatment. He certainly gave her no cause to think that he loved her. He had spoken of passion when he proposed, but that, of course was a different thing.

After they had parted company, Sarah ran up to Francesca to warn her to be ready to receive Sir Freddie. The girl stared at her with a mixture of delight and apprehension in her eyes.

'Do you think he means to ask me to be his wife?'

'I should not be at all surprised, my love. Is that not what you want?'

'Oh, yes, with all my heart. It's just that… what do I say? How do I answer? I mean, should I smile and tell him I should be pleased—should I let him kiss me?'

'I do not think there is a set rule for these things, my love. You must answer from the heart. I think he will tell you he loves you, perhaps in words stronger than mine—and you might tell him his feelings are reciprocated, if you wish. If he offers to kiss you, I see no reason for you to refuse.'

'Oh…' Francesca went pink with excitement. 'I am so lucky. I cannot believe he truly wants me. I thought he might like Miss Rowton better—or you, Sarah.'

'He is a kind gentleman and polite to everyone, but I am sure he thinks only of you. Besides, I do not think Rupert will mind if I tell you. He has asked me to marry him and I have accepted.'

'Oh, Sarah, that is wonderful,' Francesca said and hugged her. 'We shall be related and you will visit me and I shall visit you. Nothing could be better. I am so glad he asked you. I thought he liked you rather a lot, but you cannot always tell with Uncle Rupert.'

'No, you can't,' Sarah agreed. 'What shall

you wear, Francesca? What about the jonquil silk—or would you prefer one of your white-muslin gowns?'

'I think the jonquil,' Francesca said and looked nervous. 'I want to look my best, after all, and the white morning gowns are very simple. Yes, I like my yellow silk. Will you help me to change? It is almost half-past nine already. I do not want to keep Sir Freddie waiting.'

'He won't change his mind, dearest,' Sarah teased, but smiled at the girl's obvious pleasure. 'You do know your grandfather will need to give his permission and he might insist you wait for a while—but Rupert agrees that there is no reason you may not have an understanding.'

'I know Grandfather must be consulted because he has been so good to us—but I am sure he would not disagree. He must approve of Sir Freddie, mustn't he?'

'Yes, I'm certain he will,' Sarah said. 'Turn around and let me unfasten your gown. You can send for Agnes in a minute to dress your hair as you would like it.'

'I'm so happy. Yesterday, I thought everything might be ruined, but now it is all coming right.'

'Yes, it is,' Sarah said and smiled at her. 'I'm glad you're happy. We were all concerned when it was thought you might have eloped—or been abducted.'

'I was, but no one needs to know that,' Francesca said, her face aglow. 'I must be the luckiest girl in the world.'

'Weak fool!' Sir Roger looked at the younger man sitting opposite him in the inn with scorn. 'You had the girl. Why let her talk you into taking her home and concocting that stupid story to save her reputation? You should have seduced her and made sure of her. If you're ruined, it's your own fault. There's no use in coming to me for help. Unless I can pay my creditors by the end of the month I shall have to leave England.'

'I'm thinking of it,' James Monks said gloomily. 'What's a fellow to do when his pockets are to let and the girl of his dreams doesn't want to know?'

'You had your chance. Now you must take the consequences.'

'You're one to talk. If you venture back to London without a penny to your name, you'll end in the Fleet.'

'Damn you! Do you imagine I don't know that? It's why I've hung around here after… That damned woman seems indestructible. She won't listen to threats of exposure, tells me to go ahead and tell her story—and twice she's been shot at. The idiot who missed her the first time has been dealt with. He won't talk now.'

'You mean…you killed him?' James Monks was shocked.

'He could have betrayed me and I've no wish to hang.' Sir Roger glared at him. 'I had her uncle eating out of my hand. He told me how valuable those mills are. If I could have gotten her to marry me, I could have taken control and my troubles would have vanished. I even made her an offer for them because I thought she might think of marriage if they were off her hands.'

'You couldn't have paid for them.'

'No, but by the time she realised that they would have been mine through the marriage. If she caused too much trouble, I'd have found a way to be rid of her soon enough.'

'You're an unscrupulous devil. If Myers knew what you'd done, he'd kill you.'

'What's it to him?'

'According to something I heard, she's agreed to marry Rupert Myers.'

Sir Roger swore ferociously. 'I feared that might happen, but if I'm quick there may still be time to act.'

'But what are you going to do?'

'Exactly the same as you, but I shan't let her go when I have her. She may resist, but I know ways of bringing a woman to her knees. I shall rather enjoy teaching Miss High and Mighty Hardcastle her lessons—and she will learn to beg on her knees before I've finished with her.'

James Monks touched his sore nose gingerly. 'He will come after you if you lay a finger on her—and he'll kill you. I thought he was going to kill me....'

'Well, he may have a go, but I'm a pretty good shot. I would have had her the other day if someone hadn't come. I saw him from the corner of my eye and it spoiled my aim.'

'Well, rather you than me.' James pulled a wry face. 'I shan't be around, so don't ask me for help. I'm driving down to my uncle's for a visit. He's asked me to call. If he comes up with the dubs I'll be in town next Season—if not, I'm off to the Americas.'

'Coward.' Sir Roger's lip lifted in a snarl. 'I can manage without your help. Fat lot of use you'd be. You couldn't even manage a teen-age girl.'

'Fran has a lot of sense,' James replied. 'I rather liked her. If she'd married me, I'd have been good to her. I might even have settled down.'

'Violets and roses.' Sir Roger's tone was one of disgust. 'I have no such feelings for that uptight Hardcastle. I'm going to enjoy making her crawl at my feet.'

'I must go. I have some packing to do,' James murmured and rose from the table.

He was thoughtful as he left the inn and mounted his horse. Sir Roger was eaten up with bitterness, his anger against the woman who had refused him so white-hot that he was surely a little mad. He didn't really intend to harm Sarah Hardcastle, did he? An abduction that forced her to either pay him money or marry him was one thing…but there was something distinctly unpleasant about the look in his eyes.

It was only as James dismounted in the courtyard of his family home that the idea came to him. He had been feeling disgruntled because of the beating Lord Myers had given him—but Sarah Hardcastle didn't deserve the fate Sir Roger had planned for her.

What could he do? He didn't dare risk getting involved—but he might send a note warning of Sir Roger's intentions, leaving it unsigned, of course. Yes, he rather thought that might serve. He would warn her that Sir Roger meant to abduct her—and that he was a vindictive man who meant her harm. He might also give her a hint that Sir Roger was the one who had shot her.

He might have made a mistake in associating with a man like that and he rather thought he owed the family some sort of an apology for what he'd done. An anonymous letter to Lord Myers would be a perfect way of warning him of the danger without getting too involved. Lord Myers would know what to do.

Chapter Fourteen

'I've heard from Merrivale,' Rupert said the next morning. 'I had intended to leave today, as you know, but I think my business must wait. I've written to my agents and they may do some searching on my behalf.'

'Oh…' Sarah's heart caught, her pleasure marred because he stayed for his uncle's sake rather than hers. 'I am glad that you need not leave us yet.'

Rupert looked down at her, his gaze narrowed. 'You know I would not wish to leave you at all if it were not that my business is important?'

'Yes, I know.' Her heart raced as she looked up at him. The heat in his eyes made her wonder if perhaps she'd misjudged his reasons for marrying her. 'I'm glad you are staying. I was afraid the marquess might be angry with me for coming here under false pretences.'

'I fear he may—which is one of the reasons I decided to wait and leave my work to an agent.'

'Thank you…' Her breath caught in her throat and for a moment she thought he would kiss her, but then Sir Freddie walked into the breakfast room and the moment was lost.

'I was thinking of shooting a few pigeons,' Rupert said. 'Do you care to take the guns out for an hour or so?'

Sarah left them to their talk of sport and went upstairs to Francesca's room. The girl was just having her hair done and she waited until the maid had left, before telling her that her grandfather was coming down and would arrive later that day.

'Rupert has delayed his trip to be here,' she said and saw a look of relief in Francesca's eyes. 'Are you anxious about something?'

'Only that I am not sure Grandfather will permit us to become engaged at Christmas— and I do so want to, Sarah.'

'Well, you must give him a little time, but I am sure that he will agree, dearest. Once he sees how happy you are.'

'I hope he will not be angry with you, Sarah.'

'Well, I dare say he may a little, but Rupert is here—he will talk to him and I must hope to be forgiven.'

'Good afternoon, Miss Hardcastle.' Merrivale's eyes narrowed as he looked at her later that day. 'My nephew has nothing but good to say of you, and it is clear how much better my girl is for your influence—but what have you to say to me? You came here under a false banner.'

'Yes, sir, I did,' Sarah said, meeting his gaze honestly. 'It was very wrong of me, but I was not thinking clearly at the time. I am truly sorry for deceiving you by pretending to be the new governess.'

'You ought not to have done it.'

'I know and I do beg your pardon, sir.'

'Well, all's well that ends well,' he said, beaming at her. 'I can feel the difference your presence has made to this house—it hasn't been so alive since before my girl married that scoundrel.'

'That is a very great compliment, sir. I am flattered.'

'I was too old to have the care of a couple of children when she died,' he said heavily. 'I didn't know what to do with them and I fear I left them to a succession of governesses and tutors who let them down.'

'They were certainly bored and lonely, but someone had managed to teach them some lessons.' Sarah smiled at him. 'What they needed was company—and Lord Myers provided a role model for John.'

'Yes. It was a stroke of luck that he agreed to come down for a while. I've no idea why. He isn't being pursued by creditors—I know that for a fact. I dare say he fell out with his current lady-love. I thought he might be interested in getting married, but it came to nothing. Dare say he wanted a little time to lick his wounds, what?'

Sarah inclined her head, but said nothing. Had Rupert lost the woman he loved shortly before he came down—and was that why he was willing to settle for second best?

The thought made her throat tighten, but she drove it away. She'd thought as they spoke that morning before he went shooting with Sir Freddie that he might care for her, but it must have been wishful thinking on her part.

The marquess was looking at her intently. 'What do you think of this match between Francesca and Sir Freddie, then? Bit old for her?'

'There is a difference in years, but I think they are in love.'

'Are they indeed?' His bushy brows met. 'In my day we did not allow sentimentality to enter the equation. However, I can't have my girl breaking her heart so I suppose the match will have to be—but there's no rush. I've decided on an engagement at Christmas and the wedding next year, perhaps in the summer.'

'Yes, sir. Lord Myers rather thought you might be of that opinion and I have warned Francesca that she must be content to wait, because she is still very young.'

'Kick up rough, did she?'

'No, not at all. I think she just feels very fortunate to have found someone she can love—and to know he loves her.'

'Sir Freddie wants to take her to meet his mother and sister. Suggested I go, too—and you, m'dear. Seems my girl cannot be parted from you. I told him I wasn't ready for another journey just yet. He'll have to be patient for a few days. Too much junketing around isn't good for my health.'

'You must take care of yourself—' Sarah broke off as one of the footmen entered bearing a silver salver with a letter on it. 'Good morning, Sims. Is the letter for the marquess?'

'No, Miss Hardcastle. It is for you.'

'For me?' Sarah picked it up. 'Thank you. I shall read it later.'

'The boy said he was to wait for a reply, miss.'

'Oh?' Sarah tore it open and read the brief

message. It said that her uncle had been taken ill and she was to come at once if she wished to know the truth about her mother. 'No...'

The Marquess of Merrivale looked at her face. 'Is something troubling you, Miss Hardcastle?'

'I am told my uncle is very ill and asks for me to come immediately.'

'Then of course you must go, my dear. I shall send you in my own carriage with a maid and groom to accompany you.'

'I'm not sure...' Sarah was doubtful. 'I promised Francesca I would stay and, besides, I do not know who has sent this. It is unsigned.'

'Unsigned?' Merrivale's brows met. 'That is a trifle unusual, what?'

'Yes, it is.' Sarah decided she must explain. 'I was shot at and injured some days ago. I have recovered, as you see—but this might be a trap. I had a letter only three days ago and my uncle was perfectly well then.'

'In that case you are wise to think twice. How sensible you are, Miss Hardcastle. Most young women would have gone rushing off in a panic.'

'I believe that is what I was meant to do. If you will forgive me, I shall write a letter and ask one of the footmen to send it for me.'

'Write your letter. We'll send a groom with

it to discover the truth—unless you wish to go yourself. I could send an armed escort with you.'

Sarah thought for a moment and then shook her head. 'Thank you, sir, but I believe this is a trap. My enemy wishes to draw me out because I have stayed close to the house. I shall write and if a groom could deliver it and bring back a message I should be grateful.'

'Write your letter, m'dear, and I'll see to the rest. We don't want some rogue shooting at you again, do we?'

She thanked him, took her leave and went up to her room to write the letter. Her instincts were telling her that the letter was false and that meant she was still in danger from whoever hated her.

Sarah's letter had been sent and she'd asked the marquess if it might remain their secret, as she did not wish for anything to overshadow Francesca's happiness. Sir Freddie had given his love a ring, but for the moment she was wearing it on chain beneath her gown. Their engagement would not be announced just yet, even though they were to pay a visit to Sir Freddie's mother in the near future.

Sarah had not allowed her suspicions to cloud her pleasure in the company and walked in the gardens, but always in the company of her friends. Sometimes Rupert, Francesca, Sir Freddie and John, together with the dancing master, made up the little group, and on occasion the marquess joined them for refreshments outdoors.

Sarah noticed that there was usually a gardener hanging about when they spent time walking amongst the roses and various flowerbeds. The weather kept fine obligingly and they played croquet on the lawns, drank tea in the shade of some fine trees and walked, enjoying each other's conversation. Each day followed the last in a haze of perfect contentment and Sarah's feeling of alarm began to fade. Rupert was always pleasant to her, always considerate, and sometimes the look in his eyes sent her pulses haywire, but he had said nothing further to make her think that he was marrying her for any other reason than convenience.

She was determined that he should not guess she felt more than he did and her smiles for him were no more intimate than for anyone else. If he wished for a comfortable wife, it was what she would be, undemanding and good-tempered.

She'd told Rupert of her letter and her belief that it was a ruse to trap her into leaving the safety of his protection.

'You must remain here,' he had told her

sternly. 'Your uncle will write to you if it is necessary—though if you are anxious I could escort you.'

Sarah had shaken her head. 'I do not think my uncle would have sent such a letter. I am content to wait until we hear from him.'

She was returning with her friends from one of their outings some days later when a coach drew up at the front of the house. As she watched, the door opened and a man got out. Surprise and pleasure made her start forwards with a glad cry.

'Uncle William! What are you doing here?'

He turned to look at her with a frown. 'I wanted to make sure these people were treating you properly. Were you mad to run off like that, Sarah? What in heaven's name made you change places with a governess?'

'It was just a whim, Uncle. I am so glad to see you are not at death's door.'

'I dare say that was that rogue who wheedled your mother's story out of me,' her uncle said. 'I'm sorry for telling him, girl. He has a smooth tongue and I trusted him, thought he cared for you. From what Lord Myers told me in his letter, Sir Roger is a sly snake and not to be trusted.'

'Rupert wrote to you?' Sarah glanced at Rupert, for he'd said nothing to her. He was laughing with Sir Freddie and did not notice her glance.

'It's the reason I came,' her uncle replied. He looked about him, seeing the little group of curious onlookers. 'Sorry to turn up out of the blue, but I wanted to tell you the whole truth. I gather that serpent twisted the story into something ugly.'

'Wasn't it?'

'Far from it. Can we talk in private?'

'I must introduce you to the others, then we'll go to the back parlour. I am very pleased you have come, Uncle, though a letter would have been sufficient.'

'I thought I should apologise in person. It may be because of me that all this unpleasantness has happened.'

Sarah took his arm and led him towards her friends. She watched as he shook hands with Rupert, greeting him as a friend, and then introduced him to her friends.

'You must come in, Uncle. We are about to have tea.'

'This is a bit above my touch, girl. I was never one for mixing in society, you know—at least, not on this level.'

'Everyone is very friendly. I am sure the marquess will say you must stay for a day or two.'

'I couldn't do that, Sarah. I know my place

and it isn't here. I'll take myself off to the inn, though I'll call on you again tomorrow. You may have been brought up to be a lady, but I came from the lower ranks, as your father did. It was because of your mother that he had you educated as a lady.'

Sarah nodded, because she already knew what had been in her father's mind. Francesca said she would have some refreshments sent into the back parlour so they could be private and Sarah took her uncle there.

'Please sit down, sir.'

'I'll stand, if you don't mind.' He looked at her awkwardly. 'Is it right that you're to marry Lord Myers?'

'Yes, Uncle. He asked me and I said yes.'

'I suppose you know what you're doing—not always a good idea to mix the classes, but if it makes you happy…'

'It does. Why did you come all this way?'

'You've been told you were not the child of your father's wife?'

'Yes, I have. Was it a lie?'

'Your mama couldn't have children. She tried, but it almost killed her and your father wouldn't let her go through it again—but they both wanted a child.' He cleared his throat. 'Your father asked her permission to have an affair with a view to getting himself an heir. It cost her pain, but she gave it…' He paused and Sarah frowned.

'So that much is true?'

'Yes, Sarah. Your father chose a respectable widow who lived in poverty with one child. He gave her money and a house and she promised to give you up when you were born, but…and this is the part that hurts…when the time came she wept and clung to you and he had to force you from her arms.'

Sarah gave a little cry of stress. 'Oh, but that was cruel.'

'What was he to do? Your mama longed for a child and you were his. He loved his wife beyond reason and so he took you and gave you to your mama. He adopted you legally and made you his heir. Your mama never knew that he had forced your mother to give you up.'

'I see…' Sarah's eyes felt wet with tears. 'It is such a sad story. Is it true that my mother came looking for me when she was dying?'

'She came once to ask if she might see you, but your father refused. He thought she might try to steal you from him. He sent her away and he heard later that she had died of consumption.'

'Why didn't he tell me?'

'I think he thought you might despise him for

what he did. He wasn't a bad man, Sarah—he simply loved your mama too much.'

'Yes, I see that.' Sarah blew her nose on a lace handkerchief. 'Thank you for telling me. It is easier to accept than the story Sir Roger told me—though the truth remains. I was not born in wedlock and my mother was not a lady.'

'Oh, but she was, Sarah, the equal of your mother—and her husband was also a gentleman, but a terrible gambler. He left her with nothing when he died.'

'I see... How terrible that must have been for his wife. I think I understand why she agreed to the bargain.'

'Can you forgive your father—and me for telling that scoundrel? I thought he would make you a good husband, Sarah.'

'I would never have married him even had he not tried to blackmail me—but I wish I had known the truth.'

'Would it have made a difference? You could not have been more loved, Sarah. Your mama's life was so much richer for having you.'

'Yes, and I loved her—but what of my true mother? It hurts me to think Father sent her away.'

'He gave her money. She had enough to live decently for the rest of her life.'

'But she had lost a child. I think that must have been hard for her to bear.'

'Well, it cannot be changed now.'

'No, it cannot…' Sarah looked up as the door opened and a maid entered carrying a tray, which she set down close to Sarah. 'Thank you, Rose.'

'Is there anything else, miss?'

'No, I believe we have all we need.' She looked at her uncle as the maid went out. 'Will you have tea or some Madeira wine, Uncle?'

'I believe the wine,' her uncle said, looking relieved that the awkward business had gone off better than he might have hoped. 'You're such a sensible girl, Sarah.'

'I have tried to be, particularly since my father died—but I am thinking of selling the mills if Lord Myers can find a suitable buyer.'

'I made a mistake there as well,' her uncle said with a look of apology. 'I thought you'd be better without the burden of those mills—but I should have left it to you decide when you were ready.'

'I believe I may be ready now—if a trustworthy buyer can be found.'

'I reckon as Lord Myers will find you a buyer who can be trusted. Your workers won't suffer and you'll be the richer for it. That young fellow has a good head on his shoulders even if he is an aristocrat.'

Sarah laughed. 'I am glad to hear it.'

'He says you're to be married within the month. Your aunt and cousins are invited— so that will mean an expense with all the new gowns.' Her uncle sighed. 'But if he's right for you, it's worth it.'

Sarah was a little shocked, for Rupert had not told her that he intended the marriage so soon, but she merely smiled.

'I hope you will give me away, Uncle?'

'Well, if it's what you truly want…' He looked pleased, then shook his head. 'I hope this other business can soon be sorted out. Sir Roger is an evil man and he needs to be brought to justice.'

'He was wicked to tell me those lies. I do not know what he hoped to gain by spreading a false scandal.'

'Mud sticks, girl—especially when you're not out of the top drawer. No, do not look like that, Sarah. You know some of those top-lofty dames in London society will look down their noses at you, even if you are Lady Myers. They will never forget that your father made his money from trade.'

'It was a decent, honourable business and I

am not ashamed of what Father did for a living—but I think he treated my birth mother ill.'

'Well, you must make up your own mind on that—but try not to hate him.'

'No, how could I? He loved me and I loved him—but I wish he had let her at least see me sometimes.'

At that moment a discreet knock at the door heralded Merrivale's arrival. He greeted Sarah's uncle with every sign of friendship, shook his hands, insisted he must stay and took him off to speak with the housekeeper about his accommodation.

Sarah was left to the contemplation of her thoughts. She was conscious of a deep ache inside. The knowledge that her mother had been a respectable woman who had given her child to a childless woman but at the last had been grieved to part with her was painful. She wished with all her heart that she might have known her, spent a little time with her.

She needed to talk to Rupert, but knew that he would be with the others. Besides, as kind as he was, she could not expect him to understand her hurt over her mother's distress and pain.

'I do not love you the less, Mama,' she whispered. 'It's just that I would have liked to know her, too.'

Feeling an unexpected sweep of loneliness,

Sarah left the parlour by the French doors and went out into the sunshine. She knew it was almost time for tea, but she needed a few moments alone to sort out her thoughts. It was difficult to reconcile what her father had done and yet she understood. Mama had always been delicate, but so sweet and gentle. Sarah and her father had both done everything they could to please her and make her life easy and gentle. They had both mourned her desperately.

Her feelings for her mama and her father had not changed, she discovered as she walked in the direction of the rose arbour. However, there was an empty space inside her, a feeling of terrible loss.

Sarah had been wandering for some minutes lost in thought when she became aware of the rustling sounds. She stiffened, glancing over her shoulder just as a man lurched towards her. He had a thick blanket in his hands and she guessed that he had been about to pounce on her. Sir Roger had somehow found his way inside the grounds and was intent on causing her harm.

'Stay back or I shall scream.'

'You are far enough from the house for it not to matter,' he snarled. 'I've plotted and planned for this, Miss Hoity-Toity, and I've waited day after day for you to venture out alone. I was about to give up and go back to town—and now here you are.'

Sarah swallowed hard. He was right. She was far enough from the house for her screams not to be heard. Normally there were gardeners about, but she could see none. She had nothing that she could hit him with and only her wits to hold him off.

'Whatever you do, I shall not marry you.'

'If you prove stubborn, I may have to kill you.'

'What good would that do you?'

'If I can't have you and your money, I'll make certain no one else can.'

Sarah gasped. Was he mad or just driven to desperation by his debts?

'Why do you hate me so?' He had clearly lost his mind and she must play for time, try to think of a way to escape him.

Sarah heard the twig snap behind her. She thought that he must have heard it, too, but he was lost in his grievances, both real and imaginary, his eyes taking on a strange glazed look.

'I do not hate you. I love you—you must know that you encouraged me at the start.'

'That is a lie. I never encouraged you—never wished to be your wife....'

'Then I might as well kill you now.'

He dropped the blanket and suddenly there

was a pistol in his hand. Even as he lifted his arm to fire, two shots rang out simultaneously and he fell to the ground where he lay, twitching horribly.

Sarah's scream brought three men running from the shrubbery, two from behind Sir Roger and one from closer to her. She saw that one of them was a man she had thought a gardener, Monsieur Dupree and the other was the man she needed most.

'Rupert,' she said, took a step towards him and fainted.

He was there to catch her before she hit the ground.

Chapter Fifteen

Rupert bent down by her side, looking at her anxiously. It was merely a faint rather than serious injury. Pray God they had been in time thanks to the dancing master's timely warning. Rupert had but dismounted from his chaise when Dupree came rushing at him, shouting that he was sure he had seen Sir Roger lurking in the bushes.

'I saw Miss Sarah walking alone, but she looked in some distress and so I did not join her—but then I spotted this rogue lurking and came to find help.'

Summoning one of the men he had hired to protect Sarah whenever she went beyond the boundaries of the estate, Rupert had felt for his pistol and smiled because it was already

loaded and ready for use. He'd had men searching everywhere for Sir Roger without success,
but now it seemed he had come to them. His
satisfaction as he pulled the trigger and saw
it hit home flared triumphantly through him.
The devil had paid for his misdeeds and she
was safe.

He felt a rush of tears as he knelt by her side,
running his fingers over her face, looking for
signs that she was hurt. God help him if he'd
been too late.

Rupert lifted Sarah into his arms. She
moaned a little, her eyelids fluttering, and he
knew a rush of relief. She was alive. Thank
God, thank God! His darling girl was alive.

'Hush, my love. You're safe now,' he said and
glanced coldly at Sir Roger's body, which had
stopped twitching. 'Dead?'

'*Oui,* of a certainty,' Monsieur Dupree said.
'He was shot twice, in the back and the head.
Both shots might have killed him.'

'Good. The rogue deserved to die. Take him
to one of the annexes and send for a doctor—
and the magistrate. This business is messy and
must be cleared up as swiftly as possible if we
are to avert a scandal.'

'Yes, cap'n.' The old soldier saluted and then
bent down to haul Sir Roger's body over his

shoulder. 'I'll see to 'im if the Frenchie sees to the rest.'

Rupert nodded grimly, but made no reply as he strode towards the house carrying his precious burden. As he approached several people came out to meet him, Francesca running towards him, Sir Freddie close behind and the two older men standing on the steps watching.

'Is Sarah all right? We heard two shots.'

'We found her in time. Sir Roger was about to kill her—he's dead. I think the man was entirely mad.'

'It was my fault,' William Hardcastle said. 'I told him her story.'

'No, he knew it before he even met her. He was bent on getting her fortune, but when she proved too stubborn he decided to settle for revenge.'

'Good grief. Because she wouldn't marry him?'

'There's a lot more to the story. Explanations another day, if you please, gentlemen. Sarah's comfort comes first.'

'Of course, of course.'

'Take her to the salon and put her on the daybed.'

'No, take her up to her room,' Francesca said. 'She will want to be private for a while. You should stay with her until she feels better, Uncle Rupert.'

'Good girl, go up and pull the covers back.'

Francesca was ahead of him as he carried Sarah carefully up the stairs. He knew she was stirring, but she merely buried her head against his shoulder, not saying anything until he had placed her gently on her own bed.

'Please do not be cross with me, Rupert,' she said and her eyelids flickered. She sighed and then looked up at him. 'I know it was foolish to go there alone, but I had something on my mind.'

'My foolish love,' he said and bent to brush his lips over hers. 'Why should I be cross with you? I might be annoyed with your uncle, for I suppose he told you the truth, and I am furious with that devil that tried to murder you—but I could never be angry with you. I love you far too much. If anything, I am angry with myself. There was a letter on my desk warning of an attempt on your life from James Monks, but some papers of mine had covered it and I missed it. If you had died, I should never have forgiven myself.'

Sarah inched her way up against the pillows, looking at him, her lovely eyes wide open as if in surprise. 'You love me? You truly love me? I thought, but I...'

Francesca discreetly closed the door behind her as she went out. She shook her head at the small group gathered there. 'No need to worry,' she said. 'Rupert will take care of her. She will be quite safe with him.'

Inside the room, Rupert smiled down at the woman who looked at him with such dawning wonder in her eyes. 'Come, Sarah. This is not like you. Surely you knew I was in love with you? I could barely keep from carrying you off to my bed and ravishing you.'

A smile lit her face, making her look beautiful. 'I thought you might want to lie with me—but lust does not always mean love, does it? Your uncle said something about you once losing a woman you cared for?'

'Years ago when I was wet behind the ears,' he said and smiled, his fingers brushing her cheek tenderly. 'For too long I have felt little inside—transitory lust for a beautiful woman, yes, but true feelings, no, they have eluded me, until you came.'

'Why?'

'Why did I feel nothing?' Rupert frowned. 'My parents were not particularly happy together—an arranged marriage—and I asked a lady to marry me. She laughed and called me a boy, which I was at the time. I joined the army because there was a war...' His smile faded, his eyes, had he known it, wintry and bleak. 'I saw too many friends die in terrible circumstances, Sarah. A man can only take so much. I carried my best friend Harry from the field. For two days he lingered in terrible pain and then he died in my arms, begging me not to forget him and to take his things to his family, which of course I did. Some of my friends blamed me for my decision to attack the enemy position that day. Lives were lost, though we gained our objective, but some of my friends blamed me for those lost.

'After that, I shut all feelings out. When I resigned my commission I gave myself up to a life of pleasure, taking a woman if I felt like it, but giving nothing. I think that would not have changed had not a most unusual governess walked into my life.'

'Oh, Rupert, my dearest one,' Sarah whispered and held out her hand to him. He took it and pressed it to his cheek, then kissed the fingertips. 'I am sorry about your friends. I know nothing can change what happened or give you back what you lost—but when we have children of our own they may help to fill the empty places inside you.'

'You have already done that,' he said and bent to kiss her, this time a long, lingering kiss that made her sigh and cling to him. 'If you cling to me that way, I might just get in that bed with you.'

Sarah laughed, the laugh that had melted the ice and set warm blood flowing through his veins. 'If I did not think that everyone was waiting for us to go down to tea, I should invite you to keep your word. You may consider it an open invitation.'

'Shameless hussy,' he murmured and nibbled at the side of her neck. 'You taste so good, my love. I can hardly wait for our wedding night.'

Sarah touched his cheek. 'I do love you so very much.'

He caught her hand and kissed the palm. 'Do you? I was afraid you couldn't possibly love me as much as I love you. I have not exactly courted you, have I? For a long time I could not trust my feelings. I feared to be hurt or disillusioned and it was not until you were shot the first time that I began to understand how much you meant to me. Even then I was not sure that I could truly give my heart, but then I realised that my life would be nothing without you.'

Sarah smiled and caught his hand, holding it to her cheek. 'I have no need of flattery. I want you with all your faults and all your virtues. I do not think that any other man could content me.'

'That is just as well, Miss Hardcastle, because I cannot kill all your unwanted suitors.' He saw the light fade from her lovely eyes and cursed himself for a fool. 'Forgive me. It was but a jest. Sir Roger has gone now, Sarah. Nothing can harm you now. I have a special licence in my pocket and we shall marry just as soon as you are ready.'

'Tomorrow?' Sarah said, laughing up at him. 'No, no, my aunt is looking forward to the wedding. We must wait the three weeks, I think—but I do not see why we should wait in other ways....' Her cheeks turned pink and he laughed in delight.

'Wanton jade. How much I am going to enjoy being married to you, Sarah. You will set all the old tabbies by the ears when I take you to town. They will not know what to make of you.'

'I fear they may cut us.'

'Nonsense. They may be shocked by your story, but their curiosity will bring them flocking and, when they meet you, they cannot fail to appreciate that you are a true lady. Your mother was one after all.'

'I believe her married name was Harlow,' Sarah said, her brow wrinkling. 'Her husband was killed in a foolish duel, leaving her penniless—but my uncle must have told you.'

'My agents uncovered the story, dearest. I have many agents working on this business and we knew that Sir Roger had returned to the area.' He took her hand and kissed it. 'I fear I cannot give you the news you would wish for. Your mother died, just as your father was told. However, there is something…'

She gazed up at him, enquiring. 'You have discovered something else?'

'You have a brother called Harry. I had the information just this morning and intended to tell you when we had a moment to be private—which has been devilishly few and far of late, my love.'

'A brother?' Sarah stared at him, some of the pain of her mother's death draining from her. 'I truly have a brother?'

'A half-brother to be precise,' Rupert said. 'He is an officer in the army. I had thought you might wish him present at our wedding?'

'Oh, yes, I should love that. Does he know about me?'

'I think he is aware he has a sister somewhere, but not the details. I shall leave that to you, Sarah. We can make arrangements for you to meet—or you could invite him here so we might get to know him a bit before we wed.'

'Do you think of everything?'

'I am used to being in command. If I am too authoritative, you must tell me and I shall try to change.'

'I would not change you for the world,' she said and the sparkle was back. 'At least…perhaps little things…'

'And what may they be, minx?'

'You do not kiss me enough,' she whispered. 'I dare say I may find other things—'

She got no further for he decided to supply the lack immediately.

'So it is all arranged,' Francesca said and hugged her arm as they walked together in the gardens a few days later. It seemed to Sarah that her life was free of a dark shadow and the sun shone brighter than ever before, the birds singing sweeter than of late. 'You are to be married in three weeks. When you leave on your honeymoon I shall leave with Grandfather and Freddie to stay with his mama—and when I return you will be here again.'

'Yes, that is what Rupert suggested. I know I promised to come with you, but you have your grandfather and John—and, of course, Sir Freddie, who loves you dearly.'

'I shall still miss you, but you must have your trip to Paris,' Francesca said. 'I have all the rest of this year and next spring to be with you, dearest Sarah. It is wonderful that Rupert says you will make your home here with us until I am married. I cannot thank you enough for all you've done for me.'

'It was a happy chance for us both that I came here,' Sarah said and squeezed her arm. 'We have both found happiness—and I have found a brother. I have written to invite him to stay and attend our wedding. Your grandfather is to spend more time with us, and, if he can bear it, may make his home here once more.'

'Freddie says he can live with us if he chooses—or we will live here some of the time. I am sure that there is no need for him to be so lonely again.'

'I believe he knows that,' Sarah said and bent to smell a rose, picking the delicate pink bud and tucking it into her gown. 'Everything has turned out so well for us.'

'Everything is perfect.' Francesca said. 'Oh, here is Freddie. Shall we join him?'

Sarah let her go. 'Go on, dearest. I want to pick one or two more roses.'

'So you are happy, Sarah?' Rupert asked as they walked in the moonlight that night. He stopped and drew her closer, brushing his lips over hers. 'Can you look forward to our wedding without any shadows?'

'I shall always be sorry that I never knew

my mother, but perhaps my brother will tell me about her.'

'I am certain he will,' Rupert said and touched her cheek. 'You have the rest of your lives to get to know one another. We shall begin at the wedding and, if it pleases you, I would like to settle some money on him for the future, for when he retires from the military.'

'Should I not do that?'

'You will allow me the pleasure,' Rupert said. 'Your money is your own, but I shall do what I can to further your brother's career and set him up with an estate when he is ready.'

'Would you do so much for my sake?'

'I would do more,' he promised and kissed her.

'I think my mother would be happy that her children were reunited as family.'

'Then you are truly happy?'

'So happy,' Sarah said and gazed up at him. 'Of course, one thing could be better. You could kiss me more....'

She gurgled with laughter as he crushed her to him and she felt the burn of his urgent desire.

'Shall I take you to bed, Sarah? I am tempted, but with a house filled with friends and relatives I fear it could not remain our secret—and I would not have anyone think less of you.'

'Then take me to the summerhouse,' Sarah

said. 'There are cushions and blankets and we could make ourselves a bed.'

'You wicked wanton girl,' he murmured huskily. 'I might have known you would think of a way.'

Sarah turned on her side, raising her body to look down at Rupert as he lay with his eyes closed, the moonlight playing over his features. She reached up to trace the proud line of his neck and moved across his sensitive mouth—the mouth that had kissed her nearly senseless. He caught her finger with his white teeth and she laughed.

'I thought you were sleeping?'

'Just content,' he said and opened his eyes to look at her. 'You are such a warm, wonderful woman, my Sarah. I do not know what I have done to deserve you.'

'Oh, I can think of a few things,' she murmured and bent her head to nibble at his neck. 'Rather a lot of things actually. It might take a long time to tell you—and I think we ought to get back.'

'Not just yet,' he growled and rolled her beneath him into the bed of cushions and blankets. His hand stroked the satin arch of her back, his hands cupping her neat bottom and pressing her closer. She could feel the burn of his arousal and a spiral of desire curled through her. The hot, sweet liquid ran between her thighs and she knew she was ready for him again, longing to be lost in that wild passion that had overtaken them when they threw off their clothes and loved for the first time.

'I do adore you, Rupert.'

'I adore you, my darling, he whispered. 'I didn't believe I could ever love like this, but you captured my heart and refused to let go. You know I want you again, don't you?'

'Yes.' She tangled her hands in his hair. 'I want you, too. I'm yours—as often and as much as you wish.'

'I mustn't again yet because you will be so sore,' he said huskily. 'But I can pleasure us both in another way—if you wish?'

'I am yours….' She looked up at him with such trust and love that he moaned low in his throat, then bent his head and began to kiss her. His tongue stroked and caressed her, licking delicately at the hollow in her throat. His hand stroked as he cupped her breasts, gently kneading and caressing until she was arching and moaning beneath him, begging him to enter her again. Instead he bent his head lower, his tongue travelling down her navel to that soft, moist centre of herself that he had pleasured earlier. As his tongue began to weave its magic, she screamed and cried his name. Her fingers dug into his shoulder as the sensation became almost too much to bear before she exploded into flames and lay quivering in his arms as he stroked her until she came back from the heavens. 'Rupert…oh, Rupert…' she whispered and the tears ran down her cheeks.

'My hair has come down,' Sarah said and buried her face in his shoulder. 'I must hope I can escape to my room without being seen.' She laughed and sat up as he rolled away. 'I do not care. I do not care if everyone knows. I am not ashamed to let them see how much we love each other. Besides, I do not think they will care—except that it may set a bad example for Francesca.'

'I dare say that young lady has ideas of her own,' Rupert said. 'It may be as well if Merrivale allows an engagement now and a wedding at Christmas. I shall see what I can do for them. She can still go to London after all.'

'I know she is impatient and wishes her wedding was sooner,' Sarah said. 'Perhaps when we return from Paris…'

'Yes.' Rupert stood and began to dress. 'Allow me to act as your maid, my love. I dare say we can make you look respectable if we try.'

'I suppose you are proficient as a lady's maid.' He arched his brow. 'Jealous? There is no need. None of my former ladies meant anything to me.'

'I know,' she said and smiled. 'You've told me. I but tease you, dearest, as you tease me.'

'Then continue, my lady,' he replied. 'I would not have you change.'

'I do not think I can put my hair back up without my combs and brushes,' she said. 'It will have to hang loose and everyone must make of it what they will.'

'Come,' he said and took her by the hand. 'We must go in or I shall want you again.'

Sarah had once thought her wedding day would never happen, but suddenly it was upon them. The sun was shining and she rose that morning feeling on top of the world. She smiled throughout the church ceremony and the reception. It was wonderful, graced by the presence of so many friends and relatives that Sarah lost count. She could not remember all their names, but would know their faces. Some of them had come down before the wedding and so she'd had a chance to meet the most intimate members of Rupert's family and some of his close friends—all of them soldiers who had served with him and experienced the same hardships.

Now at last they were alone, not at the Merrivale estate, but at a small house that had belonged to one of Rupert's aunts and was quite close by. He had not wanted to take her away from her friends too soon, but in the end they had dashed for their carriage and been showered with rose petals and dried violets for the second time that day. Sarah could see some in her hair as she looked in the dressing mirror. She was trying to pick them out when the door opened and Rupert entered from the dressing room.

'Tired?' he asked as he came to stand behind her and look down at her reflection in the exquisite marquetry mirror. 'Let me do that for you.' He took her hairbrush and began to stroke it over her long hair, untangling the long silken strands. 'I think the knots all gone now.'

'That was lovely,' she said and then stood up, turning to face him. She lifted her face for his kiss. 'I believe it all went well, did it not? Everyone was amazingly kind.'

'Why shouldn't they be? You've made me happy. I'm a changed man, Sarah. My family and friends would love you for that—and my sister is dying to have you stay with her so she can wheedle all the little details out of you.'

Sarah laughed. 'You wrong her. I thought her sweet.'

'Don't be fooled. She'll twist you round her finger if she can—as she does me. Jane has been trying to find me a bride for years, but I was not of much help, because I kept refusing to meet her candidates.'

'Fortunately for me,' Sarah said and leaned forwards to kiss him. 'It would have been terrible had you been taken.'

'There was never any chance of it. I was waiting for you, my love.'

He lowered his head and kissed her, then bent to sweep her up in his arms and carry her to their bed. She lay looking up at him, a smile on her mouth.

'I am so very glad,' she murmured. 'For otherwise I should have had to be your mistress.'

'Now she tells me,' he said in a mocking tone. 'I might have been spared all the expense of the reception. I thought they would never stop eating and drinking.'

'Oh, Rupert…' Sarah laughed as he threw off his robe and revealed that he was wearing nothing and was fully aroused '…never stop loving me.'

'Never,' he vowed and then he joined her on the bed. They moved together as one, lips meeting in a burning kiss. Flesh to flesh they held one another, looking into each other's faces, and for a long, long time there was no need of words.

* * * * *

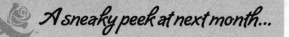

A sneaky peek at next month...

HISTORICAL

IGNITE YOUR IMAGINATION, STEP INTO THE PAST...

My wish list for next month's titles...

In stores from 3rd May 2013:

☐ The Greatest of Sins – Christine Merrill

☐ Tarnished Amongst the Ton – Louise Allen

☐ The Beauty Within – Marguerite Kaye

☐ The Devil Claims a Wife – Helen Dickson

☐ The Scarred Earl – Elizabeth Beacon

☐ Her Hesitant Heart – Carla Kelly

Available at WHSmith, Tesco, Asda, Eason, Amazon and Apple

Just can't wait?

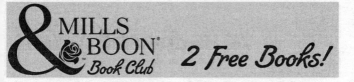